One and Only

Brotherhood of Blood, Book 1

A deadly crash changes the fate of one lonely vampire.

Vampire enforcer Atticus Maxwell stands at the edge of his own oblivion...until the faint heartbeat of a desperately wounded mortal woman calls him back. The terrible crash that almost took both their lives has brought him a charming, intriguing woman who just might give him a reason to live again.

Lissa was headed for a conference at a resort in a last-ditch attempt to find a job. Instead, on a rain-slick mountain road that almost killed her, she finds the love of her life. A love with the most eligible, reclusive vineyard owner in Napa Valley—one that isn't quite human.

No barrier—not even breaking the news to Lissa's friends—seems too great to hold back their blossoming love. Until they learn the accident that brought them together wasn't an accident at all, but a murder attempt by an unknown enemy.

Atticus saved Lissa once. Can he keep her that way in the face of a renewed threat?

Warning: This book contains graphic language, hot neck biting, outdoor loving and a hot man with a killer smile.

Rare Vintage

Brotherhood of Blood, Book 2

She would give her life to save his, but can he save her from himself?

As the new Gal Friday at Atticus Maxwell's winery, Kelly is grateful for the much-needed job, and delighted to be working with her best friend Lissa. What she doesn't need is the exasperation brought on by Marc LaTour's constant flirting. Yet she can't deny she is drawn to the mysterious, unsettling Master vampire.

After six hundreds years of searching, Marc has resigned himself to the fact that he'll never find his One. Kelly is under Atticus and Lissa's protection, and therefore off limits. Yet the desire to possess her is too strong to resist. Curiosity leads to lust—and the surprising discovery that they indeed could be destined mates.

But a dark cloud hangs heavy over them. A rival vampire has challenged Marc for leadership—a challenge that involves a fight to the death. The cost of survival could forever poison any hope for a future together, but if they can both pass the final test, they could find love that will last for eternity.

Warning: This book contains graphic language, hot neck biting, outrageous flirting and undeniable lust.

Phantom Desires

Brotherhood of Blood, Book 3

This time, the creature under the basement is real. And dead sexy.

Computer expert Carly is tired, burned out and ready to downgrade her hectic lifestyle to something simpler. Her solution—pull up stakes and move to an old farm house in the middle of Wyoming. Her new house is full of old-time charm, and it comes with an unexpected surprise. Dmitri Belakov.

Dmitri, a Master Vampire, had an agreement with the former owners of the house to let him live peacefully beneath it in his hidden lair. Now there's a new owner, and he may have to risk revealing his presence to negotiate a new contract. He moves cautiously because if she won't deal, he'll have to kill her once she knows his secret. Carly's mind is unusually hard to influence, but he makes inroads when she is asleep.

Their shared dreams are more erotic than he ever expected, firing a hunger within him to know her feel and taste in the flesh. But doing so risks far too much. Even if Carly can't deny the attraction arcing between them, loving him will force her to make a choice. An eternity in darkness with him—or life in the sun without him.

Warning: This book contains graphic language, explicit sex, very naughty dreamwalking and passionate neck biting.

Brotherhood of Blood

Bianca D'Arc

A SAMHAIN PUBLISHING, LTD. publication.

Samhain Publishing, Ltd.
577 Mulberry Street, Suite 1520
Macon, GA 31201
www.samhainpublishing.com

Brotherhood of Blood
Print ISBN: 978-1-60504-543-6
One and Only Copyright © 2010 by Bianca D'Arc
Rare Vintage Copyright © 2010 by Bianca D'Arc
Phantom Desires Copyright © 2010 by Bianca D'Arc

Editing by Bethany Morgan
Cover by Angela Waters

One and Only, ISBN 978-1-60504-264-0
First Samhain Publishing, Ltd. electronic publication: November 2008
Rare Vintage, ISBN 978-1-60504-381-4
First Samhain Publishing, Ltd. electronic publication: February 2009
Phantom Desires, ISBN 978-1-60504-485-9
First Samhain Publishing, Ltd. electronic publication: April 2009
First Samhain Publishing, Ltd. print publication: February 2010

Contents

One and Only

Dedication

To my family. For believing in my dream even when I didn't.

Chapter One

What was that noise? It was subtle, yet it grated on the ancient one's sensitive hearing. A metallic twang-slap-grind that set his teeth on edge and made him wonder just how mechanically sound this old shuttle bus really was.

Once again, he marveled at how a being as powerful as he still needed to conform to the expectations of mortals—especially in the brave new world of technology. It was becoming harder and harder to reinvent himself now that his image was captured routinely in a myriad of different official ways. The next time he had to "die" and come back, he'd have to alter his appearance drastically. Mortal memories might be short, but photographs, it seemed, lived forever.

Of course, that was supposing he'd bother to come back this time.

Atticus Maxwell had been alive longer than he believed any being rightly should. The centuries had become endless. The business of living was tedious, with no one to share it with. Atticus had always been a loner, but had held a secret hope that someday he'd find at least one person in all the world—and all the centuries—to share his life.

It was the dearest goal of many of his kind. After a few centuries, most bloodletters settled down and began the search for the one person who could complete them. It was a serious business, and a quest he didn't take lightly, but after all these years, he'd almost given up hope.

Atticus had searched longer than most, but he was still alone.

Lissa hadn't wanted to board the shuttle bus, but there was no other feasible way to get to the mountain retreat where the business conference was being held. The place was on a rocky hillside that bordered wine country. The views were said to be magnificent and the five-star cuisine was not to be missed. Or so the travel agent had promised.

She was at a crossroads in her career, having just lost her job as an account manager due to company downsizing. This professional conference was supposed to help her network for new contacts in her field and also had the advantage of hosting a small job fair of sorts. She had two interviews lined up for tomorrow, in fact, but she couldn't seem to shake the feeling of foreboding she'd had when boarding the hotel's private shuttle bus.

It happened that way sometimes. She had a very small psychic gift that had helped her avoid trouble in the past, but tonight she was getting mixed signals from her sixth sense. She didn't want to board the bus, but she didn't know if that apprehensive knot in the bottom of her stomach was due to the shuttle bus, the passengers or the conference that awaited her.

Then he'd appeared.

A man. Out of the night. He'd stolen her breath, and all her senses—both mystical and mundane—had gone on alert. He was dangerous, she could tell just by the aura of power around him, but he was also the most handsome and enticing being she had ever encountered. Her sixth sense pulled her toward him. It made her yearn for him in a way she had never yearned before. Something about him was arresting and fearsome at the same time, yet he drew her as a moth to a flame and she was powerless to resist.

So she boarded the bus, even encroaching on his personal space to the point where he stumbled over her foot, crushing her toes for a short moment while her cheeks flamed in embarrassment.

"I'm so sorry." Alarmed blue eyes met her gaze for a brief moment as shock passed over his features. "Please excuse me," he said.

His voice rolled over her, rich and deep. It rumbled through her very being, awakening every synapse in that brief moment that was over all too soon.

She smiled at him and mumbled her acknowledgment, but he'd already turned to claim his seat farther back in the crowded shuttle bus.

And that was the extent of their contact. So little to build such a lasting impression. Lissa knew she would never forget the man as long as she lived, though she'd probably never even know his name.

Atticus pondered the small woman he'd unwittingly touched. She was a drab little thing in her buttoned up navy blue suit, but there was something very appealing about her. He had sought the mountain retreat that overlooked his own land in the valley far below for a bit of peace, but his thoughts were in more turmoil now than they had been in many decades.

Who was that woman? And why did she claim so much of his attention?

He really should be concentrating more on the strange sounds coming from the van's undercarriage, but he couldn't bring himself to look away from her. He could just see the top of her head and lustrous brown hair over the top of the seat a few rows in front of him.

Lightning flashed close by, distracting him, and the bus swerved on the slick mountain road. The driver pumped the brakes and the grinding sound elevated to a screeching metallic twang ending with a sickening snap. Quick as that lightning flash, the bus slid sideways on the wet pavement, overturned, then tumbled over the edge of the ribbon of road into the void.

The shuttle bus rolled violently down the steep ravine. Atticus was thrown from side-to-side, top-to-bottom in a violent thrashing of metal against soft tissue that had no chance at all against such devastation.

The shuttle bus came to rest, after long moments of sickening freefall, at the bottom of a cliff, deep in wet foliage. The only sound was the creaking of metal as it rocked to a stop and the steady drip of soft rain on the leaves of the forest.

He was going to die.

Finally, after over a thousand years of walking the earth, his life was going to end. Atticus almost welcomed it.

But the girl would die, too, and that bothered him. He thought it odd. By now he probably shouldn't have a conscience left, but the thought of her death—when he could, in all likelihood, save her—plagued him.

His thoughts seemed very far away while lying in a pool of his own blood, with some kind of support beam making a hole in his chest. Atticus felt his immortal life slipping away, but the faint, struggling gasps for breath issuing from the small woman called him back. She was alive. For the moment.

Everyone else on the shuttle bus was dead. Atticus knew they were gone when their heartbeats ceased echoing in his ears. He no longer sensed the motion of their blood swishing through their veins.

They were all gone. All except for the quiet girl who'd smiled so kindly at him after he'd accidentally stepped on her foot while boarding.

Atticus never touched mortals, except to feed. Such acute hearing and senses made it painful to get within touching distance, unless they were under his thrall. Yet, somehow, this quiet, shy woman had invaded his personal space earlier that night. She'd crept up on him without his knowledge. Or perhaps it was Atticus who had invaded her space. He couldn't be sure. But whichever way it happened, it had shocked him.

He hadn't been so surprised in years. Centuries even.

Yet this nondescript woman, with the soft-looking, mousy brown hair and hazel eyes, somehow managed to invade not only his space, but his thoughts as well. Incredible.

And now she would die, alone in the night, on the side of a deserted mountain road, along with the rest of them.

Unless he fought against the darkness. And won.

Regardless of what he was, with such injuries as he'd already sustained, it would not be an easy battle.

When Lissa Adams woke, darkness engulfed her. Straining to see in the absence of light, her breath accelerated as she panicked. Her apprehension only grew when she realized another person lay beside her. A soft dripping sound echoed through what she supposed was some kind of underground chamber or cave. That's what it sounded like—and smelled like. She felt rough rock and scattered grains of sandy dirt beneath her palms.

She knew the mountains were dotted with such places, but she couldn't remember how she'd gotten here. Or why she was so groggy.

She tried to sit up, but the effort it required nearly blacked her out again. The being beside her stirred at her movement, and she felt more than saw the person rise to lean over her.

"Where are we?"

"I moved us to shelter."

Rich and warm, his voice bathed her senses in a dark and dangerous way.

Sexy, she thought. She'd heard that voice before.

It was accompanied by flashing eyes and chiseled features. A man's face flickered through her mind. She'd been fascinated by him and instantly captivated. She remembered thinking he was quite possibly the most striking man she'd ever seen.

"You stepped on my foot."

He chuckled at her innocent observation, setting her insides aflame.

"Indeed. But that was more than twenty-four hours ago."

He stroked a gentle finger down her cheek and she shivered, not in fear, but in surprising arousal. If just the brush of his finger could elicit this response, she wondered what he could do if he really tried.

That thought stopped her cold. Men like this one didn't usually go for women like her. Better to focus on the peculiar situation she found herself in than daydream about her rescuer.

"What happened? I remember the bus swerving..."

"Ah, yes. Just before we rolled down the side of the mountain. You hit your head very hard, I'm afraid. That's probably why you're still a bit fuzzy."

"Where's everyone else?"

He paused only slightly. "Dead."

Her breath caught in shock as her mind raced. "How did we...?"

"Relax, sweetheart." He moved closer. "I pulled you from the wreckage and found shelter, but I was badly damaged in the accident as well. I'm sorry for it, but I need your essence to speed my healing."

"My what?" Hot breath bathed her ear as he settled closer to her side. His strong arms enveloped her shoulders as his mouth stroked over the line of her jaw and lower.

"Don't be afraid. I won't hurt you, but I need your blood, and I'm too weak to cloud your mind. You'll have to trust me." His words whispered against her shivering skin. He dragged sharp teeth back and forth over her jugular as if savoring the moment before the feast.

She barely had time to take in his words before he struck. A piercing pain registered only for a flash, followed by the greatest bliss she had ever experienced. Intensely sexual, it engulfed her in a way she'd never known. He sucked at her neck, licking at the essence of her, swallowing like a thirsty man in the desert. Yet reverence and gentleness communicated through his tender handling of her bruised and battered body.

Oddly, she didn't object. She knew she should be afraid, but an intense arousal overwhelmed her. She didn't have the strength to voice even the faintest protest.

He drank for what seemed a long time, his hands moving over her body, molding her breasts and stroking her skin. Only then did she realize she was naked. She gasped as his long fingers stroked down between her legs, angling inward, invading her most intimate places as his mouth caressed the tender skin of her throat.

He knew his way around a woman's body. Those skilled fingers knew just where to stroke, just where to pinch to drive her excitement to the highest possible point. She teetered on the precipice as his fingers slid in the arousal he drew from her body. His mouth sucked at her neck, his breath feathering through her hair, his pleasing masculine scent teasing her senses. And the feel of him. He was hot and heavy against her, hard as only a man could be and muscular in a way she hadn't expected.

One hand cupped her breast, teasing her nipple as his fingers finally pierced the imaginary boundary, sliding inside her, where few men had ever been. But this man—though she'd known him only a few minutes, really—was like no other man she'd ever encountered. He fired her senses like no other, sending slick, hot arousal to her core. Even the thought that he was some sort of dark creature out of legend couldn't stop the most intense sexual experience of her life.

That one tantalizing finger pumped into her, stretching her. He added a second digit as she whimpered in need. She hadn't had sex in a long time. She was tight, but her body remembered pleasure, and this man—this vampire!—proved himself a master at manipulating her responses. He *owned* her pleasure.

Two long fingers stroked within, his thumb teased higher, rubbing in perfect counterpoint. She came with a wrenching jerk of hips that threatened to dislodge him, but his great strength kept her easily in his clutches. He continued the stimulation, extending her orgasm for long, intense moments while his upper body covered hers, his lips feeding hungrily from the small incisions he'd made in her neck. The pleasure washed over her in the most intense waves she'd ever known and right then she didn't care if he was a vampire, werewolf or Indian chief. All she knew was his mastery. And she already knew she wanted more.

Gods! She was sweet. The sweetest woman he'd had in all his many centuries.

And he'd had many.

Temptation lured him to drain her dry and take all of her precious essence, but he hadn't gone through the trouble of saving her—and himself—for nothing. He'd had a hard time dragging himself off the makeshift stake that had only narrowly missed his heart and then hauling her out of the wreckage in a very weakened state.

He wasn't about to kill her now.

Not when he wanted to taste of her again and again. No, he would keep this female around and keep her healthy. She was fast becoming an addiction.

He realized, belatedly, that he'd never healed as quickly as he had in the past twenty-four hours with her blood in his system. He'd taken her blood out of necessity before he could find a safe place for them to seek shelter. Luckily, she hadn't bled much in the crash, but her brain injury had looked serious. He would need more of her essence to heal himself before healing her more fully. Already, he'd reduced the swelling in her skull somewhat with his healing gift. She would be much better, if not fully recovered, after a second session. But to do that, he must be stronger.

Her blood energized him. And her responsive body tripled the energy he derived from her blood. She'd been potent before, but now that she'd come so beautifully for him, his energy level peaked. He was near full strength. As she would be, as soon as he found the strength to tear himself away from her juicy neck and give her the healing she needed.

But she was so sweet!

With a groan, he backed off, using a light zap of his healing touch through his tongue as he licked the sensitive skin of her neck. She squirmed deliciously under him, but he knew he had to finish her healing first, before satisfying other needs.

Settling the unaccustomed hunger for her blood—and her body—would come later.

"Are you all right?" He nuzzled her neck a moment longer.

"I'm..." She gasped as he moved upward to kiss her lips. "I'm okay. Please..."

"Please what?" He lifted to look down at her expression, which held a hint of dismay, a huge helping of bliss and a smattering of residual fear. "Please *please* you again? I'd be happy to, but it will have to wait until I can heal your wounds a bit more."

In the darkness he saw the faint elevation of color in her cheeks. It made him hard to realize that even after the blood he'd taken from her beautiful body, she could still blush. He'd always liked modest women—something that was becoming increasingly hard to find in this modern world.

"Heal me? So you're not... You're not going to kill me?" Her beautiful eyes were wide with apprehension and he didn't like her looking at him that way.

"No, sweetheart." He stroked her hair, trying to impart reassurance with a gentle touch. "I wouldn't have bothered carrying you from the wreckage if I intended you harm. I'm a healer. Even before I became...what I am...I had the gift of healing. I only want to use it to make you well. What comes after that is in the hands of fate."

"What are you?"

Atticus sighed. He should have expected the question. He'd left himself wide open for it, but he hadn't thought beyond the need to comfort this small mortal woman.

"I'm immortal."

"Like a vampire?" Fear clouded her words, but he also sensed fascination. It was a good sign.

"Some call us that, though it's not a term I prefer. There's too much incorrect mythology associated with the word and too much fear as well. We're mostly peaceful beings, only seeking to co-exist."

"But you feed on human blood, right?"

He nodded, sitting up by her side. The light in the cavern was dim, but he could see her plainly. He suspected she could make out his form as well, from the way her gaze tracked his movements, though without doubt her vision was less able to cope with the dark than his.

"As you experienced yourself, we do need blood to survive. Blood and sex. We are creatures of energy, and the psychic power released during orgasm is ambrosia to us."

"So that's why you made me..."

"Come? Yes, sweetheart." He liked teasing her, oddly enough, though he usually didn't waste much time conversing with his mortal prey. "You came beautifully for me and increased my strength. You helped heal me and I will do the same for you in turn."

He wasn't a man who often indulged in the pleasures of the flesh. He had many gifts to bring prey to him. Clouding mortal minds so they never knew of his feeding from them had proved to be one of his most powerful abilities. He had often brought females to orgasm as he fed from them, because it usually doubled the potency of their blood, but he didn't take pleasure for himself. He hadn't even considered doing so in a very long time. Just one more thing to fall by the wayside as the malaise of his endless existence festered and grew.

But this small woman had ended all that. With one look, she'd sparked a fire that brought him back to life. Back to passion. She fed his hunger like no other. He didn't regret the impulse that made him save her. He didn't regret living, though only the day before he had welcomed death. She gave him reason to go on, a flicker of hope in his increasingly dark world.

She might even be the One.

His breath caught at the enormity of the thought. He searched her pale features. She was beautiful to him, even covered with smudges of dirt and her hair in disarray. He knew she experienced more than a little pain from her head injury, but she seemed content, still a bit warm and fuzzy from the climax he'd given her. Strange pride filled him at having put that dreamy look in her eyes.

Each immortal searched for their One—the single person in the entire world who completed them. Most never found their mate. Many went insane and became true monsters. But a few, like him, walked the earth for centuries on end, searching.

The idea that he might have found her, just when he'd been ready to end it all, astounded him. He hardly dared believe. But there were signs...ancient signs that led him to believe that she might just be his One.

First, her blood was more potent than any he had ever had, and her orgasm fueled his own desire in a way he hadn't experienced in many decades. He wanted to come inside her to see if the rest of the legend could possibly be real.

Could they share their minds?

Could they truly become One?

Healing would have to come first, but he had to go slow. Brain injuries needed special care. He'd taken the risk of drinking from her and giving her pleasure because there was no way to restore his own health without her blood. As he'd absorbed her essence, his strength had returned and he'd been able to block the worst of her pain and make her focus on the good sensations he gave her. It had been a risk, but there had been no other way and he was confident in his ability to heal her completely, now that he was fired up with the life that ran so beautifully through her veins.

Chapter Two

"How old are you?" Curiosity overcame Lissa's better judgment. The idea that she was sitting naked, in a dark cave with a friendly vampire was simply too weird.

"I've walked the earth far longer than you, sweetheart," he replied with a chuckle. From the sound of his voice and the vague shadows she could just make out, he'd moved away.

"My name is Lissa." She tried to sit, making it only to her elbow before her head started spinning.

"Lissa." The rumble of his voice cut off her next question. She'd been about to ask his name, but it didn't seem to matter when he was beside her, his warm breath wafting over her skin and his voice rumbling through every pore. "A beautiful name for a beautiful woman. Here." He supported her shoulders and took her hand, placing some kind of small basket in her grasp. Or was it a cup? She couldn't make out much in the murky darkness of the cave, but she could both hear and feel liquid sloshing around within the small receptacle she now held. "I collected some water for you. This cave has a little spring near the back that should be safe for you to drink."

"What is this?" She touched the rim of the cup, feeling branches and leaves.

He settled beside her. "I wove some twigs together and lined it with leaves. It's not entirely waterproof, but it works well enough. Drink, Lissa. You need fluids."

She found a smooth spot on the rim where leaves had been

folded over the twigs and tried a sip. The water was cold and incredibly refreshing. She drank the whole cup, smacking her lips as she lowered the makeshift container.

A shock went through her system when he leaned down and licked her lips, turning the caress into a kiss that was sweeter than anything she'd ever tasted.

"You are beautiful, Lissa, and you taste good enough to eat." His whispered words caressed her face as he lifted away, a millimeter at a time.

Her head swam as he let her go and her vision clouded. The man was potent, but she was still feeling the effects of being knocked around the interior of the shuttle bus as it careened down the mountain. He laid her back on the thin padding of their ruined clothes, and stroked her cheek with light, comforting motions.

"I'm sorry, sweet Lissa. You need to rest."

"Don't leave me." She clutched at his arm as he made to move away. She had no idea where the impulse came from, but she didn't want to be alone. In particular, she didn't want this compelling man—creature of the night though he was—to go far from her. She needed his warmth, his presence at her side. He made her feel safe, though just why she should feel safe with a vampire, she couldn't say. Logically, she should be trying to escape him, but logic had nothing to do with the terror in her heart at the thought of his leaving her.

"I won't. I promise you. But you need to rest more before I attempt the next phase of your healing. As do I. Healing takes something out of the healer and I was injured in the accident as well."

"Oh no." She hadn't truly understood before, her thought processes clouded by everything she'd had to deal with since waking. "Are you all right?"

"Don't worry for me, sweet Lissa." He brought her hand to his lips and kissed her knuckles with an old-world flair. "I'm much recovered since tasting of you. Just a few minutes rest will have me at full strength and ready to give some of that energy back to you. But I want to be sure to do this right. Brain injuries can be difficult. I want to make certain we're both ready when I attempt to heal you completely."

Silence descended as he settled beside her. He held her hand, offering warmth and comfort she wouldn't have believed possible from a vampire.

"I thought you guys were supposed to be cold."

He gave a long-suffering sigh. "The myths about my kind are seldom correct."

"Then what is true? I already know you drank my blood—unless I was hallucinating that part."

"No, you weren't hallucinating. Though I normally leave the mortals I drink from with no memory of the event. They don't tend to handle the idea as well as you have."

"I must've gotten my brains scrambled by the accident," she admitted. "I don't understand why I trust you, but I do. Maybe it's stupid of me to tell you that, but I can't see how my situation could be any worse."

"Oh, it could be worse, little one, but lucky for you, your trust—amazing as it is—is not misplaced this time. I want only to protect you. Of course, even if I were an ancient *Venificus* killer, I might still tell you that, to keep you cooperative."

The irony in his voice comforted her. Something in her deepest mind liked him. Not only liked him, but trusted him. It was the same place the feelings of mixed dread and elation had come from when she'd been about to board the shuttle bus. She understood the warning now. The dread was most likely a premonition of the accident and the death that would visit all those innocent souls in the vehicle. The elation might have something to do with her rescuer. From the first sight of his handsome face, she'd been drawn to him.

Destiny wasn't something she often tried to fight. She was just talented enough psychically to understand things sometimes happened as they were meant to happen. Fighting against fate only made life more difficult.

His words caught her attention, the niggling of her second sight alerting her to something important. Or perhaps it was something that would be important later. Either way, she trusted her abilities enough to investigate.

"What's that word? Veni-something?"

"*Venifucus.*" The foreign word rolled off his tongue, but a shiver of premonition set her nerves jangling. "It's an old word. A name for a group of killers who left this realm eons ago." He was quiet for a moment, as if reflecting. "I'm not sure why that popped into my mind now, when I haven't thought of them for centuries."

Lissa knew enough to tuck the information away for later consideration. Her gift sometimes guided her to learn strange tidbits that became useful months, sometimes years, later.

"Centuries?" The thought gave her pause as he sighed. One of his warm hands stroked her shoulder, offering comfort.

"I was born in what you would call the Dark Ages, though to us, they were just hard times. My family owned a small vineyard, as I do today."

"You make wine? But...?" She didn't know how to ask him the questions running through her mind. A vampire businessman? It seemed too weird to contemplate.

"I can drink wine. In fact, it's a delicacy to my kind, though we can't ingest much else without consequences. But the fruit of the vine is our one last link to the sun. It heals us and invigorates us. I've always enjoyed the winemaking process and in one form or another, I've been involved in wine production since about the fourteen hundreds." He sounded as proud as any successful businessman talking about his career. "My main vineyard lies in the valley below. In fact, we're not too far from my land here. Perhaps tonight I can venture out and get some clothing and food for you. Or if you're well enough, you can come to my home and get cleaned up. We'll call the hotel from there and let them know you're all right."

"I was on my way to a conference, looking for a job. Guess that's out now, all things considered." She didn't want to think about her dwindling bank account or the bills that had been piling up.

"You won't make the conference, but try not to worry. I have a lot of business connections. Perhaps we can find you a job, once you're healed."

Tears gathered in the back of her eyes at this man's incredible kindness. Not only had he heroically dragged her from the wreckage and saved her life, but he was talking about helping her get her career back on track. He was almost too good to be true and under other circumstances, she probably would have been very wary, but she'd been drawn to him from the first. Fate, it seemed, had thrown them together, and for better or worse, her destiny was intertwined with his—at least for the foreseeable future.

Atticus lay beside her, attuned to her moods as he'd never been with any other being, mortal or immortal. It was as if he could sense her emotions, though he'd never had any kind of empathic abilities before.

She was a complex woman. Her surface thoughts were chaotic after the trauma she'd been through, but he sensed an inner core of strength he'd seldom encountered in any being, and almost never in a female. She was remarkable in every way.

He could feel her fretting over her lack of a job. Atticus didn't want to frighten her by being too forward, but she had nothing to worry about. If necessary, he'd create a job for her— if she really wanted one. Although the longer he was in her presence, the more he thought seriously about keeping her. He had enough money to support an army. He could keep one small woman in style for the rest of her natural life.

But that was the sticking point. She was mortal. He'd never made a practice of keeping mortal pets around his home as some of his brethren did. It smacked of slavery to his mind and he didn't hold with that. For the first time, he was considering asking a woman to stay with him who knew full well what he was and what he'd want from her. There was no way he could keep her under his roof and not want to taste her blood again and again.

It was a momentous step.

He'd have to think carefully about the consequences before he broached the subject. There was also the improbable, but tantalizing idea that she could actually be his One. He'd find the answer to that question before he went any further, but he didn't dare get his hopes up too high. He'd searched the world over for centuries. He'd almost come to terms with the idea that he would never share his immortal life with one special woman. Almost. But there was a small part of him that still yearned for that impossible dream. Perhaps this woman was the answer to his quest. Perhaps.

But he had to heal her first, then take her, to be absolutely certain one way or the other.

Atticus leaned up on one elbow, looking down at her lovely face in the darkness.

"Don't fret, sweet. It will all work out. For now, let's concentrate on making you well, all right?"

Her expression lightened, much to his relief. "All right. I just wish everything would stop spinning." She chuckled and closed her eyes, likely unable to see much more than shadows in the dim cave.

"I can help with that." Gently, he placed his hands around the points of impact on her skull as he gathered his renewed strength. Using his healing gift, he directed pulses of energy to the places in her badly bruised head that were still injured. He'd done a lot of the repair work already, but the finer points had been beyond him the night before. He'd stabilized her, but left the finesse work until he was stronger.

Concentrating, he set to work. It took quite a while, but when he finally released her, she was healthy once more.

And ready for what he planned next.

"How does that feel? Is the headache any better?" His deep voice drifted down to her from above. She felt so good with his hands on her face, in her hair. Her eyes had drifted shut of their own volition while he'd touched her, her unconscious mind trusting him in ways she'd never really trusted another being. Even with the few lovers she'd had in her life, she'd never fully let go and let them control her body or her responses. With this strange, startling man, giving over all her power was second nature.

Her body recognized him on some intrinsic level that she didn't bother to question. She knew from past experience with her psychic gift that some things defied logical explanation. Her uncharacteristic response to this imposing male creature was undoubtedly one of them.

Her eyes flickered open. She could see him a little better in the dim light that filtered into their underground sanctuary from somewhere behind her. His form was less fuzzy than it had been. She took that as a good sign as she raised one hand to touch her head.

"The pain is gone. My head doesn't hurt anymore and I think my vision is clearer, though I still can't see much in this darkness. But it's better. I feel much better. Thank you."

"You're quite welcome, my dear." She could just make out his eyelids lowering as if he was fighting fatigue.

"Are you okay? I mean..." She tried to see his expression in the darkness. "I hope you didn't overtax yourself. Will you be all right?"

He brought her hand to his lips for a gentle salute. "You are sweet to think of my comfort, beautiful Lissa. It's true that healing takes a great deal of energy, but I'll be fine."

"Is there anything I can do?" She grew concerned by his quiet words, his restrained tone.

He paused before answering. "There is something you—

we—could do to strengthen us both, my dear, but I hesitate to ask."

"What is it?" She tried to rise on one elbow, but he moved closer again, forcing her to remain beneath him.

"I told you I can gain strength from sexual release." His eyes actually sparkled. She could see them twinkle in the dim light. "I can pleasure you—and myself—if you'll allow it, and bring us both back to full strength."

"You want to...uh...*be* with me?" Her hesitation stood between them as he gazed down at her. She wanted to be sure she understood him perfectly. It would be all too easy to build impossible dreams around a man like this.

"I want to make love to you, sweet Lissa. There is quite a difference." He leaned in, nibbling on her bare shoulder.

"But I'm not on anything." Her face flushed with embarrassment. "I mean..." she was at a loss for words.

"Never fear, sweetheart. You can't get pregnant with me. Not unless..." He didn't finish the thought, but she sensed wistfulness in his words.

"What?"

"The only way I could make you pregnant is if you were my one, true, destined mate, which is highly unlikely. I've searched for centuries and never found her." Silence stretched before he continued. "You can't catch anything from me. We don't suffer from or carry mortal diseases. You're safe."

Lissa was uncomfortable with the direction of the conversation, but he didn't let up. If anything, he moved closer.

"I've pleasured many women in my years but have not sought my own pleasure in a very long time. I didn't want to. Not until I met you."

"You don't have to lie to me." Hurt seeped into her words regardless of her desire to hide her feelings. They were too close to the surface. This incredible situation and incredible man were doing things to her emotions that she couldn't control.

He drew back, his face hovering above hers where she could see more of his expression. His eyes were clear, gleaming orbs in the darkness, the tight lines around his mouth showing clearly how tense and tired he was.

"I do not lie. When we first touched, I knew there was something different about you. You drew me, Lissa, unlike any woman in many, many years. I wanted you from the moment I saw you, though I'd planned only to track you down at the hotel, cloud your mind and drink of your essence. But now that I've tasted you, I doubt I could've stopped there. Had we not been in the wreck I would still have found you and wanted to bed you. Your warmth and energy are tantalizing to me."

"Really?" Her voice was small, her feelings unsure, but she was fascinated by the idea of what he'd have done if they hadn't been in a wreck. He might've come to her and she would have had no memory of this elegant, strong, incredible man.

All in all, she was glad now for the wreck, if only because he hadn't been able to cloud her mind. She wanted to remember every moment with this man, to hold against the years in the future. She was sure she would never meet another like him.

His very existence proved to her that magic was real—not only the magic of the vampire, but the magic of him. He was everything she'd ever dreamed of in a man, and never dared hope for. She knew there was no future for them, but for this one moment out of time, she could experience what it was like to be held in his arms, to be made love to the way she'd dreamed of all her life. It was worth the risk to her heart, though she suspected it would be very easy to fall in love with him. But it was a chance she was willing to take.

Whenever he touched her, unearthly flames licked over her senses, warming her soul. Lissa didn't understand it at all, but reveled in the feel of his hands, his quiet strength. She wanted this dark stranger. She wanted him inside her with a passion unknown to her.

"Yes, sweet Lissa." His voice drifted over her. "I would have ravished you in the dark, given half a chance."

His words ignited a frenzy of need in her body. She could no more deny him than she could deny the fire racing through her veins. She reached for him, needy, yearning.

"Please," she said simply, suspecting he could see every nuance of her thought process in her expression. It was obvious now that he could see much better in the dark than she. It was yet another tidbit of memory about this experience she would file away to recall later, when he was gone from her life.

He bent, kissing the smile from her lips, inflaming her with a fever she'd never known, but had always yearned for in her dreams. His fire licked over her senses as his tongue dueled with hers. His teeth were sharp, reminding her of the way he'd bitten her and made her come, but she wasn't frightened. Far from it.

"Your skin is like silk, sweet Lissa," he whispered against her skin as he moved down her body, placing nibbling kisses down across her collarbones and onto the swell of her breasts. His hands stroked lower, first circling her hips, then delving between her legs, urging her to spread them for his passage. Lissa was beyond shyness, beyond any thought of demur. This man aroused her passion unlike any other man she'd ever known. She knew she was already slick and when his fingers encountered the evidence of her desire, he raised his head to stare into her eyes. He was so close, she could see the excited sparkle in his gaze, pinning her beneath him with the gentlest touch.

"Please..." she gasped. She wasn't sure what she was begging for exactly, but she knew he could provide it. He was the answer to all things at that moment.

"Yes, sweet Lissa. You're ready and I can't wait. I have no finesse. Forgive me." He slipped one finger into her channel. "But I need to know." His words registered dimly as he kissed her again, thrusting his tongue inside her mouth the way she wanted him to thrust himself inside *her*. The lascivious thought made her squirm as that first finger was joined by another, sliding in rhythm in and out of her channel. She wanted him bad and his stroking only made the yearning worse.

"Please!" she cried out.

"Say yes. I need to hear it from your lips."

She could barely talk, let alone think. He'd driven her passion higher, faster, than she'd ever experienced. Yet, his patience was impressive. He waited, even though it had to be clear she was his for the taking. His hard cock rubbed against the skin of her thigh as he moved closer, bobbing, stroking and driving her insane. She had to have him now, but he waited for her permission.

He removed the fingers tormenting her, moving over her so he could fit his hard length into the space made for him. She tried to move down onto him, but his strength denied her. Her frustration level rose higher and higher as she strained toward him. Finally, she could take no more.

"Yes! Dammit, yes!" She panted against him. "Come into me now."

With an animalistic growl, he pushed forward, breaching the tightness of her body with a slow, firm, inward thrust.

Even in his passion, he moved carefully, lest he hurt her. He'd felt how tight she was with his fingers. He knew she'd have trouble taking him at first, but she'd adapt, and come to love his possession. He'd make her sing out in joy when she came around him, and he could hardly wait to bring her with him, over the edge into bliss.

But first, he had to get fully inside. He thrust shallowly, reveling in the feel of her passage. She was tight, but her maidenhead was absent. She'd had other men before him. With a wave of dominance, he was glad she'd have something to compare him with. This way, she'd know their joining was nothing ordinary.

No, this joining would be of epic proportions. He felt the heat rising already. Things were churning inside him in a way that was new to him and the boost to his energies coming from their joining spiked higher, like nothing he'd expected.

It was even better than the best he'd ever had. Stronger, more fulfilling and hotter than hell.

He let himself dare to hope that she might be the One. He didn't need the final sign that would come with climax, to know it in his heart. She was his One. He could feel it in his bones as he began to thrust deeper, keeping time with her cries of passion.

"Are you with me, sweetheart?"

He needed her to look at him, even though she could barely make him out in the darkness of the cave. But he needed to see her sparkling eyes as his body joined fully with hers this first time.

"I'm with you." Her words were faint gasps of air as she climbed ever higher with him.

"My name is Atticus," he told her, thrusting hard and deep, fully embedding himself as if he would never leave. "Say my name, Lissa. I need to hear it on your lips."

She panted. "Atticus." Her inner muscles clenched around him as she rose higher still. "Faster, Atticus. I need it harder." Her words were heated whispers of delight and yearning.

He complied with a groan of satisfaction, seating himself deep. He pumped hard, reaching into her mind with his to know when and how she wanted him to thrust. But her thoughts were in perfect alignment with his and he noted the ease with which he accessed her mind as yet another sign that she was his One.

The thought brought him to a trembling precipice. She was right there with him. With a final push, he tumbled over the edge, his body spurting inside her as she screamed in ecstasy, clenching around him.

He hadn't come so hard in years, if ever. And she loved

every minute of it. He could feel the satisfaction in her mind—a mirror of his.

Magnificent, joyous union. At last.

Pathways opened between their two souls, joining them together for all time. He realized with a blinding flash that he had full access to her memories now, as if they were his own. He wondered if she would have the same access to his mind. The thought gave him pause. Some of his memories were too grim to share with such a kind and gentle woman.

She was such a bright beacon of hope in his otherwise dark world. He didn't want to subject her to his memories, including centuries of living in a world that had been sometimes harsh, and even inhuman. He doubted she could accept the more sinister parts of his long existence.

"Don't think that, Atticus." She shocked him with her words as she stroked his chest with trembling fingers. "There is no part of you that I couldn't accept."

"Then you share my mind?" His heart opened in joy at the thought. He'd found her at last. Joined in mind, they were truly One.

"How could I not? I was more than a little psychic even before the wreck. I knew there was something different about you the moment you stepped on my foot."

He chuckled and moved his heavy weight off her, settling at her side.

"Psychic?" He stroked her shoulder as he contemplated the ramifications. He hadn't realized she had any kind of extrasensory abilities, but he could read now, the way her gift had helped her in the past. His new mate was full of surprises that he would spend the rest of their years discovering.

"It runs in my family. But I've never experienced anything like what just happened, or what I'm learning now, seeing inside your memories. It's amazing. And a bit overwhelming." Softened with awe, her voice washed over him.

"Do you understand what you see in my memories? Do you

understand that you are my One? My *raison d'etre*? My everything?" Anxiety filled him as he waited for her all-important reply.

She rose to lean over him this time, stroking his bristly cheek with reassurance. "When we climaxed together, it all came to me in a blinding rush. I'll admit, there are some things I'll have to think through and sort out, but the most important thing is that my heart recognized you, Atticus. Not only am I your One, but you're mine." She leaned down to kiss his lips sweetly. "And I want you to bring me over."

He sucked in a breath of shock. "Are you sure?"

If she drank his blood, she would become immortal too. They would share eternity—together.

He'd planned to talk her into it in time. It was a big change for a human, and he hadn't wanted to push. Now she'd broadsided him with her decision and her delighted chuckle told him as clearly as the mischievous thoughts in her mind that she enjoyed it.

"Yes, I'm sure, Atticus. I love you."

The vacant place in his soul suddenly filled with her blindingly bright light.

The most sacred quest of his long lifetime had ended, and now he could get on with living and enjoying his immortal existence with a woman he loved by his side.

"I love you, Lissa. And I always will."

She lightened his heart as he pulled her over him. With a sharp thrust, he brought them together once more, both ready for more. Sharing minds made all aspects of life better, they discovered as his cock drove home where it belonged, right up inside her, as far as nature allowed. She squirmed in delight. Her body knew his. It recognized its other half.

It was a slow joining, a lazy thrust and return that they both wanted to draw out.

"When you make me a vampire, will I have to suck other people's blood?" She didn't sound too thrilled with the idea, and he easily read the aversion to touching other men in her mind, which pleased him greatly.

"Now that we are One, you need only drink my blood. Our love and our blood will sustain us both now."

"So no more biting the necks of women you don't know?"

He grinned as he brought her higher with a deep thrust. "No, love. Just you. And I'll bite," he pulled her down so her heavy breasts were inches away from his mouth, "only you. All of you. From here to forever." He reached up with his tongue and licked her nipples, pulling each deep into his mouth in turn, as she moaned above him.

She began to ride him, her breath hissing out as her pleasure rose, and he reveled in the wicked thoughts in her mind. His girl liked it a little kinky, it seemed. They'd have centuries together to explore all their shared desires. Atticus liked the wicked thoughts in her mind that marched so well with his own tastes. That they were compatible in this way was only more proof that she had been made just for him.

"You're a naughty girl, aren't you?" He liked the way Lissa gasped, her skin heating. He knew she was both embarrassed and enthralled by the idea of playing sexy games with him. "Answer me, sweetheart." A tinge of dominance filled his tone and he felt her clench around him. No doubt about it. She liked it.

"Yes, Atticus. I've been bad."

"Very bad," he agreed with a satisfied smile. They were definitely both on the same page. "Now what do we do with bad girls?" He let the words draw out as he slowed his upward thrusts, holding her on a knife's edge of pleasure. She moaned and he sensed words were beyond her at this point. "Do you want to feel the force of my hand on this pretty ass, sweetheart? Is that what you want? Do you want a spanking?"

Her eyes closed as she clenched and threw her head back. "Yes!"

That's all he needed to hear. Atticus swatted her ass and

urged her to ride him faster. She began to whimper and moan on every deep thrust and every hard spank. Atticus tongued her nipples then grazed his fangs over the soft flesh on the side of one full breast, drawing just a bit of blood that he greedily lapped up.

She loved it. He read the exciting flash of sexy pain that thrilled her, and the resulting pleasure as he stroked his tongue over her soft skin in her chaotic thoughts. He smacked her ass then moved one hand around to search out her little clit. Unerringly, he grasped the tiny button, squeezing hard and making her come with a delicious shout that echoed through the dark cavern.

He followed her into madness as he shot his seed deep inside his mate.

His One and only.

Chapter Three

By nightfall, they were both back to full strength, though Lissa knew she would bear some black and blue bruises from the accident for the next few days. Atticus had discussed their next move with her and they'd decided to leave some evidence of her adventure for the human authorities to see. They would, no doubt, have been searching for her since the wreck that had claimed so many lives. Luckily, no one but the driver had known Atticus was on the shuttle bus, since his decision to go up to the resort had been a last minute thing.

As a result, they decided to placate the authorities with a story that made some sense, though it was admittedly sketchy. They arrived at Atticus's home just after sunset. To say it was a mansion was an understatement. The European-styled villa was set in the midst of a picturesque vineyard and both the house and manicured landscape took her breath away.

Opening the grand door, Atticus whisked her into his arms and carried her over the threshold. It was a romantic, old world gesture that brought tears to her eyes.

"Welcome home, love." He paused to kiss her, keeping her in his arms as he kicked the door shut and carried her into a spacious living room. The kiss grew bolder as he lowered her to a soft, wide couch. She could feel the conflict inside him. He wanted to call the authorities on one hand, to begin the process of making her completely well. On the other hand, he shared the raging desire burning in her own blood to make love here and now—to claim her without further delay.

"Yes, Atticus. Yes." She stroked his skin, taking the decision out of his hands. "Make love to me."

"Are you certain?" He pulled back only slightly. "I don't want to hurt you. I hated to leave even one small bruise on your skin when I could easily have healed them all."

"You could never hurt me," she reassured him. "And we needed to leave some of the bruises to show the nice ambulance men," she teased with a coy smile. "But I want you now, Atticus. I don't want to have to wait until they let me out of the hospital. I can't go two minutes without wanting you. I'm addicted to you." She laughed to ease his strain, cupping his cheek and looking deep into his mesmerizing eyes.

"You do the same to me, Lissa, and it's an addiction I pray never to quit." He swooped in for a devastating kiss, aligning his body with hers on the plush sofa. "I can't resist you. But we do this my way. I don't want you in any pain whatsoever."

"Whatever you say... Master." She gave him a saucy smile as she read his need for domination in their shared minds. She was getting better at reading him the more they were together, though the idea that they were One still boggled her mind.

He growled and nipped her neck playfully, then worked his way down her body. They were both naked and he took full advantage, pausing to lick one pointy nipple into his mouth, then the other until she was writhing on the soft fabric.

"Please..." she moaned in need.

"Don't move." Atticus left her sensitive breasts, nipping the swell of her tummy next as he worked his way downward. Strong hands pushed her thighs apart until one foot rested over the back of the sofa, the other on the floor. Then his mouth was on her, sucking her, his tongue stroking with flickering little licks that set her on fire.

Her passion rose like a skyrocket, bursting into a little explosion even as he pushed one long finger into the slick heat that was more than ready for deeper invasion.

"Atticus!" He rode her through the tiny storm, letting the waves break only to build again, stronger than before. She could feel him holding back, letting her pleasure override his own through their bond, and she loved him for it. He was so afraid he might inadvertently hurt her. The care he showed her was a beautiful thing and she was humbled by it, but she wanted him. She didn't want to wait any longer for his possession.

Atticus growled as he sat up. "This isn't going to work." He ran one hand raggedly through his hair. The gesture was endearing considering his frustration was all because of his care for her. Lissa followed him, crawling over him until she was seated on his lap. She'd never been so aggressive in lovemaking before, but she knew he liked it. He was probably as surprised as she was by her actions, but definitely fired up as she straddled his straining erection.

"I know you wanted to do this your way, but I like my way better." She stroked his cheek with hers, rubbing against him like a cat. She felt so sexy in that moment, it was a wonder she didn't purr. The silly thought brought a smile to her lips as she licked over his firm jaw and down to his neck. Two could play the neck nibbling game, though her teeth were admittedly not up to the task the way his were. Still, the sensation of her blunt teeth over his skin seemed to inflame him.

"Harder," he urged her, when she bit down on the muscle where his neck met his strong shoulder. She obliged, noting the little dents her teeth made in his skin as she pulled back.

"I think I'm going to love biting you after you change me."

He stilled. "You really want that? You'll join me in my darkness?"

"I'll join you in the dark, in candlelight, in the ocean, in an airplane. Anywhere you are, I'll be there." She gave him a shy look from under her eyelashes, playing with him. "If you want me."

"If I want you?" He growled and flipped her over his legs,

ass up. He swatted her butt and made her squeal with pleasure. "Woman! How could you doubt it? I'll gladly join the mile high club with you. I have a friend with a very nice jet he'd be willing to loan us. Just name the date."

She giggled as he rubbed her stinging bottom, then spanked her again.

"Are you laughing at me, Lissa?" His mock outrage made her laugh harder as her breathing sped. His hand came down in sharp slaps against the fleshy part of her ass, driving her higher.

She loved it. She didn't understand it. She'd never been spanked by any man before Atticus, but with him, it just felt right...and really, really exciting.

"I asked you a question, wench."

She had to think back to remember what he'd been saying as his hand landed a few more times. She was more than hot at this point. She was steaming and ready for anything he could give her.

"Um..."

"What was that? I asked if you were laughing at me, sweetheart."

"No. No, I'm not laughing at you." She gasped as his fingers began to travel the crack of her ass, dipping within the slick heart of her to tickle and tease, making her yearn for more. "Please, Atticus! I need you now."

"Are you sure? Do you think you've been a good girl? Do you deserve a treat?"

She could have slapped him when he laughed, but she knew it was all in good fun. Still, she wasn't feeling very humorous at the moment. No, at the moment, she needed him inside her. She needed him. Period.

He toyed with her, his fingers driving her crazy—a poor substitute for what she really wanted. She wiggled and moaned, but he was merciless.

"Atticus... Please."

He finally took pity on her, lifting her up and placing her on her back, positioning her like a rag doll. He was so strong, he took her breath away. Yet he was as gentle with her as if he handled the most delicate crystal. He paused above her, his hard cock so close to where she wanted it most, but he made her look into his eyes as he braced himself above her on his elbows.

"I love you, Lissa."

Her heart melted. "I love you too." Her pledge was spoken in a whisper, stronger for its emotional depth. She felt their words ringing through the bond they shared, making it stronger. "Come to me, Atticus. I need you."

"I'll always need you," he confirmed as he took her lips and claimed her body with one smooth move. He pushed inside her, sliding easily in the thick arousal he'd caused. She moaned as she felt him slide all the way home. Where he belonged.

The ride was only just beginning. Atticus paused for just a moment as he kissed her long and deep, but soon he was thrusting in long sweeps, almost pulling out only to plunge home again, over and over. She cried out and wriggled under him as his motions drew her higher. He knew just how to move to give her the most pleasure.

That this spectacular man was all hers only heightened her passion. She'd known him such a short time, but time meant little to something as powerful as their love. Their joined souls meant they knew the core of each other's personality without even trying. They were truly One.

She felt his raging desire as a reflection of her own as he drove them both faster and higher. She clutched at his shoulders as he lowered his head, stroking his tongue over her neck as the sharp points of his fangs dropped to zing her with little pinpricks of unexpected pleasure before sinking deep into her jugular.

The moment he struck, her orgasm began and it went on

and on while he sucked at the sensitive skin of her neck. She felt him come as he pulled her essence into himself, bathing her in a wash of his pleasure. Lissa cried out at the wonder of their shared souls, their shared passion, their shared bodies. She loved this man more than anyone or anything she'd ever known and would for the rest of their days.

Atticus withdrew his teeth from her skin and licked over the wounds, sparking closure of her wounds so there was no mark left to mar her skin or betray his predilection for biting her. She was too sated to do more than follow when he lifted her over his body, changing their position so she'd be more comfortable as her eyes closed and sleep overtook her.

"I've been granted a miracle, Lissa. I love you more than life and I'll never let you go. Never." He kissed her temple as he settled her over his heart.

The last thing she heard as she drifted off was his words of love. She slept against her mate with a smile curving her lips.

Much later, Atticus placed calls to both the resort and the police, spinning a tale about how Lissa had just shown up on his doorstep out of the blue. Atticus brought her to the bedroom he kept above ground and gave her some of his clothes to wear. She had just enough time to clean up while an ambulance was summoned. His shirt was too large for her as she emerged from the bathroom of the master suite and she looked adorable in it.

"They'll be here soon, my love. Undoubtedly, they'll want you to go to the hospital, maybe even keep you there until tomorrow." He took her hand, drawing her down to sit beside him on the downy bed. "I regret I cannot go with you, but it wouldn't make much sense to the authorities. I don't want to raise any sort of suspicion. Plus, it's bound to take a while for them to reassure themselves that you're all right. Likely they won't let me be near you while they run their tests and it could take all night." He shrugged. "The police will likely want to take my statement and check my land, so I'll need to be here to show them around. I could cloud their minds, of course, and the people at the hospital, but crowds are tricky. If I miss even one mind, I could be putting us both in danger of discovery. It's safer for me to remain here, all things considered. Being caught out in the sun is dangerous for my kind, as it will be for you once you are turned."

She smiled, assuring him of her love. "I'll enjoy the sun for a few days yet, but I won't miss it too much, if I can have you in return."

"You'll always have me, my love." He drew her knuckles to his lips in a gentle kiss. "Once you square things away with the hotel, I want you to come back to me. Tomorrow night, I want you to lie beside me, here, in our home."

"I want the same thing, Atticus. I'll get my stuff from the hotel and be knocking on your door right as the sun goes down."

He drew away to reach into his trouser pocket, producing a set of keys as they both stood. "You don't ever have to knock. What's mine is yours. This is your house too. You will make it a home as it has never been...until now." He pressed the ring of keys into her palm, closing her fingers around the cold metal while her eyes filled with tears.

She hugged him close, burying her face against his chest. He held her for long moments, until at last, he heard the buzzer that indicated a vehicle was at the gate leading to his estate.

"They're here."

"I know." She pulled away with a sad expression on her lovely face. "But I don't want to leave you."

"I will be near, Lissa. Wherever you go, from now until eternity, all you have to do is reach out with your mind and I'll be there. We are One. In time, we'll learn how to manage the joining better, but for now, just think of me and I will be with you."

"Same goes for me, Atticus."

She drew back and they walked from the bedroom, down a

long hall and into the main area of the house. Atticus flicked a button on the way, releasing the gate so the authorities could make their way up the drive. They'd have to act like mere acquaintances while the humans sniffed around their home. Atticus had lived long enough to know when the wiser course of action was to play by human rules and this was one of those times.

His new mate was human and had family and friends. They had to be careful how they managed her conversion so she could keep her human contacts for at least the length of her normal lifespan. After sufficient years had passed, they could reinvent themselves, as Atticus had done many times in the past. It was tricky to manage turning a human without cutting them off from all previous ties, but for Lissa, he would do anything. She deserved to keep her friends and family in her life and he wouldn't make her chose between them and him—if a true mate really had a choice. He knew full well, she didn't. Neither did he. They were destined for each other.

The police car came into view and Atticus went to meet them at the door. He paused before opening the portal, turning to look at her as she climbed under a blanket he'd spread on the wide couch.

"I love you more than I can ever express."

Her eyes filled again as her gaze met his. "Me too, Atticus." She sniffed, wiping her eyes with the back of one hand as she pulled the cover up to her chin. "Let's get this over with. The sooner I leave, the sooner I can return...to you."

"Atticus?"

"Here, my love." His deep voice purred through their shared minds. *"How are you holding up?"*

"They've got me in a private room. Things have quieted down a bit, but I had a few X-rays, plus a team of doctors checking me over in the emergency room. I think they're satisfied that I'm okay. As you suspected, they admitted me for the night. A nurse

is supposed to wake me up every hour to check my eyes or something."

"They're probably concerned about the bump on your head. Does it hurt?"

"Not much. But you were right to leave a little bit of the damage from the crash. They're already marveling over how well I came through the wreck that killed everybody else."

"I'm sorry I had to leave a single mark on your beautiful body, but we have to be careful if you want to continue to live your current life."

"I appreciate all the thought and effort you've put into this, Atticus. I love my family and friends, but I love you more, especially for going out of your way to preserve my relationships with them. You're a special, amazing man and I can't believe you're in my life."

"Same here, my love. And of course we need your family and friends, otherwise who will we invite to our wedding?"

She paused, the flavor of her shock, delight and awe coming through loud and clear. "You want to marry me?"

"Oh, yes. A wedding like you've always dreamed of, Lissa. With all the trimmings, including a big bridal party. I guess I'll have to come up with groomsmen to balance out your old college friends, eh?" His chuckle sounded through their minds. "But we'll have to have an evening wedding, of course."

"I can't believe it."

"Believe it, my love. I never thought to marry, and in the eyes of my people, we are already mated, but I know from your thoughts how important this is to you. I want you to have the ceremony and the reception of your dreams. That is, if you'll consent to be my wife. Sorry, I should have asked that first. Will you marry me, Lissa, and make me the happiest of men?"

"Yes! Yes, I'd be delighted to marry you, Atticus. I love you."

"Hold that thought, love, for this evening. Dawn approaches and I must seek shelter for the day. Will you be all right today?"

"I'll be fine. They let me call my friend Jena. She's a doctor. She should be here any minute, though she's not on staff at this hospital. She'll gather the rest of the group and they'll take good care of me. I'll get my things from the hotel and be at your place as soon as I can ditch my friends."

"Our place, Lissa. This vineyard is your home now too. Or we could move someplace else if you want. I'll live anywhere, as long as you're there."

"I know how much you love the vineyard, Atticus. That you'd be willing to give it up for me means a lot, but there's no need. The place is a dream. The house is lovely and the grounds are gorgeous. I'll be happy living there...with you."

"Good. Then hurry home, love. I'll be awaiting your return."

Jena entered Lissa's hospital room shortly after dawn, waking Lissa with her presence. Not long after Jena assured herself that Lissa really would be all right, their friend Kelly arrived with a change of clothes for when the doctors sprung Lissa later that morning. As Lissa had predicted, the troops were rallied and her friends circled around her, taking turns sitting with her and talking until the doctors let her go with a few words of instruction and a bottle of pain relievers.

Over their objections, Lissa had her friends take her first to the resort to collect her bags, which had been sent ahead. That accomplished, they took her home and stayed for lunch. Lissa laid the groundwork for her new relationship with Atticus by telling them of her plan to visit the man who'd rescued her, to return his shirt.

"Should you be driving after that knock on the skull?" Kelly wanted to know.

"The doctors said I'm fine, right, Jena?" Lissa turned her gaze on the doctor and Jena had to admit she was right. "Besides, I'm just going to drop off the shirt he let me use. Believe me, if you'd seen this man, you'd want to do the same."

"He's that good looking?" Jena asked as she poured tea for

them all in Lissa's small kitchen.

"Better," Lissa said with a grin. "His name is Atticus Maxwell and he has lovely, mysterious eyes."

"Maxwell? *The* Atticus Maxwell who owns the most exclusive winery in the entire valley? They say he's a bit of a recluse, and eccentric too, though he bottles some of the best wine in the country—maybe even the world. It's won all kinds of awards," Kelly said with surprise widening her eyes. "Honey, he's one of the richest men in the valley. You showed up on *his* doorstep?"

"I didn't know whose house it was. It was just the first one I saw after walking away from the accident in a daze."

"You were very lucky, Lissa. And blessed. Somebody upstairs was watching over you." Jena's voice dropped to a hushed whisper. "I'm so glad you're okay."

A group hug followed and soon after, Lissa was able to usher her friends out the door of her apartment with promises to call the next day, or sooner, if she needed anything. Lissa set about packing her belongings, but only a few. She couldn't do anything too obvious yet. Atticus had cautioned her that they had to move slowly. But she filled a suitcase with clothes and shoes, taking a few mementoes that she wanted to have with her at his house. She watered her plants and closed up the apartment so it would be okay for a few days. It was unlikely she'd be back anytime soon. She wanted to spend every moment with Atticus and she knew he felt the same.

She threw the suitcase into the trunk of her car and headed out of town toward Atticus's place in the valley, about an hour away. He'd given her the keys and codes for the alarm system and gate. She didn't feel like a visitor or trespasser when she let herself into the big house. Instead, she felt very much as if she were coming home.

Lissa made dinner for herself in the sparkling clean kitchen. Atticus had a few canned goods and packaged foods in his cupboards, though she knew he didn't need to eat. Like many things about the giant house, it was stocked for the occasional mortal guest and designed to give Atticus every appearance of normalcy. His kind lived in secret and had for centuries. Atticus had explained earlier about the lengths he'd gone to give every appearance of being a normal man and there was no doubt he'd become very good at putting up a façade of mortality.

The kitchen was a dream—big and airy with every modern convenience—as was the rest of the house. She loved the Mission style furniture and earth tones that dominated most of the décor. She gave herself a tour of the above-ground rooms, pleased to find an art studio, a small home gym and a very busy-looking office. He found her there, while she was perusing his calendar, which was lying open on the desk.

She sensed him even before his muscular arm snaked around her waist from behind, drawing her back against his hard chest. Warm lips traced the skin under her ear with just a hint of pointed teeth scraping against her, making her hotter than she'd ever been for any other man.

"Good morrow, my love." His deep voice sounded near her ear, sending shivers down her spine.

"Atticus." His name was a sigh of pleasure as he cupped one of her breasts, tugging and exciting her every nerve.

"I love to hear you say my name just that way." His warm chuckle skittered along her senses as he turned her in his arms. "Waking up to you in our home is a miracle, Lissa. One I never thought I would experience. I feel as if heaven is smiling on me for the first time in many long years."

The kiss they shared then was one of coming home, of undreamed of love, of safety and hope. Lissa didn't know how much time had passed when Atticus finally released her lips, but her head was spinning and she had to hold on to him for balance. He'd made her dizzy with just his kiss.

"How do you like the house?" He moved further back, once he seemed sure she was steady on her feet. "I sensed your pleasure as you toured earlier, but as we're new to this joining, I thought we'd start slowly."

"How so?" She perched on the edge of his desk, since he seemed to want to talk.

"I have a lot more experience traipsing through people's minds than you, my dear." He gave her a sly smile. "I thought it best to give each other a little room to interact as any normal mortal couple would...in the beginning at least...when we're not making love. When I'm inside your body, I can't help but want to be in your mind as well."

Lissa remembered the way they'd joined the night before and shivered. There was nothing that could compare with the way they'd shared minds and bodies in the ultimate pleasure.

"I agree." She tried to smile, but her mouth was dry from the heat of her memories. "And I'll admit it's hard to get used to the idea of sharing our minds. I'm a little psychic, but I've only ever gotten the odd premonition here and there. I've never been able to read someone's thoughts, though it was rumored my grandmother could."

"Really?" Atticus seemed intrigued. "She must have been an amazing woman. Even without trying to enter your mind, I can feel the love and respect you have for her. Keeping the connection partially blocked will help us when we need to act normally in the company of mortals. Your friends, for example. At some point, I'll need to meet them."

Lissa laughed, thinking how her buddies would drool over Atticus. It wouldn't be too hard to convince them she'd fallen head over heels for the man in such a short amount of time.

"Give it a week or two. I have a standing dinner with the group a week from Wednesday. We get together every month to share gossip. I'll start getting them used to the idea that we're an item then."

"I see you've been giving this some thought as well." Atticus's approval washed over her senses. She'd never been all that empathic before, but she could feel his emotions, even if she wasn't directly reading his thoughts. "As for my friends," he lifted the calendar from the desk, "you'll meet one tonight. I've asked the Master to come meet you, since it's such a rare occurrence that one of us finds his mate. Marc and I have been friends a long time. You'll like him."

"You really call him Master?"

"Sometimes. It is his title, since he rules the bloodletters in this region. I'm in the hierarchy as well. I'm his second, actually. We have a small circle of friends, all of whom rank highly in the supernatural hierarchy hereabouts, but Marc is our leader. Hence the title of Master. But he's a good man. Not at all lord-of-the-manor. You'll see. I think you'll like him. He's got a wickedly sharp sense of humor."

She felt the genuine affection Atticus had for the other man and was intrigued. There was a devilish sparkle in his eye when he spoke of this "Master" that boded well. If Atticus liked him, chances were, she would too. They were aligned like that. Perhaps because they were mates.

Lissa felt cheated that they didn't have time to make love before Marc arrived, but as Atticus told her, it was better to get the formalities out of the way before they got too distracted. They would spend the rest of the night caught up in each other, she knew. And Atticus was talking in terms of centuries together, which still overwhelmed her. They would have time.

Marc LaTour was handsome as sin and sharp as a tack. He greeted Atticus with a backslapping hug and then turned his arresting, assessing gaze on Lissa. She wanted to squirm under his inspection until she saw the very real awe in his expression. He seemed genuinely happy for Atticus and at the same time a little afraid of her. That dichotomy made her want to put him at ease.

Atticus poured wine for them all and Marc raised a toast to them. "I'm happy for you both," Marc said, sitting at ease in the cozy living room. "Between us, Lissa, I was growing concerned for my friend Atticus. He took chances he shouldn't have in recent years. Hopefully with you here, he'll be more careful. I value his friendship."

"As I value yours, my friend." Atticus tipped his wineglass in Marc's direction. "But please don't frighten my mate. All that matters now is that she *is* here and we are together. What came before matters not."

Lissa placed her hand over his, drawing his attention. "What came before made you what you are, Atticus, and I love every part of you. But you can rest assured," she transferred her attention to Marc, "there will be no more taking chances with his life. That carelessness is over."

She could see hints of the things he'd allowed to happen, the desolation in his life that led him to that shuttle bus and to the brink of death. Even with their connection moderated by his incredible psychic control, she knew he'd been near the end of his rope, but now that they'd found each other, his entire outlook had taken a radical turn.

"And glad I am to hear it." Marc stood, helping himself to a second glass of wine from the sideboard, clearly at home in Atticus's house. "But I have some news I must impart that makes it even more critical. I hesitate to say this in front of you, Lissa, for I don't mean to worry you, but as new mates, I've heard there's no way to really keep you from knowing what he knows, so..." Marc shrugged elegantly. Everything about the man was both devilish and suave.

Atticus sat forward. "What is it?"

"Ian looked over the accident site and the vehicle wreckage at my request. When he reported back at sunset, I went over there myself before coming here. Atticus, that was no accident, though the mortals will no doubt rule it as such. There was the faint scent of magic around the vehicle. I have no doubt it was tampered with."

"What flavor of magic? *Were*? Mortal? Fey? Or something else?" The rigidity in Atticus's spine and his narrow-eyed gaze alerted Lissa to the seriousness of the situation. She felt a hint of disbelief at their casual use of the term "magic", but then, she hadn't believed in vampires until a day ago either.

"It was something very old, indeed." Marc's eyes took on a faraway cast as he seemed to search for an answer. "It felt fey, but not quite. And ancient. It's something just tickling my memory, but I'm not altogether certain I've ever run across this particular kind of thing before. It's damned odd, to say the least. Ian's organizing surveillance in case the magic-user returns to the scene of the crime."

"Who were they targeting? Do you have any idea?"

"That's the hard part. The magic wasn't attuned to our kind, but neither was it attuned to any particular mortal that either Ian or I could discern. Plus we were working with only traces. Whoever cast the spell was skilled. Very skilled indeed."

"Nobody knew I was on that bus. It was a last minute decision on my part to go up to the resort. There were only a few other passengers—all mortal. Love," Atticus turned to Lissa, "you said you felt something as you boarded. Tell Marc what you felt. It might help solve this puzzle."

Lissa put her wineglass on the low table. "If you like." She turned to Marc and tried to put into words the feelings of dread that had hit her when she set foot on that shuttle bus. "There was a strong urge not to board, but it was generalized. I couldn't be sure, and the moment I saw Atticus, he intrigued me. Distracted me really." She sent Atticus a soft, teasing smile. "From him, I felt a different kind of energy—like I had just met my fate." Atticus squeezed her hand in encouragement. "The two instincts were in conflict, but my desire to follow Atticus was stronger than the feelings of dread."

"Thank heaven for that," Marc said with feeling that surprised her. "If you hadn't been on board and survived the crash, I doubt my good friend would still be among the living. No," he held up a hand to stall Atticus's response, "don't object. I've sensed what was in your heart for months, brother. Without your One, you were nearly lost to us. Fate plays a bigger hand than we know. You were on that shuttle bus for a reason, Lissa, though you knew it was dangerous, you boarded anyway. That is significant."

"You think so?" The idea was startling to her, but it felt right.

"I do. I also think, until we know more about who and what caused the crash, you both need to be careful. It's unclear who the target was, but that wreck was no accident and quite a few innocents paid the price."

Lissa was struck with renewed sadness at the reminder of the loss of life. That she'd survived when everyone else died was nothing less than a miracle. A miracle named Atticus. And if Marc was to be believed, if she'd succumbed to her injuries, Atticus would have had no reason to save himself. They would both be dead.

The idea that someone deliberately caused the wreck by magical means was nearly overwhelming, but she'd been exposed to a number of strange happenings in her life. The existence of vampires was only the latest—and admittedly most astounding—of many odd things she'd seen. The idea that magic was real was somewhat easier to accept, given her recent experiences.

"You think whoever did that might have meant it for one of us?" Lissa's eyes widened at the thought. "I don't have any enemies that I'm aware of. Particularly not of the magical kind."

"I'm sorry, my dear, but you yourself said you were psychic. Certain beings would have been able to sense your power and some might even target you because of it. The supernatural world is a more brutal place than your mortal one sometimes. We try to preserve a delicate balance between those of us who would leave humanity to their own devices and those who would seek to dominate and even enslave them. And there are even a few groups of mortals who are aware of certain aspects of the supernatural world and seek to eradicate it. If someone knew of your abilities, you could very easily have been the target of the magical tampering."

Lissa held one palm over her racing heart. "I can't believe it."

Atticus squeezed her other hand, turning toward her on the couch. "But you must, my love. You must believe that the threat could be to either of us and act accordingly. For starters, I want you to move in here. We'll go over to your apartment together and retrieve your things."

"But not tonight." Marc interrupted Atticus and stood to leave. "Ian is coordinating surveillance on Lissa's apartment and a few other places. I want to know who the target of the wreck was and why. Tipping our hand too early might cause them to scurry away. If one of you is still being targeted, we'll find out. The vineyard is well protected, but Lissa's place is not. It makes sense for you to stay here then, milady, though it might seem odd to your mortal friends. You'll have to inform them of a whirlwind romance and perhaps an impulsive wedding can be planned? You two can decide how to best handle that, but leave the dangerous part to me."

"I hardly know what to say." Lissa was at a loss. Marc was indeed a powerful man with a dominant way that she'd never encountered. Atticus was the strongest man she'd ever met. Before meeting him, she'd never dreamed the kind of man she fantasized about even existed. Atticus was perfect for her, but Marc...he was every bit as handsome, commanding and powerful as her new mate, though without the soft side that tempered her lover. He was formidable.

"Stay with your mate and be happy, milady. Let me handle the threat—if there is, indeed, any. We may come to find that another was the target and now that he or she is dead, the threat may vanish. Either way, it is far better to be safe than sorry."

Atticus rose and stretched his hand out for a brotherly shake. "I can't thank you enough, Marc. Lissa's safety is the most important thing in the world to me."

Marc nodded once. "Understandable. Even admirable. I envy you, my friend, and I aim to see that nothing threatens your future happiness. I'll be in touch when I know more. For now, rest here and stay safe."

They saw Marc to the door and Lissa was impressed by the low-slung, shiny black sports car he drove. That car had to cost more than ten years of rent on her apartment in the city and it purred like a big cat. These men—these vampires—were wealthy sons of guns.

Chapter Four

Atticus locked up the house, arming the security systems and making certain all was as safe as he could make it. They had hours until sunrise and he wanted to spend many of them making love to his new mate. But before they let passion carry them away, they had some planning to do.

He led her toward the indoor pool housed on the back side of the house. It had a glass roof that he could open to the night sky in warm weather. The pool was surrounded by lush, tropical plants and had a small waterfall to make it look and feel like a naturally occurring grotto in some exotic destination.

"This is gorgeous at night. I saw it earlier today, but it's even more beautiful now." Lissa moved toward one of the large bird of paradise plants and stroked its leaves as she gazed out over the water.

"I'm glad you like it. I spend a lot of time out here, stargazing and contemplating the infinite." He moved to the small bar and poured two glasses of deep red wine. Replacing the bottle, he brought them toward the plush lounge chairs nearby. She sat and accepted one of the glasses, before he took the space next to her on the wide chaise. "Now, of course, I can sit out here and ponder you."

She laughed and sipped at the wine, smiling at him over the rim of the crystal glass. He wanted to make love to her right then and there, but they had a few things left to discuss first. He could wait. But not too long.

He put one arm around her as they leaned against the low back of the long chair, putting their feet up. He'd never been so comfortable in his entire existence.

"Do you think your friends will accept that I swept you off your feet so quickly?" Atticus had seen the close relationship Lissa had with the small group of women she'd befriended in college while sifting through her memories during their initial joining. He kept the mental block between their minds in place for now, because he knew it was more comfortable for her to learn him slowly—and they truly had eternity to do so. He'd savor this time of learning her as she got used to him and his abilities.

"After they meet you, I think they'll understand." Her sexy tone teased him. Tantalized him. But they had to talk first, before he lost all caution and reason.

"I'd prefer to elope, but I know you want to have your friends at the wedding. How about we plan a ceremony for here at the vineyard? The grounds are beautiful at night. We could dress it up a bit with candlelight and soft music."

"Sounds perfect. And when they see the setting, they'll understand why we're holding the ceremony at night. It's so much more romantic."

"I hoped you would think so. I'll start the preparations with my staff as soon as it's feasible."

"You have a staff? Do any of them know what you are?"

"No, my dear. We keep our secret as close as possible. My on-site employees in the production areas don't come to the house. It's fenced off for privacy and they know not to trespass on my eccentric wish to be left alone. I have a business office in the city. I go there sometimes—especially in the winter, when night falls earlier—for late meetings with the marketing staff. I also make appearances at charity dinners and such, keeping up the appearance of a wealthy businessman who works for fun and not necessarily every day. I have something of a playboy reputation which helps explain why I work from home and am seldom seen during the day. Once in a while, I'll brave the daylight and hold a meeting here in the media room. It's on the interior of the house and safe from the sun. I designed it so the interior core of the house is accessible without having to pass near rooms with windows. All exterior rooms open onto a hall that separates the interior sections and allows me to move about without difficulty during the day."

"Then you don't have to sleep all day?"

"Like anyone, I do need some sleep, and I'm lethargic during the day, but I can stay up if necessary. It's not the easiest thing, but I am ancient, my dear. Over time, I've gained abilities my younger brethren cannot claim. I can be awake during the day and can even stand low levels of indirect sunlight for short periods, every once in a while. I don't dare go out of the house during the day, but I can always invite people here. Though I admit, I do look tired. My rare mortal guests probably attribute the circles under my eyes and the occasional giant yawn to my carousing lifestyle." He chuckled.

"You like having that bad boy reputation, don't you?"

He pretended innocence, enjoying her teasing. "It's a cross I must bear."

She turned in his embrace to face him. "Well no more, Atticus. You're a reformed rake now, and you'll be spending every night with me. Newlyweds are allowed a lot of leeway. I'll keep up the illusion around the house during the day—at least until I become...like you." She drew back to look up into his eyes. "Speaking of which, I want you to do it on our wedding night. I want it to be my wedding gift to you."

The very idea stole his breath. That she'd be so willing to give up the sun for him was humbling. Atticus kissed her, unable to put his thoughts into words and needing to express his undying love in the most elemental way.

He lowered her to the plush padding of the overstuffed chaise, coming over her in a way that made her feel delicate and cherished. He had such a commanding presence, he overwhelmed her in many ways, but it was a delicious sensation and one she was surprised to discover she really enjoyed.

Atticus pulled back, smiling down at her. "So you like being my woman, eh?"

Lissa blushed as she realized their thoughts were twining as closely as their limbs. At times like these, the mental barrier Atticus held in place between them broke down. She felt his delight with the thoughts running through her head about his possessive actions. She also read the naughty images he sent her way—images of submission and tantalizing pleasure she'd only dreamed of to this point.

She considered herself a widely read woman and had even delved into a few erotic works of fiction. Some of the things that had intrigued her in those books surfaced in her mind as she saw the vivid images in her mate's mind. He'd done more than just read about those things, though he was cautious enough to withhold specific memories of other women from her. It was a wise decision on his part, considering their position.

Still, the thought of his vast experience rankled. Compared to him she was the next thing to a virgin.

"But I like virgins." Atticus leered at her in a comical way and she had to join him in laughter, punching his arm in a playful way. "Shall we play school girl and lecherous uncle? Or harem girl and sultan? Name your pleasure, sweet, and it shall be yours."

Unbidden, an image formed in her mind, even as her cheeks heated. His eyes flared with heat as he moved over her with predatory motions. She was his captive, and they both knew it.

"Ah, I see. You want to play captured lady and pirate rogue." He grinned and she could've sworn his eyes gleamed in the semi-darkness of the grotto. He looked around for a moment as if considering his options. "The setting is perfect, don't you think? I've taken you prisoner and we're hiding out in the lee of some Caribbean island. I like the way your mind works, my dear."

"Well it is rather...tropical in here."

"And you've read a good many pirate books, haven't you?" He winked at her. "I'll have to investigate some of those tomes. Purely for research purposes, you understand."

She laughed. "I'd be delighted to assist with your...uh...research." He swooped in to nibble on her neck playfully, then retreated with an abruptness that left her gasping.

Atticus stood and offered her a hand up from the lounge chair. She followed where he led, more than willing to let him guide her in this secret fantasy.

He tugged her into his arms and looked down into her eyes, suddenly serious. "I'll spend the rest of my days fulfilling all of your fantasies, my love, as you've already fulfilled mine, just by existing and being here with me."

"You say the sweetest things, Atticus." She stood on tiptoe to place a gentle kiss on his lips.

When she pulled back, he bent and scooped her into his arms, carrying her toward the lush foliage surrounding the well-camouflaged pool. He made a beeline for a young palm tree that had numerous vines growing around it.

"You're my captive, milady," he said as he dumped her onto her feet and placed her back to the tree. He tugged one of the vines free and used it to tie her hands behind her back around the tree. "In short, you're mine. Best get used to it."

Leaning back, it wasn't uncomfortable. The tree supported her and the vines were strong, but soft against her skin. A few quick tugs told her it wouldn't be easy to get out of the bindings. The vines were stronger than they looked.

Atticus backed off slightly, surveying her. She was wearing a lightweight cotton dress that was like many she owned. This one had buttons down the front, all the way to the hem.

"A real pirate would tear that pretty dress off your luscious young body," Atticus mused. "But we haven't any spare female clothing aboard and I don't like my men lusting after what's mine. They'll do that enough just having you here. No need to make it worse by having you traipse around naked."

He was getting into this role and Lissa found it easy to believe he might've once been a pirate. As the thought flashed across her mind, she saw a tall ship in his thoughts.

"You *were* a pirate!"

"You'll soon discover that once a pirate, my dear..." he winked at her and tugged at the bodice of her dress, "...always a pirate."

He made short work of her dress, unbuttoning it completely and pushing it down her shoulders to tangle on her bound arms. She wore a bra and panties beneath. The bra had a front closure, so it followed the dress, sliding down her arms and getting stuck about halfway to bunch between her shoulders and the tree. The panties, he slid down her legs, kneeling before her as he lifted first one foot and then the other to remove them completely. With a devilish grin, he tucked the pink satin into his pocket, and remained on his knees before her.

Lissa shifted on her feet, uncertain. He had that pirate gleam in his eyes again.

"Atticus?"

"You're to call me captain, wench!"

Lissa jumped at the steel edge in his voice. He was staring at her crotch. When she noted the direction of his interest, he licked his lips, making her squirm. Reaching out, he slid one hand between her thighs, coaxing them apart. That hand rose up the inside of her thigh, tickling, teasing, tantalizing, until it reached the soft curls at their apex. He pet her then, watching her reactions as she trembled.

"Do you like this, wench?" Atticus slid one finger into her folds, stroking the nubbin that was already excited and awaiting his pleasure—and hers.

"Yes, captain."

"Say 'aye'," he corrected her in a throaty purr.

"Aye, captain."

"Good girl." He stroked her more firmly in reward, making her gasp. His fingers moved deeper into her secret folds, spreading, testing and pinching her with practiced finesse. "You're very wet, lass," he observed. "I think you've done this before, haven't you? I'll lay odds you're not virgin. Tell me, has your sniveling betrothed back in England been in here?" He rammed two fingers into her wet hole. "Has he had his cock in this wet pussy? *My* pussy?"

"No!" she keened, her head rolling from side to side against the trunk of the tree as he pulsed in and out of her tight core with his fingers.

"No?" He didn't let up, but redoubled his efforts. "Then who was it? The footman?" She continued to shake her head. "The stable lad?" He pushed her harder, driving her higher. "The deck hand on the ship I took you from?"

Lissa climaxed on his hand, unable to stop herself. She came in a rush, gasping for air as he watched in approval.

"Ah, so it was the deck hand after all. Tell me, milady, did you like it? Did he make you come like I just did? Or was it a fast screw against the wall?" He took his fingers from her core, but moved closer, using both hands to spread her lips wide. "Did he lick you like this?" Dipping his head, he made her gasp as his tongue licked over her clit, stirring her passions once again. He ruled her pleasure. It was as if her body knew only his touch and would respond to him in ways it had never responded for any other.

He delved deeper with his tongue. She could feel his teeth beginning to elongate into the fangs that would pierce her skin and bring the brightest climax she'd ever known. He was gentle, but firm, and careful with those sharp fangs. He gave her just enough, never too much, but always just the right stimulation at the right time.

"Such are the benefits of sharing our thoughts," he said in

her mind as he continued to drive her passions upward once again. *"And now it's time to fulfill the rest of this little fantasy."* He drew away just as she would have peaked, shaking his head and clicking his tongue in disapproval.

"You're a greedy wench, aren't you? With a greedy pussy that needs to learn who its new master is. Get on your knees, girl!"

Lissa was confused at first, but managed to sink onto her knees, her arms still drawn behind her around the tree, her dress pooled around her and under her knees, providing some padding. By necessity, her legs were spread, her ankles finding space on either side of the wide trunk.

When she looked up from securing her position, Atticus had undone his pants and was using one hand to stroke his hard cock, hovering just in front of her face. He smiled that devilish smile at her and she was lost.

"I can see you want this, wench. Tell me, did you suck your deck hand's cock? Did he give it to you day and night?"

"Aye, captain," she said boldly. It was time she started participating in this fantasy, she decided. Maybe there was a way to turn the tables on her lover. Eyeing him with a new, saucy attitude, she looked forward to trying.

"Naughty wench." He chuckled as he stepped forward, placing the tip of his cock against her lips. "You know what to do with this then. Swallow me down, girl, and do your best. If you please me, I'll go easy with the lash."

He'd surprised her with that last bit. Was he going to whip her? The thought should have sent her running for the hills, but coming from Atticus, the threat made her hot. There was something seriously wrong with her, but it felt too good to worry about it now as she opened her mouth and took him deep.

Atticus groaned when she used her tongue on him. She teased the crown of his impressive erection, licking and sucking until he was ready to come. She felt the tremble in his limbs, but he refused her. He pulled from her mouth with an audible popping sound as she sucked hard to the last second. She was disappointed, but it was forgotten when he reached behind her and released the vines holding her wrists and untangled the dress and bra to let them fall to the ground.

He lifted her to her feet and turned her around to face the tree trunk.

"Hold on, wench. I promised you the lash and the lash you'll get for being such a disobedient tart."

"What did I do, captain? I'll be a good girl. I promise." She was getting into the fantasy as he pressed her nude body against the rough bark of the palm.

"You gave your virginity to some slobbering deck hand. You gave away what was mine, wench." He used the vine to smack her bare back. It stung, but it didn't hurt too bad. Lissa was shocked to feel her arousal, which had faded a little while she pleasured him, return tenfold. "You need to learn your place and how to please me, wench." Another lash with the ropey vine landed on her backside, stinging the soft flesh and making her hotter.

"From this day forward you will fuck only me. And those I give you to," he added as an afterthought before the next blow landed on her upper thighs.

"You'll give me to others, captain?" she couldn't help but ask.

"Impertinent wench. Do not think to question me. That's earned you another lash." And the blow landed in the middle of her back, lighter than the others, but just as exciting. "You won't question me again, wench. If I tell you to suck my first mate's cock while I fuck you from behind, you'll do it and no question. Do you understand?" Another blow landed while he awaited her answer.

She was gasping with excitement by the time she managed to answer. "Aye, captain."

"And you'll spread your legs for any man I choose to give you to while I watch, whether it be my first mate or my cabin boy. Do you hear me, wench?"

"Yes!" she shouted when he landed the next blow right over the crease of her ass.

"And you'll take me up the ass while the cabin boy licks your pussy if I ask it, won't you, lass?" He used the vine differently this time, bending it in half and riding it up the inside of her thighs, pressing hard against her pussy as she rubbed all over the tree, the vine, anything she could to give satisfaction to the flame burning her alive from the inside out.

"Aye, captain!" She cried out as he pulled the vine away and lifted her by the waist, positioning her on her hands and knees in front of the palm. In less than a minute he was pushing inside her, thrusting deep from behind.

"You're a feisty wench, love, but I'll tame you. You're mine, do you understand?"

"Yes!" She cried out as he pulsed within her, stroking deep and fast and hard, just the way she needed it. She was so close, it would take little to push her over the edge of the most intense arousal she'd ever known.

"Say it, wench! Say you're mine." He bit down on her neck from behind, taking her blood and stealing her sanity.

She screamed as she came, hurtling toward the stars in an explosion of passion unlike anything that had come before and took Atticus along with her. She felt the wet spurts of his climax as she twined her mind with his, experiencing his bliss as she shared her own.

"I'm yours."

They stayed that way, both panting and basking in the glow of a magnificent climax for a long time before Atticus stepped back. He lifted her in his arms and took her over to a chaise lounge off to one side. They lay there together for long minutes, basking in the afterglow of the most glorious love she'd ever made. The wide chaise lounge was soft under her bare body and Atticus was warm against her.

"Were you really a pirate?"

Atticus chuckled in reply. "Until recently, passage by sea was the only way to get from one continent to another. So, yes, I've sailed, but it wasn't a profession or way of life for me. Spending the daylight hours in the hold was often uncomfortable and hard to explain."

"I hadn't thought about that. Is it so hard? To live without the sun?"

"Sometimes it's the most difficult thing in the world. But sometimes...like now, since I found you, I wouldn't trade my existence for anything. You are my sunshine, Lissa. All else matters not."

"I love you, Atticus." She kissed his cheek and rested her head against his chest, closing her eyes, secure in his love. She drifted to sleep dreaming of the life they would have together.

Chapter Five

"How's the job search going, Kel?" Jena asked over crisp noodles in a local Chinese restaurant. Lissa and her friends were having dinner together, as they had every few weeks since college. The old group had stuck together remarkably well over the years after graduation. Their married friend, Christy, had even managed to make their dinner this month, though she was subdued as usual. Carly, owner of a small but successful software company, sat next to her, picking at appetizers as the conversation focused on Kelly.

"Not good," Kelly responded, dunking a noodle in duck sauce. "It's the wrong time of year to get a teaching job. If only that other teacher hadn't decided at the last minute to come back from maternity leave. The school bent over backwards to accommodate her and hung me out to dry."

"That stinks," Carly said as she sipped her iced tea.

"You got a raw deal there," Jena agreed as the waiter brought their entrees.

"How's it going at the hospital? Did you get the cut in hours you wanted?" Lissa asked Jena after the waiter had gone.

"We made a compromise. I get more on-call time and less on-duty time, but the hours are still about the same. Killer. I think it'll be next year before I can really scale back the hospital obligations and pay more attention to my private patients."

"You know, even when you own your own company, it's hard to scale back." Carly sighed as she sat back in her chair and looked at her friends with weary eyes. "I'm thinking of taking a breather from the installations."

This was big news. Lissa knew all about Carly's work, designing and installing custom software packages. The job took her all over the country and she'd be away on an installation for weeks at a time. Lissa thought Carly had enjoyed the work and the travel, but she could see the lines of fatigue around her friend's eyes and the shadows beneath.

"You work too hard, Carly. I think it's a good thing to delegate some of the work to the people you hired. That's why you hired them after all." Jena wasn't shy with her opinions.

Carly nodded. "I think you're right, but it isn't that easy to get out of entanglements. I've got one more contract I have to work on myself out in Wyoming. I liked the area when I went to make the proposal. Maybe I'll stay there for a while and get away from it all."

"Sounds like a good idea," Lissa said, though this was the first time Carly had spoken about moving to another part of the country. Still, it didn't sound like she planned to stay there permanently. An extended vacation would be good for her.

They talked a bit more about their respective occupations, but Lissa kept mostly silent while the others griped. She had to break her news at just the right moment and was worried about how to phrase it, though she'd been rehearsing this scene for days in her mind.

"So what's new with you, Lis? Any more news on that hunky guy who saved your life?" Carly asked. She'd been filled in on the whole scenario, though she'd been away on a job when Lissa had been in the wreck.

"Actually," Lissa patted her lips with the napkin and realized her time had come, "I have quite a bit of news on that front. He asked me to move in with him."

Exclamations sounded from around the table. Some were disbelieving, some excited, but all were surprised. Lissa had been so caught up in Atticus these last days, she hadn't spared a whole lot of time talking to any of her friends except to reassure them that she was healing well when they called to check on her injuries.

"Well, are you?" Kelly wanted to know.

"This is kind of sudden, isn't it?" Jena, ever the most levelheaded of the group, seemed suspicious.

"Actually, I've been spending a lot of time with him since that first day I got home from the hospital. He's...um...I'm in love with him and he loves me too. We're going to get married and I want you all to be bridesmaids." The words came out in an excited rush.

Squeals of delight drew attention from around the restaurant as her friends jumped from their seats to clobber her with awkward hugs. Jena still seemed skeptical, but congratulated her along with the rest. They talked more about Lissa's news and the plans she and Atticus had made so far for the wedding.

Lissa was careful to explain that Atticus worked odd hours and would probably be available for a dinner one night soon to meet them all. In fact, she told them, he'd asked her to arrange a dinner party at the vineyard so her friends could see where she would be living.

Atticus and Lissa had discussed the plan at length. While the vineyard was kept private and as secure as possible, Atticus didn't think letting her friends visit under controlled conditions would be too much of a problem. They agreed to ease her friends into the idea of them as a couple, starting tonight. Atticus would pick her up at the restaurant, taking a few minutes to be formally introduced to the tight-knit group. It was one of many meetings they had planned for the next few weeks during which time the women could learn more about him.

When dinner was nearly over, an hour and a half later, Lissa gave Atticus a little wave. He was in perfect time to pick her up and meet her friends.

"Is that him?" Kelly asked, following the direction of Lissa's greeting. "Invite him over for dessert. We have to look him over and be sure he's good enough for you, Lis." Kelly's tinkling laughter followed her teasing statement.

Lissa rose, placing her napkin on the table. "I'll be right back."

She stopped on her way to ask the waiter to add another chair to their large table, then walked straight into Atticus's waiting arms. He kissed her with just the right amount of passion and discretion for such a public place, but refused to let her go completely as they walked to the table.

This was the perfect set-up as far as Lissa was concerned. Atticus could join them for an after-dinner drink. He wouldn't be required to eat anything, yet he'd be seen at a restaurant, which helped maintain his façade of mortality.

"You're getting good at this covert stuff, my love," he said in her mind as they neared the table.

"Every little bit helps, Atticus. I want to help keep you safe and if pretending to be mortal achieves that goal, I'm all for it."

He bent to kiss her temple with a soft brush of his lips. *"You're too good to me."*

He pulled out her chair and smiled at the group of women as Lissa made the introductions. Atticus was at his most charming and he easily won over Lissa's closest friends. Jena, the doctor, was the last to fall under his spell, but fall she did and by the time they'd drunk their after-dinner wine and nibbled on a few fortune cookies, they'd not only agreed to serve as bridesmaids, but Kelly had promised to help Lissa pack her belongings for the big move.

Lissa and Kelly had been packing all day at her apartment as it neared dusk. The plants were boxed, as were all the dishes and her mother's crystal. Everything but the kitchen table and the bigger pieces of furniture, which would be taken out by a moving company later in the week. Atticus had arranged it all. Or rather, his staff had seen to the details once Atticus had introduced her to them at a hastily called dinner meeting last week.

"Any news on the job front?" Lissa asked Kelly as they finished wrapping the last of the knickknacks from her faux mantle.

Kelly sighed, sounding disappointed. "No luck yet. It's a bad time to be looking for a teaching job. I just hope I can pay my rent until the job market opens up a bit."

"Kel, you know if you need a loan, all you have to do is ask."

"Thank, Lis, but the situation isn't that dire yet. I'll let you know if it comes to that point, but for now I'm still okay."

Lissa would have said more, but the doorbell rang. She dropped the newspaper she'd been using to stuff boxes of breakables and went to answer it. She looked through the peephole, but the man waiting in the hall didn't look familiar. Still, the movers were supposed to send a guy out to measure things today and he hadn't shown up yet. Maybe this was him, running late.

Deciding that must be it, Lissa opened the door, but before she could even ask the man for identification, he pushed the door inward with a violent shove, sending her flying backwards. Lissa stumbled, just barely able to stay on her feet, though it was a close thing. Kelly came running as Lissa felt a splash of something douse her.

"I'm going to kill you this time, bitch!" The man shouted as he stalked forward, bearing down on her as she backed away in shocked confusion.

Everything became clear as time seemed to slow. Only the stumble had saved her from being hit in the eyes. She had no idea what the clear liquid was, but it didn't hurt. At least not yet.

"Atticus! Oh God!" Lissa screamed for him in her mind

when Kelly jumped in front of her to face the madman.

"*What is it?*" Atticus was there, in her mind, quick as a flash, seeing through her eyes and sharing her thoughts.

"*This guy's crazy, Atticus! He's threatening—*"

"*I see him, Lissa. Be careful. He could be a magic-user.*"

The man threw a chair aside as he stalked toward the women, as they retreated behind the small dining table in one corner of the apartment.

"What are you doing?" Lissa screamed, hoping someone would hear the commotion inside her apartment and call for help.

"You're dead, witch. Your kind are not allowed to live." Insanity looked at her from his wild gaze.

"*Stall him, Lissa! I'll be there as soon as I can. And I'm bringing help. Remember, you'll have to invite us inside, otherwise we won't be able to enter.*"

"*Just hurry!*"

"*We're almost there. Just a few more minutes.*"

"I don't know what you're talking about! Get out of my house this instant!"

Lissa's strong words seemed to slow the man. He stopped in his tracks and looked at her with narrowed eyes.

"You can't fool me, witch."

"Why are you calling her that?" Kelly asked. Lissa could see her friend was furious, confused and scared out of her wits. It was a combination she understood because she was feeling much the same thing.

The man looked over at Kelly, pausing for a moment. He traced some kind of pattern in the air in front of Kelly's face, then stepped away from her. "You're in the wrong place, girl. With no power of your own you can't rely on this one to protect you. I'm warded against her kind of evil."

"Evil? What in the world are you talking about?" Kelly drew the man's attention again.

"You really don't know what she is?" The man seemed suspicious as his wild-eyed gaze slid from Kelly to Lissa and back again.

"No, I don't. Why don't you tell me?" Kelly was backing away and Lissa saw her friend fumble behind her back for the phone that sat on the credenza.

"Stay where you are, girl." The man's hand shot out and Kelly halted as if frozen in her tracks. Lissa felt a hum in the air that disturbed her. It felt cold and slimy, though she'd never experienced anything like it before in her life. It felt evil.

Kelly's eyes widened as she struggled to move but failed. Lissa was shocked. The man had done something that made Kelly literally freeze in her tracks. All with just a flick of his hand.

"Atticus." Her voice was a mere whisper of fright through their shared minds.

"I saw, love. He's the mage. Try to stay as far away from him as you can, but tread carefully. We're almost there. Just a few more seconds."

"Hurry."

The man turned back to her. "Now you die, witch." His features were grim, his expression maniacal. Lissa had never been so scared in her entire life.

"I'm not a witch." She had to stall. Atticus was almost there. She just needed to buy him a few seconds more.

"Then how did you escape my magic. You should have died in the crash, regardless of how hastily I set the spell. When I scented your power on the street, I acted quickly, but that spell never fails. You should have died."

"But fail it did." The man whirled toward the open door to the apartment and Lissa knew Atticus waited there with his friend Marc.

"Who are you?" The man sniffed and growled. "Bloodletter." The word was said like a curse as the man started to make furious motions with his hands. Lissa felt the oily hum grow again to almost deafening proportions.

"Invite us in!" Atticus shouted in her mind.

"Come in, Atticus! Come in, Marc! Help us!" she cried, sobbing as the hum escalated, driving her to her knees.

In a furious blur of motion, Atticus leapt on the intruder. Lissa couldn't follow it all. Atticus and Marc both moved too fast for the human eye to follow, but in a matter of moments, the intruder was slumped on the floor, bloody and unconscious.

Atticus dropped him the moment it was safe and reached for her.

"Lissa, my love, are you all right?"

"Atticus." She sagged against him, burrowing into his strength as she shook in reaction. She'd never seen anything so violent as the fight nor felt anything as malevolent as that man's magic. It sickened her.

"He splashed her with something." Kelly's voice came to her from beyond the comforting circle of Atticus's strong arms. "You'd better wash it off in case it's corrosive or worse."

Atticus drew back, examining her wet clothing. He smiled as he touched, smelled and even tasted the residual wetness on her skin. "It's Holy Water. Nothing more. Such a thing cannot hurt you. You're not evil and never could be." He hugged her close for a moment more, then stepped back, turning them both to face Kelly.

But Kelly's wide eyes were trained in dawning horror on the intruder and the man who bent over him on the floor. Marc's lips were bloody as he drew away from the attacker's wrist. There was no way he could hide what he'd been doing. Marc had fed on the man's blood and even now, licked his lips as he grinned at them.

"Magic blood is potent, indeed," Marc said conversationally as he dropped the unconscious man's arm back to the floor with a soft thud. "I have his essence. He'll never be able to escape."

"What are you?" Kelly seemed fascinated and not as

distraught as Lissa would have expected. "What are you talking about?"

"I'm sorry, Kel." Lissa tried to catch her friend's attention, but she seemed mesmerized by the Master vampire.

"I regret you saw this, little one," Marc said, moving to stand in front of Kelly and touching her face with one long finger. "But there's no hope for it now. Much as I'd like to cloud your memories of this, I sense already that your mind is too strong to be swayed for long. If you weren't so close to Lissa, it might work, but you'll see her, and Atticus...and me, from time to time and the memories would resurface. You must swear to keep our secret or face the consequences."

"Atticus, is he threatening her?" Lissa asked him privately.

"Yes." The short answer came in her mind. *"It's the only way to preserve our people and prevent even more bloodshed. Kelly will have to be watched from now until the end of her days. She knows about us and that knowledge must be kept sacred."*

"Watched by who?"

"One of us. Most likely Ian. He's our enforcer."

"What if we watched her? I mean, she's looking for a job. You could give her one at the vineyard, couldn't you? Would Marc accept that?"

"It could work." Atticus's tone was speculative as he placed a gentle kiss on her hair. *"I'll talk to him about it once this is settled. Ian's on his way. He'll take charge of the magic-user. We need to question him to find out what he knows. Right now, I want to get you out of here and back to the house where it's safe."*

"I'm all for that. But we need to take care of Kelly too."

"Marc, may I have a word?" Atticus left Lissa's side and took Marc off to a corner of the room while Lissa went to Kelly.

"What the heck was all that, Lis? Is your boyfriend a...vampire? Or am I losing my marbles?" A shaky smile hovered over Kelly's mouth.

"No, you're not losing your marbles, Kel. I know it's a shock, but Atticus is immortal. He saved my life after the wreck and we're joined. We can share our minds. He's my other half, Kel. My perfect soul mate."

"God, Lis. A freaking vampire?"

That startled a laugh out of Lissa. "I know, it sounds crazy, but it's not. I called to him in my mind and he came, didn't he? He saved our lives, I think, from Crazy Guy over there."

"This is all because of your psychic ability, isn't it? Damn, girl. I always knew you were spooky with the things you could see sometimes, but this is just too much."

"It's part of it, I think, but Atticus tells me he's been searching for me for centuries. We're getting married and sooner or later, I've told him, I'm going to let him make me like him."

"You'd give up daylight for this guy?" Kelly looked duly impressed.

"Kel, I'd give up anything and everything for Atticus. He's my soul mate."

"Oh, Lis." Kelly reached out and pulled Lissa into a hug. Both of them were still shaking from the traumatic events of the evening, but it felt good to have Kelly's support. "I'm happy for you, though I admit it'll take a while to get used to."

The men returned as they let each other go.

"Forgive me, *ma petite.*" Marc bowed slightly in Kelly's direction. "I'm Marc LaTour. I regret frightening you. That was not my intent." Marc's sparkling eyes hardened. "But it was important that one of us retain a connection to this man. By attacking Lissa, he has, by extension, attacked her mate, Atticus, as well. And where Atticus is involved, so must the Brotherhood be."

"The Brotherhood?" Kelly repeated.

"A loose organization of our kind in this region. I am the

current leader. Atticus is my second. We protect each other and defend our privacy with zealous intent. Now that you know about us, you will be expected to hold our secret closer than any other you possess. Can we count on you? If not for us, then for love of your friend, Lissa?"

"I would never hurt Lis. She's like a sister to me. I promise not to tell anybody about what I've seen here tonight." Kelly laughed with a short, almost hysterical sound. "Besides, who in the world would ever believe me?"

Marc stepped closer, crowding Kelly's personal space. "There are those who would most certainly believe, *cherie*. Those that would hunt us and murder us simply for existing. That, I cannot allow. And so you must be watched for the rest of your days."

"Watched? By who?" Kelly's shoulders squared in agitation and Lissa feared the confrontation she suspected was brewing. She reached for Kelly's hand, drawing her attention.

"It's not as bad as it sounds. Atticus and I will be doing the *watching*. You need a job, right? Well, it just so happens, my fiancé here has a job waiting with your name on it. You can earn a living, work with friends and be *watched* all at the same time." Lissa looked from Marc to Atticus and back at her friend. "What do you say?"

"It is an elegant solution to all our difficulties," Marc put in.

"Okay," Kelly said, her gaze still suspicious.

"Great." Lissa hugged her to her side for a quick moment. "I'll like having you around the vineyard every day. Heck, maybe you could move in. We have tons of room."

Kelly held up one hand. "Let's take this a step at a time, Lis. For now, I'll take the job. You know how badly I need it. And thank you, Atticus." She looked toward him.

Any response he would have made was halted by the arrival of another tall, powerfully built man at the threshold of the apartment.

"It's Ian, love," Atticus said in her mind. *"You need to invite*

him in."

Lissa waved at the man at her doorway. "Come on in, Ian. Thanks for coming over on such short notice." She felt strange to be exchanging small talk while an intruder lay on her rug, unconscious.

Ian nodded, making short work of lifting the dead weight of the crazy guy off her floor and onto his broad shoulders. Without a word, he turned and headed back out the door.

"Handy man to have around," Kelly commented with wry amusement. Lissa was glad to hear some of her usual humor creeping back into her conversation. The events of the past hour had been jarring, but it looked like they'd all be okay, including Kelly, thank goodness. She was taking all these revelations remarkably well.

"You have no idea," Marc agreed. "Now that we're all secure here, might I suggest we finish and head for the vineyard? We've had an eventful start to our evening and I think we could all use more peaceful and secure surroundings to talk things through."

Marc and Atticus helped them set the apartment back to rights and carried Lissa's bags out to her car. When Lissa looked around, trying to figure out how the men had gotten to her place, Atticus intercepted her thoughts.

"We flew," he said in a whisper in her mind.

"What?"

"Marc and I are very old. Over the centuries, we've developed many skills. One of the more useful is the ability to shapeshift. When needed, we can become whatever we need to be to get where we're going or accomplish our goals."

"That's amazing."

His wry chuckle sounded through her mind. *"Glad I could impress you, love."*

They headed back to the vineyard in two cars. Marc rode

with Kelly in her compact while Atticus took the wheel of Lissa's sedan. An hour later, they pulled through the gate and onto the winding drive that set the main house far back from the road.

They gathered in the living room to talk through the events of the past hours. Lissa knew from Atticus's mind that this debrief was for Kelly's benefit as much as anyone's. The men would take her measure while they talked and they'd also help calm her and show her that they weren't monsters. Lissa was glad they were taking time with Kelly. Her friendship had always meant a lot to Lissa and she hated to think that Kelly's life would be adversely affected simply by being her friend.

Atticus was pouring wine for them all when the doorbell chimed. That was odd enough, given the fact that nobody could enter the estate except by being admitted to the gated driveway. Nobody *normal*, that is. If someone could fly, for example, all bets were off.

"Good reasoning, love," Atticus said in her mind as he went to answer the door. *"It's Ian. And yes, he can shapeshift into some amazing forms, including a rather fearsome dragon."*

"Now that, I have to see." Lissa resisted chuckling aloud, though she had to bite her lip to do it.

Atticus returned to the living room with Ian in tow.

"What happened?" Marc wanted to know.

Ian's lips thinned into a hard line. "The bastard put up one hell of a fight. He resisted questioning and when I gave him just a little leeway, he turned around and attacked me." Ian's clothes were scorched in places, Lissa noted. "He tried to send a magical message to his brethren. I can't be certain I stopped him in time."

"He's gone then?" Marc's expression turned grim.

"No way to avoid it, unfortunately. I'm sorry, Marc. He was stronger that I expected and more than a little unhinged. He killed himself, in the end. His power turned in on himself and fried him to ash before my eyes."

"Damn." Marc twirled his wineglass idly in one hand.

"Did you learn anything before he died?" Atticus asked.

"Only that he was as mad as a hatter." Ian helped himself to a glass of wine at the sideboard. "And that he wasn't operating alone. He had at least one, possibly more cohorts. He also said he'd come upon your lady by chance. He was going to a conference at the hotel and noted her power as he waited to board the shuttle bus. Apparently psychic power is anathema to his particular sect of loons."

"That's a bit of a relief. It means he didn't know about you in advance. You were just a target of opportunity, not someone he'd been stalking." Atticus stroked Lissa's hair as he sat on the arm of her chair. "If he'd had more time to plan, you might not be sitting here tonight."

"I can't help but feel terrible that all those people died because one nutball had it in for me." Lissa felt the heavy weight of guilt settle on her shoulders.

"No, lass," Ian spoke from across the room. "Evil the likes of which you encountered tonight needs little excuse to kill. I have no doubt that madman had the blood of many innocents on his hands. The crash was in no way your fault. I've learned over the years, that some things are simply a matter of fate."

Chapter Six

Kelly was given a guest room for the night when Lissa and Atticus finally retired sometime in the wee hours of the morning. Marc had stayed late, doing his best to charm Kelly, though she seemed somewhat immune to the handsome Master's charms. Ian left before Marc, but not by much, and he promised to return the next night to go over Atticus's security arrangements. Things would need to be updated now that Lissa was going to live in the big house as well.

Over the next weeks, Kelly went to work at the vineyard, performing organizational tasks for both Atticus and Lissa. Lissa moved in and Kelly was hired ostensibly as her assistant. Kelly took to her new role as liaison between Atticus's existing staff and the couple very well. Of those who worked for Atticus, only Kelly knew his darkest secret, and that one little fact, they discovered, made her invaluable to him in a short amount of time.

Kelly took over keeping the social calendar for both Lissa and Atticus. They attended a few evening events together and Atticus's business associates began to recognize her as his fiancée. Lissa kept odd hours. She'd sleep late after staying up all night with Atticus, but she did still go shopping and even sunbathing a time or two with Kelly and her friends. She wanted to enjoy her last weeks of sunlight before joining Atticus in his dark world.

It was easier, having Kelly to talk to about the changes she'd agreed to make in her life. They worked together in the house during the day. Kelly would work in the outer room of Atticus's home office, settling into the personal secretary's role, while Lissa moved her belongings over to the mansion and redecorated here and there. The women would meet for meals in the spacious kitchen or go out to enjoy the local bistros.

All in all, it was one of the most enjoyable times of Lissa's life. She was planning the wedding with Kelly's help and enjoying time with her friends and the love of her life. It was tiring, to be sure, but she wouldn't have traded a moment of it.

By the time the wedding finally rolled around a few weeks later, Lissa would be a well-established part of the limited social scene Atticus enjoyed. The couple had established themselves as somewhat eccentric people who valued their privacy, but were still upstanding members—albeit on the fringe—of the local business community. They attended a few charity functions together where Atticus introduced her around and she furthered his façade of normalcy by appearing at a few daytime events, carefully chosen to enhance both of their reputations. It was a master plan, carefully crafted with Kelly's help and able assistance. Kelly, too, was established as not only a trusted member of Atticus's staff, but a close personal friend of Lissa's. When Lissa became immortal, they all agreed that Kelly would carry on her good works in the daylight hours.

It fell into place even better than anyone could have anticipated. But by the week before the big wedding, Marc had become a bit of a thorny issue. He'd started visiting the vineyard more often than he had in the past. He'd arrive just after sunset to bedevil Kelly with barely veiled innuendos and flirtatious banter.

"Argh!" Kelly walked into the living room from the front hall, Marc following close behind, grinning like a fool. "Atticus, will you please tell your friend to leave me alone?"

Lissa stifled a laugh at Kelly's exasperated tone.

"Marc, leave Kelly alone." The smile on his face belied the serious tone of his words.

"What did he do?" Lissa wanted to know as Kelly flopped onto an overstuffed armchair that dwarfed her petite frame.

"He bought me a car. A Lamborghini no less. It's out in the driveway."

"What?" Lissa was shocked. She knew these men were rich, but she'd had no idea the Master vampire had enough money to give away expensive world-class sports cars to women he barely knew.

Marc grinned as he sauntered into the room. "Kelly and I were talking about cars the other night and she said she liked Italian sports cars. I thought she should have one, so I called Karl at the motor shop." He shrugged, seating himself on the arm of Kelly's chair.

She jumped up and put space between them. "While I like a gift as much as the next girl, I can't accept a *car* for God's sake. I couldn't even park that thing in my neighborhood. You'll have to take it back."

Marc gave a long-suffering sigh as he slid sideways into the chair she'd vacated. "How about I keep it for you? I think I have one empty bay in my garage. You could come visit your car every few days and share a glass of wine and some cordial conversation with me while you're there."

"In your dreams, LaTour." Kelly's gaze could have killed a lesser man, but Marc was made of sterner stuff.

"But you are, *ma petite*. My dreams are the only place where you're civil to me."

Kelly threw up her hands, and fled the room in a huff.

"I don't think I've ever seen Kelly at such a loss for words before," Lissa said, smiling as her friend disappeared out of the room.

"No?" Marc asked with a speculative gleam in his eye as he watched the empty doorway through which Kelly had left. "That gives me more hope than it rightly should." He shook his head.

"I have never met a more confusing, annoying and tantalizing woman."

Lissa nudged Atticus and he tightened his arm around her shoulders. He had to know from her worried thoughts how deeply the Master's words troubled her.

"See here, Marc," Atticus said. "I hope you're not thinking of messing with one of my betrothed's best friends."

"Messing with her?" Marc focused his attention on Atticus, his brows drawn and lips curved in an expression of puzzled amusement. "To be perfectly honest, I have no idea what I'm thinking of when it comes to the lovely and intriguing Kelly. She fascinates me and that is a rare enough occurrence that I'm driven to try to understand why. It could be that she is the first mortal woman in centuries to know what I am. That is a novel experience."

"Marc." Lissa sought his attention. "I think you should redirect your fascination." She took a deep breath for courage, but this needed to be said. "Kelly is one of my closest friends. I don't want anything bad to happen to her."

"I don't wish that either, *ma petite*." Marc's gaze measured her determination but she refused to back down.

"She's showing all the signs of being attracted to you, but I don't think it's a good idea for you to tease her. You could hurt her badly with very little effort on your part. Kelly seems tough on the outside, but trust me, she's got a gentle heart that bruises easily. I don't expect you to understand, but I'm asking you to leave her alone. She's had enough heartache for one lifetime already."

Marc's eyes narrowed as he studied her, remaining silent until she was about ready to fidget. Only Atticus's strong presence at her side kept her still and her gaze unwavering as it met Marc's. At length, he stood from the chair, nodding once in an old-world gesture of formality before he turned to leave.

"I'll keep your words in mind, *cherie*, but I can promise nothing except that I will try to comply with your wishes."

Atticus stood, gesturing for Lissa to stay where she was while he saw Marc out. Opening her mind a little, she saw through Atticus's gaze the sleek yellow car that sat in the darkened drive. It was a beauty, but much too extravagant for a simple school-teacher-turned-executive-assistant like Kelly.

Marc drove off in the fantasy machine and Atticus returned to the living room. Lissa met him at the doorway and slipped under his arm to stand at his side. He hugged her close as she wrapped her arm around his waist.

"Do you think he'll leave her be?" Lissa worried a little as Atticus and she headed for the more private wing of the big house for a little alone time.

"I think he'll try, but I'm not certain he'll succeed. To be honest, I've never seen him like this before and I've known him for centuries. Never has a woman gotten under his skin the way your friend Kelly appears to."

Lissa didn't like the sound of that, but relegated it to think about later as Atticus guided her toward the more private parts of the house.

He led her to the master bedroom, which was in fact, only a façade. Inside, a hidden panel guarded the entrance to the underground complex and the protected chamber in which he slept. He would go there for the day, but for tonight, he planned to take advantage of the plush master suite and the giant bed he rarely used.

"Do you know how much I truly love you?" he asked, each of them undressing as they stood before the extravagant bed.

"I can see it in your eyes and read it in your thoughts, Atticus. I'm more certain of that than of anything else in this world. And I know you can be just as certain of me. It's probably the most amazing thing about this relationship we have. No uncertainty. No ability to hide our true feelings. I love knowing that the man I love, loves me in return just as much."

"If not more," he agreed, sliding out of his own clothing

while she removed the last of hers.

When they were both naked, they came together in a blistering kiss that rocked their combined world off its axis and in a totally new direction. There was no play this time, no teasing, just desperate need on both their parts.

Atticus had never known such pleasure. She nurtured something in his soul, shone her light on the seed of hope that had never taken root before he'd met her. Now it blossomed into a healthy, living, growing thing and his dark world was brighter for her influence.

He drew her down onto the plush bed, settling her beneath him in the way he knew she liked. He could read in her thoughts how she liked feeling small beneath his body, how she liked his heat and his gentle touches. He gave her all she could take and more. He worshiped her with his mouth, his teeth elongating and scraping over her sensitive skin, making her shiver. He loved the way she responded to him. He'd spend eternity exploring new ways to make her moan and quiver beneath him.

The thought made him smile. He looked upward to find an answering grin on her beautiful face.

"This will only get better the longer we are together," he promised, licking her navel as her abdomen rippled in reaction to his touch.

"I can hardly believe it could be any better." Her words were a breathy sigh.

"Believe it, my love." He nipped her belly before rising to seat himself between her thighs. She was more than ready. As was he.

Atticus spread her legs wide, holding her knees propped up on his arms. He eased downward, holding her gaze as he took possession of her hot channel, joining them both in body and in mind. After the first few pulses, he wasn't quite sure where he left off and she began. He felt her pleasure and his own, the mingling of their minds combining and multiplying the rapture he felt whenever he was with her.

As they drew near the peak, he bent closer to her, folding her legs back to give him even greater access to her body. The angle changed when he bent even lower to sink his teeth into her neck, bringing them both to orgasm at the same moment as they shared minds, blood and ecstasy.

They lay together on the large bed, wallowing in the aftermath. Lissa stroked his powerful chest as she rested against him. She could still feel his mind joined with hers as it had been in those moments of shared pleasure—as it would be once she'd become like him and learned how to manage their mental link.

Her thoughts turned to her friends and how they would handle her marriage. Kelly was already getting into the groove of the vineyard and they'd talked about having her move into the big house so she didn't have such a long commute every day from the city. She would understand Lissa's new life better than any of the others.

Carly was going to Wyoming, so at least for the first few months, she would be out of the picture and wouldn't notice the changes in Lissa. Christy was habitually quiet and had to be dragged out of her house most of the time. Chances were she wouldn't notice any changes in Lissa because she wouldn't see much of anything.

Jena was another story. Sharp eyed and inquisitive by nature, Jena would notice things that others might not. Kelly would come in handy, standing with Lissa against any questions Jena might pose. But in the end, they were all her friends and they wouldn't hassle her if she was happy. And she *was* happy.

"And glad I am to hear it," Atticus said, giving her a lazy grin as she pulled back to look at his face. "Now still your racing thoughts, my love, and let me bask in this bliss for a few more minutes."

She wanted to be grumpy, but she felt the wonder in his mind of what they shared and she couldn't be mean. She settled her head on his shoulder again and closed her eyes, trying to relax her mind and release her thoughts.

A vision came to her out of the blue, shocking her breathless.

Pain. Terrible pain and weakness. Danger and sorrow. Ripped, rended flesh and blood. Lots of blood. The smell of it was in her nostrils. The smell of death. Death and...wine?

Lissa shook out of the vision with an abrupt jolt as she sat up straight in the bed. Atticus rose beside her, his face clouded with concern.

"Oh no!"

"Was that a vision? Is that what you see with your psychic gift?" Atticus wanted to know.

Their minds were still joined, she realized, so he'd seen what she had. Looking up at him, she nodded, biting her lip to keep from crying. He gathered her close and rocked her in his strong arms.

"It's never been so strong before," she whispered. "Never like that. Atticus, did you see?" She trembled, remembering the face she'd seen through the haze of blood and pain. If only she knew what it all meant. The vision was nothing more than a warning of pain and blood to come, but it didn't give her anything solid to go on...except the smell of wine and the lone face in her vision.

"I saw her," Atticus confirmed in a grim tone.

"How can we save her?"

Atticus held her tighter. "I don't know yet, my love, but we will do all in our power to help prevent *that—*," the anger and surety in his tone comforted her, "—from happening to your friend. I promise you."

Rare Vintage

Dedication

With deepest appreciation to my family, who have stood by me through all my career choices. Thanks also to Bethany for her great advice and steady hand at the reins. And to my readers, who make each day a joy and give me a reason to keep writing.

Chapter One

Kelly sat back in her office chair, staring at the computer screen. A heavy sigh ruffled the wisps of hair fringing her forehead. Things at the vineyard had been in upheaval since the Master vampire of the region, Marc LaTour, had moved in. Well, at least for her.

The blasted man seemed to be there every time she turned around, watching her with those dark, mysterious, ancient eyes. Since she worked in the evenings to be on call during most of the hours when her best friend, Lissa, and her new husband, Atticus, needed her, she had precious few moments of daylight when Marc couldn't corner her.

Just last night he'd dangled that damned yellow Lamborghini in front of her again, revving the engine as he brought it out of the mansion's twelve-bay garage.

"Just taking your car for a spin, *ma petite,*" he'd called to her from the driver's seat. "Wouldn't you like to join me?"

"No, thank you." She'd been as firm as possible and turned away as he laughed. The hardest part was she'd have loved to take a drive in the expensive machine. It was the man she needed to avoid if she wanted to keep her sanity.

She'd heard the sports car roar down the driveway a minute later. Marc infuriated her. He'd attempted to give her the car as a gift, which she'd flatly refused, but he persisted. He was like a dog with a bone, and she was the one whose nerves were being chewed on.

Kelly had moved in to one of the many guest rooms at the mansion a few weeks after Atticus and Lissa were married. Her lease on a small apartment in the city had come up for renewal, and she took the opportunity to move out. She'd never enjoyed the hour-long commute each way from the city to the vineyard. She'd been working for Lissa and Atticus since shortly before their wedding as the couple's assistant. It made sense for her to move into the mansion where she worked and one of her best friends lived. They certainly had plenty of room in the grand building.

Things had rolled along well until Marc showed up with the yellow sports car and a suitcase in tow. Marc had apparently decided, in his high-handed way, that he needed to move in with his friends while his own house was being renovated. Atticus and Marc were long-time associates and close friends.

They were also both immortal.

They'd known each other longer than Kelly had been alive. Centuries, in fact. It still boggled her mind to think that her best friend, Lissa, was now as immortal as her new husband. The thought of living forever was intriguing—even mildly tantalizing—but not practical for Kelly. Just the thought of drinking blood made her shiver. No, she preferred to live a normal life without the need to drink blood. Well, as normal as it could be when one of her best friends was a vampire.

Kelly returned to work, whiling away the hours until sunset when Lissa and Atticus would awaken. Marc, too, unfortunately. Not that he was unattractive. In fact, he was one of the most devastatingly handsome men she'd ever met, but he was way out of her league.

She sat back, staring at the screen again, lost in thought. Kelly jumped when a breath of warm air sizzled past her ear.

It was Marc, of course. He was hovering close, just over her shoulder. She could feel him, though he hadn't made a sound as he approached. Only now did she hear his slow breaths and the deliberate way he inhaled her scent as if he was smelling a rare perfume.

"I thought they made it clear to you that I'm not a snack."

"*Mmm*, I quite agree." He dipped his head lower, his stubbly cheek rubbing along her neck, raising goose bumps. "I imagine you'd be a full seven-course meal." He punctuated his words by licking the sensitive skin just over her rapidly beating jugular. "Ah, *l'aparatif c'est marvelieux*. A very satisfying feast for the senses at that."

The man had licked her! She could hardly believe it. She was barely suppressing shivers that wanted to course down her spine. It was devastating to realize they were shivers of excitement, not revulsion.

This had to stop. The man was a steamroller and if she wasn't careful, she'd end up flat. Flat on her back, that is, with him possessing every last inch of her body, her blood and her sanity.

"Mr. LaTour!" She twirled her rolling office chair around, making him move back. "For the last time, I'm not on the menu."

His dark gaze blazed down at her, humor in its depths. "My proper title is Master, but you can call me Marc, *ma cherie*."

She rolled her eyes, putting on a brave front. "I call no man master."

"Ah, but, *ma petite*, I'm not just a man. For centuries now, I've been something more...and less." He turned thoughtful as he reflected on just what he was at this point in his long, lonely existence.

"I know what you are." Kelly jumped to her feet, emphasizing her words with a rudely pointing finger, but he liked her fire. "You're a womanizer, a scoundrel and someone who believes rules don't apply to him."

She was working up a fine head of steam, and Marc enjoyed the show. Kelly was adorable when she was in a temper. It was just one more thing that fascinated him about this petite, complex, mortal woman.

"Sadly, you're right about some of that. I've never followed rules, *cherie*, because for many years, I've been the one who makes them. Alas, I admit to being a bit of a scoundrel as well, but I do object to the term 'womanizer'. While it is true I enjoy taking my sustenance from females more than males, I always leave them well satisfied and with no complaints. In fact, they rarely even remember me." Again, that odd pang of something that could be regret sounded through him. He shrugged it off and stepped into her personal space, crowding close and tipping her chin up so he could look deep into her pretty eyes.

"I bet you would remember me though, *ma petite*. It would be difficult to cloud your fascinating mind, and I believe I like the idea of you thinking of me years into the future, for I will most certainly be thinking of you. You are..." his voice dropped to a low whisper, "...eminently memorable, *mademoiselle*."

He leaned in, dipping his head as if to kiss her. Her eyes widened, but she didn't pull away. She was as trapped as he was. He'd been dreaming of her for weeks now—wanting to know the taste of her lips, the feel of her tongue and the passion of her kiss.

"Is there anything I can help you with, Marc?" Lissa's loud voice sounded from the doorway, startling Kelly back to her senses and away from the outrageous invitation in his eyes. Kelly moved, putting space between them as quickly as she could manage on wobbly legs.

Lissa strolled into the room to stand next to Kelly, indicating without words that she would protect her human friend, even from the Master. Kelly knew it was a gutsy move, considering that Lissa was newly turned, and Marc had centuries of experience on her. But the two women had been friends since college and were closer than sisters. They'd watched each other's backs for many years. Kelly knew Lissa would do anything for her, just as she'd do anything for her friend.

Kelly was the only one of their old study group that knew what Lissa had become, though the others had dutifully inspected her new husband and wished them well. They were all close, but Kelly and Lissa were best friends. It had always been that way, since the moment they'd met in an advanced math class all those years ago.

"No, nothing you can help me with, fledgling." Marc's smile was respectful, but just a touch mocking as he reached out and raised Kelly's hand to his lips. "Until later, *cherie*." He left the room as silently as he'd come, leaving the two women to themselves.

Kelly dropped into her office chair with a troubling mix of relief and frustration. "Thanks, Lis."

"If he gives you any trouble, you tell me, okay? I may not be up to his weight class, but my Atticus can certainly kick his butt—and will—if he doesn't abide by our rules in our home."

Kelly reached out to touch her friend's hand. "I'm okay, but I appreciate the offer. I'll let you know if he gets too far out of line."

Chapter Two

"My bride is not very happy with you, Marc." Atticus poured two glasses of deep red wine and handed one to his companion. The fermented fruit of the vine was the only thing that connected their kind to daylight—that was both their yearning and their pain. It was the one thing that could offer them ease and a modicum of healing. "Can't you just leave her little mortal friend alone?"

Marc schooled his expression, but felt the turmoil of conflict in his heart. "I'm not really sure I can. She calls to me in a way I've never experienced in all my years." He shook his head as if to clear it. "But I won't hurt her. You know me better than that. Besides, I have bigger fish to fry. Atticus, I need you to step into the role of Master of this region."

"Isn't that your job? You know I'm enjoying every moment I have with my new mate. We're still newlyweds after all. If I were Master of this region, the job would require a lot of work away from Lissa, and I'm a little too selfish to part from her for very long."

"Don't you see? Having found your mate makes you the perfect candidate to replace me. The rest of our kind see you as more stable and more powerful just by virtue of having found a mate. That upstart Gibson would never dare challenge you, though the time is fast approaching when he will challenge me. I don't want to have to kill him. The job just isn't that important to me anymore. I'm tired, Atticus. I've earned my rest."

"That sounds suspiciously final, Marc. Don't tell me you're considering—"

"Don't say it." Marc wearily raised one hand. "No, I'm not suicidal, but I want what you have, Atticus. You've found your one and only. You have purpose and happiness in your life. It's been far too long since I've truly enjoyed my endless years on this earth. Being a Master used to be enough, but after seeing you and your mate together, I realize how empty my world truly is." He polished off his wine and sat back. "I want purpose. I don't want to just exist anymore. I want a little joy in my life, a little happiness. Is that wrong?"

Atticus regarded him with serious eyes. "It's not wrong, Marc, but I'll share with you what I've never told another soul. When I found Lissa, I was ready to die. I was nearly gone in fact." Marc wasn't as shocked by the revelation as he should have been. He'd sensed Atticus had been reaching the point of no return, even as he neared it himself. "As you know, everyone else aboard that mini-bus died in the initial few moments of the wreck. I took a support beam through the chest, very near my heart."

"*Sacre bleu!*"

"Only Lissa lived of those on board, and I was ready to let myself bleed out and end it all, but then I thought about her. I barely knew her, but she'd caught my attention during the short drive. Still, I had no idea she would turn out to be my mate. I just knew I didn't want to see her die. I pulled that beam out of my chest and brought her to safety. I struggled to save her, but the moment I tasted her essence, I knew she was special. When we made love..." Atticus trailed off, seemingly lost in the memories of that moment, "...our minds, our hearts, our very souls joined and I knew she was the One I'd been waiting for through all these centuries." Atticus shifted his gaze back to Marc. "My point in telling you all this is that I didn't expect to find her. I'd given up hope. Much, as I suspect, you are on the verge of doing. My advice to you is to just not give up."

"I will try, my friend, but I do not dare hope that lightning will strike in the same place twice. You have found your mate after centuries of searching. I fear my search is not yet at an end, but my patience and willingness to go on alone is nearing that point."

"Don't give up, Marc. She's out there."

"I had hope..." Marc hesitated, which wasn't like him.

"What?"

"When I first saw your wife's friend, Kelly, I had hope that she might be—" Marc turned away, reaching for the wine decanter with less than graceful movements. "But it is a silly hope. I could not be that fortunate."

"Marc, there's something I think you should know."

The somber, tense tone of Atticus's voice alerted Marc to the serious nature of what his friend had to impart.

"You know Lissa has some psychic ability," Atticus began, seeming unsure of how to break his news. Marc grew even more concerned. "Shortly after we met, Lissa had a vision. We were closely linked at the time and I actually saw it too. Marc, the vision was of Kelly—covered in blood. She was dying, and we both felt that it was no accident. She is in very real danger."

Marc felt his tension level double, then double again. Nothing and no one would threaten Kelly. He would see to it.

"It's one of the many reasons we convinced her to move in here, where we could keep an eye on her," Atticus continued while Marc seethed. "Aside from the fact that she has knowledge of our existence and had to be watched anyway, Lissa hoped that keeping her close would help us protect her."

"You should have told me at once!" Marc exploded, unable to hold his temper any longer. Atticus didn't deserve the full brunt of his outburst. Marc did his best to rein it in. "I expect to know the minute your mate sees anything else. And from now on, I will be keeping a close watch on Kelly. Nothing must happen to her. Do you hear me?"

"I do, old friend." Atticus looked at him with both compassion and sadness. "But what if you are the threat?

Marc, she was covered in blood and her neck—" Atticus swallowed as his eyes glazed in memory. "Her throat was in shreds as if an animal had savaged her with his teeth. Lissa didn't recognize it, but I've seen that once before in my years."

"Alexandra," Marc said knowingly, flopping into his chair, defeat in every line of his body. "When Viktor went mad and savaged her. I remember it too, my friend. It was a sight so horrible, I will never forget."

"In the vision, Kelly had the same wounds, Marc. And there was too much blood. I don't see how we can save her life if that is truly to be her fate. Even turning her might not save her with that kind of trauma."

The men were silent for a moment, lost in their own thoughts.

"We will keep her safe," Marc said finally, the steel returning to his backbone even as his stomach tensed with worry. "Between us, we can keep watch over her. If it is as you suspect and one of our Brotherhood will attack her, it cannot happen during the day. And if both of us watch her by night, if either one of us is the threat, the other can subdue him."

"I am mated, Marc. Forgive me, but I have no reason to attack Kelly. In fact, being that she's my wife's best friend, I have every reason to protect her."

"Then you believe I am the threat." Marc watched Atticus, glad to know his old friend would speak honestly with him after all these years—even on a topic as unpalatable as this.

"I believe you could be. You, or any of our brethren."

Marc sighed. "So the problem remains. To be safe, she should have two watchers at all times."

"She will not agree to it, Marc. She is as stubborn as my wife. Perhaps more so."

"Then we don't tell her. But starting now, we will watch her. Your mate can help too. Kelly will not be alone if we can help it."

"And we also have electronic monitors in all the rooms. She

doesn't know about them."

"*Dieu!* I didn't know about them either, Atticus. Since when did you become James Bond?"

Atticus laughed. "Don't try to tell me you're not having your home wired for sound and pictures as we speak. I'm sure you're upgrading whatever you had there to begin with during this renovation. You'd be a fool not to."

"You know me too well," Marc agreed with a grin. "All right, I assume you'll let me in on your monitoring system?"

Atticus surprised him by tossing a small black box his way. It was about the size of an old transistor radio and had similar buttons and knobs.

"I intended to get your help on this all along. There is simply too much time where Lissa and I are—*ahem*—otherwise occupied. We need help if we're to keep Kelly safe."

"You mean while you're off making love to your wife, Kelly's vulnerable." Marc's mouth thinned into a grim line as he thought of the unknown threat. "I'll get help on this. Perhaps Ian would be suitable to take a turn on monitors while you and Lissa are offline."

"Better yet—" Atticus spoke as he poured more wine for both of them, "—Dmitri will be in town for a few days. I've invited him to stay here. Since he'll be close and has a reasonable excuse for being here, we'll ask him to help. He's always been a trustworthy man. When he goes home, Ian can take over."

Chapter Three

Professor Dmitri Belakov, history teacher and Master vampire of his own domain in the Midwest, arrived a few days later. Atticus, Lissa, Ian, Marc and Kelly—since she couldn't be left unguarded, though she had no idea the men were taking turns looking after her—met Dmitri at a private air strip not far from the vineyard. He'd flown himself in a very costly small jet that allowed him to travel from the middle of the country to the West coast in a matter of a few hours.

Marc had to be on hand to greet his fellow Master. The Brotherhood was a loose organization, but they did like to observe tradition. When one Master arrived in another's territory it was only polite to make his presence known through official channels. More than that, Dmitri and Marc were old friends. They'd lived and worked together in centuries past, before settling in the United States and becoming Masters in their own right.

Atticus and Ian had been part of the old group as well. They'd spent a few merry centuries cavorting across Europe and the Middle East, settling for decades at a time in different cities along the way. They'd watched each other's backs and shared both pleasure and peril too many times to count. They'd formed strong bonds of friendship that could never be dismissed.

"It's good to see you again, *mon ami.*" Marc gave Dmitri the traditional European greeting of a kiss to both cheeks.

"It was time to visit my old friends. It's nice being Master of my domain, but there are not many of our kind on the prairie." The men laughed and then led the newcomer over to meet Lissa and Kelly, who'd waited by the cars.

Dmitri—much to Marc's amusement—made a fuss over Lissa, annoying Atticus in the process. It was all part of the game these old comrades had played many times in the past. Of course, now things were different. One of their group had found his mate, and all the others were both happy for him and jealous as hell. Such a drastic change deserved a little good-natured ribbing.

"*Enchante, madame,*" Dmitri purred, lifting Lissa's hand to his lips for a lingering kiss. Marc had watched his friend perfect that Slavic charm over the centuries, and it didn't hurt that Dmitri was easy on the eyes. Women had fallen for his dark good looks for a long time, and Lissa seemed to be no exception as she murmured a return greeting.

"You ride with Marc in the Lamborghini. I think we'll all be happier at the house where we can relax." Atticus made a show of appropriating his wife's hand and tucking it firmly into the crook of his arm.

Atticus ushered his wife into their car, and Kelly got into the back seat, but Marc noticed the look of longing she directed at the yellow sports car when she thought he wasn't looking. He could see how much she wanted to ride in it, or better yet, drive it, but she denied herself the pleasure—denying him in the process.

The car had come to represent something bigger. It had come to symbolize the ongoing struggle between them. He tempted her, and she refused. He flirted with her, and she rebuffed him. He wanted her, and she pretended to be unaffected, but he knew it was just an act. The true victory would be when she finally broke down and admitted it.

It hadn't taken long for Dmitri to realize something was going on between Marc and Kelly. He asked about it during the drive to the vineyard.

"So who's the girl?" Dmitri's question was not unwelcome, but Marc preferred not to discuss the more annoying aspects of his relationship with the delectable Kelly. Still, he understood Dmitri's interest in how Kelly fit into their little group. He knew Lissa was Atticus's mate, but Kelly was unclaimed and yet part of the intimate circle. Marc should have expected the question sooner or later.

"She is Lissa's best friend. She had the unfortunate luck to see me feeding from a man who had attacked Lissa before she moved in with Atticus. Her mind is too strong to cloud sufficiently, considering that Lissa refused to break ties with her, or any of her mortal friends for that matter."

"So you're watching her?"

"She's working for Atticus at the vineyard and yes, we are watching her, but for more than just her knowledge of our existence. There is a further complication that I wished to discuss with you before we get to the house."

"I'm all ears."

"Lissa is slightly psychic." Marc glanced over to gauge his friend's reaction to the news. "She had a vision of Kelly, covered in blood, her throat savaged—most likely by one of our kind."

"And you think to protect her from this possible future?"

"I must!" That came out a little more emphatically than Marc would have wished, but Dmitri only raised one dark brow in his direction. "We decided to have two of us with her at all times during the dark hours. Atticus and Lissa are the two most unlikely to be the culprits, so they are primarily responsible for keeping tabs on her, but they are also newlyweds..."

"Ah, I see." Dmitri nodded with a wide grin. "Say no more. It will be no hardship to help keep an eye on the lovely Kelly."

"So long as it's just an eye. She is Lissa's best friend, and I have been strictly ordered to keep my hands to myself. That goes double for you, my friend."

"You? The great Master? Ordered around in your own

domain. What has this world come to?" Dmitri burst out laughing as Marc had intended. Better to treat this all as a laughing matter, as long as Dmitri got the message.

"Laugh if you like, but you'll soon see that Lissa has sharp fangs when it comes to her mortal friends, and Atticus will do just about anything she asks. Since I am living with them while my house is being renovated, I can do no other than follow the rules they lay out for their house. They've put Kelly firmly off the menu."

"A shame." Dmitri gazed out the window at the passing scenery. "She is a beautiful woman."

Marc felt his hackles rise and did his best to fight the reaction.

"Beautiful, yes. But also off limits. *N'est-ce pas?*"

"*Oui, mon ami.* I understand and will abide by your wishes in your territory."

At the vineyard, they gathered in the large living room while Atticus poured out one of his prize-winning vintages for them. Kelly felt a little conspicuous being the only mortal in the room, but Lissa had asked her specifically to stay so she wouldn't be the only woman present. Six of one or a half dozen of the other, Kelly thought, realizing that women in general were probably far too preoccupied about being the odd woman out in any situation.

She shrugged, accepted the delicious wine and sat back to listen to what promised to be a fascinating conversation. Kelly had thought a lot about immortality since Lissa's wedding and subsequent change. She'd worked at the vineyard for some time and dealt daily with Atticus, Lissa and even Marc, but she'd never really had the opportunity to just sit and observe Atticus talking with his friends—especially not friends this old.

"So what brings you to California?" Atticus asked Dmitri as he handed him a glass of burgundy.

Dmitri frowned as he accepted the crystal goblet. "My

house was sold."

"What?" Marc was the first to voice the confusion that filled the room.

"I thought it was clever to keep my stronghold beneath that old farmhouse," Dmitri said with a trace of bitterness. "I had an agreement with the farmer and his descendents and it worked well for centuries, but the last of the line never married and recently passed on to the next realm. His land was sold before I could act. Damned lawyers." The curse was muttered into his glass as Dmitri took a bracing swallow of the delicious wine.

Atticus laughed, drawing attention. "Now, now, Dmitri. I seem to recall you played at being a barrister once upon a time."

"That was a very long time ago, Atticus, as you well know. I'm a professor of history now."

"So where were you that you didn't know of the goings on until after the sale?" Ian asked. "I thought the University kept you close to your territory most of the time."

"I was on sabbatical last semester, visiting friends in Europe, supposedly researching a book on the Tudors."

"A lusty lot they were, eh? Nothing like the current insipid batch," Marc said, the spark of memory in his eye. It floored Kelly to think that these men might actually have known those long-dead kings and queens of England.

"You've got that right," Dmitri said, raising his glass to Marc. "To Henry."

The men repeated the toast, and Kelly shot a wide-eyed look to Lissa, who looked just as surprised. Lissa shrugged and raised her glass as well, joining in the toast as Kelly did the same.

"Ah, but I see we've shocked the ladies. Forgive me." Dmitri bowed his head slightly in Lissa and Kelly's direction.

"Come off it, Dmitri," Marc chastised his friend. "We all know you were going for shock value. It's so rare that we get to speak freely among mortals, or recent converts." He nodded to

Lissa. "Dmitri currently peddles his knowledge of the past as a history professor, if you can believe it."

"I am writing a book on Henry and his descendents for the University, but I didn't really need to do research on the subject. My trip was more for pleasure than anything else," Dmitri clarified.

"So you actually knew Henry the Eighth of England?" Kelly asked, feeling brave.

"Damned right he knew him. This fool," Marc gestured toward Dmitri with his goblet, "was sent to England in hopes of marrying into the family. Just because he was born the nephew of old Ivan."

"Who wasn't so Terrible," Ian and Atticus said in unison, deadpan. A moment later all four men burst into laughter. It was apparently an old joke among them.

Kelly had always liked history and if she remembered correctly, Ivan the Terrible had been coroneted the first Tsar of Russia at roughly the same time that Henry VIII died in England. Was it possible she was speaking to Russian royalty? Judging by the sparkle in Dmitri's eyes as he held her gaze, it was more than possible. It was fact.

"I can only assume by the charming look of horror on your pretty face that you've figured out just how old and decrepit I truly am," Dmitri said, giving her a jaunty salute.

The man was hardly decrepit. He was a hunk. Gorgeous, aristocratic features, sparkling, lively eyes and a muscular figure that was everything masculine proved he was anything but decrepit, though he was very, very old.

Kelly realized that everyone was looking at her expectantly. She had no idea how to respond, but she had to come up with something.

"I take it none of the Tudor heirs would have you for a husband, so you must've still been...mortal...at that time." She'd almost said "human", and she knew by now how much they hated that distinction.

"Ah. You see to the heart of the matter. I was indeed mortal when I went to that sceptered isle. When I eventually returned to Mother Russia, I was not. But that is a tale for another day." Dmitri polished off the remainder of his wine and rose to pour himself a refill.

"So what are you going to do about your home?" Marc asked, and Kelly was grateful for his change of subject.

She'd unwittingly hit on a sore point of some kind. Or maybe it was just too personal a thing to share with a new acquaintance. She wasn't sure if the story of how someone became a vampire was a taboo subject or not. She'd have to ask Atticus about it the next time she caught him alone. Or better yet, ask Lissa to ask her husband.

Dmitri settled into his chair in a lazy sprawl. "I have no choice but to wait and see who moves in above me, then gauge my next move from there. I won't give up my home easily, but if there is no other way, I may soon be looking for a new place to live."

"Isn't it kind of...uh...quiet, living out on the prairie by yourself?" Lissa asked. Kelly had talked with Lissa about the way she seemed to know all kinds of things she shouldn't and was shocked to learn that Lissa and her new husband shared their thoughts. It seemed Lissa was calling once again on the knowledge of her new spouse.

"I value my privacy," Dmitri answered in gentle tones. "There are not as many of us out there and my territory is larger, if less populated. There are lots of other supernaturals though, and therefore safety is something I cannot take for granted. That's why I built my home underground. There is little possibility anyone—be they *were*, fey or mage—could sneak up on me where I currently live. I like the arrangement, and I will be very put out if the new owner proves troublesome."

Kelly didn't like to think about the poor person who'd unwittingly bought the Master vampire's lair. Dmitri might be handsome and urbane on the surface, but she had no doubt he could be every bit as savage as Marc. She would never forget the sight of Marc's fangs, red with fresh blood as he lifted them out of a man's wrist.

Sure, the man had been crazy and he'd tried to kill both Lissa and Kelly only moments before, but still, it was a rude introduction to the world of the supernatural. Kelly had just had another. Dmitri's casual mention of "*were*, fey or mage" made her wonder just what—or who—else might be out there. But she wasn't going to ask. No, she'd already made enough waves for one night.

Chapter Four

When the party broke up about an hour before dawn, Marc found Kelly on the veranda. The night was still, the stars cold in the dark sky. It was the time of night he loved best.

"I see we had the same idea." He spoke in low tones to compliment the quiet of the pre-dawn hour, but Kelly still jumped. He'd snuck up on her again, much to his amusement. He loved the way she gasped when he caught her unawares.

"What are you doing out here?"

He liked the breathless quality of her voice. It made him think of forbidden things. Things he'd like to do to her and with her that were put firmly off limits by Atticus and Lissa. Marc would be a poor guest indeed if he took advantage of their hospitality—and their other guest—but oh, how he wished he could forget his principles for a few minutes. Just long enough to see if Kelly's lips tasted as luscious as they looked.

"Now is that any way to talk to a fellow lover of the night?" He moved to stand next to her at the wall overlooking the peaceful vineyard in the distance. "You do love it, don't you? The dark right before dawn. The silent hour of the night becoming day. I mean you no harm, Kelly. Surely you know that. Don't fear me."

"I'm not afraid of you, Marc, but you do make me uncomfortable." Kelly turned her gaze to the vineyard. "To answer your question, I do love this time of night. I never realized how beautiful it was before. I was always asleep at this time, before I came to work for Atticus."

"And your world has been turned upside down by the discovery of the supernatural."

She sighed, and he longed to put his arm around her. The instinct to comfort this puzzling female was different and unlike anything he'd felt in centuries.

"What did Dmitri mean when he talked about '*were*, fey or mage' tonight?"

"Caught that, did you?" Marc liked her quick mind. It was one of the more enticing aspects of her personality he'd come to appreciate during his time at Atticus's home. "We are but one of the many kinds of supernatural beings that inhabit this realm. There are *were*creatures of all kinds, a few fey who occasionally visit or some that even prefer this mortal realm to their own and a very few mortals who have magical abilities. Your friend Lissa has a tiny bit of magic within her. You call it psychic ability, but it's really just a manifestation of mortal magic."

"Psychic ability is magic." Kelly repeated his statement as if considering its flavor. "Huh. But she's not a magician. She can't produce a rabbit out of a hat on command."

"It's true, Lissa doesn't seem to have control over when or how she receives visions, but there are some mortals who are very adept at controlling their inner magic and some gifted people who can tap into the magic of other realms."

"That's amazing. When you say *were*creatures, you mean like *were*wolves?"

The warring notes of fear and fascination in her voice both amused and alarmed him. "Wolves, hawks, big cats, all kinds of predators. If you ever encounter any of these other supernaturals, be very careful, Kelly. Like us, not all are good, and most have strict rules of behavior that aren't anything you're used to in the mortal world."

"How so?" Kelly faced him without a shred of her usual reserve. Marc liked the way she sought his opinion and asked questions. This was perhaps the first real conversation they'd had since they'd first met. He liked it. More than he probably should have.

"*Weres* live by archaic rules. Most are predator species and as such, they have pecking orders, so to speak. Most have Alphas that rule the rest."

"Sort of the way you're Master over all the other vampires in this region?"

"Almost like that, but our Brotherhood is a much looser arrangement than the *were* hierarchy. We choose to abide by the Master's will wherever we choose to settle. The *weres* have familial packs, tribes and clans, dictated by their species and location. They seldom travel far from their home and within the group, leadership is often chosen based on bloody battles between competing Alphas. Many are fights to the death."

He could read the growing unease on Kelly's face and knew it was time to change the subject. In all likelihood, she'd never come across a *were*. There were a few in the area, but they tended to give bloodletters a wide berth.

"We don't interact much," Marc said, touching her cheek and drawing her gaze to his. "Most of the supernatural beings don't get along with each other. Few, if any, get along with us in particular because of what their blood does to us."

"What does it do?" He dropped his hand as she spoke, but he was glad to have her full attention. Just hours before, she would have been screaming bloody murder for such a simple, yet intimate touch.

"Shifter and mage blood is considered a delicacy. It's rare that we get a chance to sample from either of those unless the person in question agrees. They seldom agree." He cracked a smile, charmed when she returned the gesture. "Fey blood is too strong for us, generally speaking. The power it packs can act as a poison, but the lure is great. Half-fey, now, that's another story. The magic of the other realms flowing through half-fey blood is diluted enough for us to drink, but potent enough to give us a boost of power few of us ever experience.

It's a temporary effect, according to legend, but it's rumored to be the biggest rush an immortal can experience in this realm. But half-fey are even rarer than mages or shifters and they are more powerful than either of the others. Unless they are willing—for whatever reason—to share their blood, there's almost no chance for one of us to ever sample that kind of power."

"You mean fey as in fairies? Little pixies like Tinkerbell?" Kelly's nose scrunched up in the cutest way when she was puzzled. Marc had to resist the urge to kiss the freckled tip.

"Actually, they are fairly normal looking to our eyes, at least as they manifest themselves in this realm. The half-fey are, of course, also half-human, so they look just like you or me, but perhaps more beautiful than the average person. There is a Glamour of magic about them that makes them very visually appealing."

"That's fascinating."

"No, Kelly." He cupped her cheek, unable to resist the pull of her presence any longer. Marc moved closer, aligning his body with hers. "You're fascinating. You're the most beautiful mortal I've encountered in many years—inside and out."

He dipped his head, placing a chaste kiss on her upturned nose, as he'd longed to do. Her quivering response made him dare more. Pulling her into his arms, he went lower, to kiss her lips as he'd wanted to do for weeks.

She was just as delicious as every dream he'd had of this moment. And he'd spent a lot of time dreaming about the delectable Kelly.

As the kiss deepened, so did his desire. He'd never been so enflamed by a woman, so devastated by a mere kiss. She tasted of honey and wine, a rare combination that tempted his senses almost beyond reason. She tasted of life.

The only thing that could make this moment better would be if she allowed him to taste of her essence...her blood.

It was too much too soon. Marc knew that deep in his soul,

where his restraint was rooted in long years of patience. He would have her, but it would be elsewhere—away from his friend's home, where he wasn't beholden to respect the rules Atticus had set forth.

But she tasted divine. Marc lost track of time as he kissed the only woman he'd been this attracted to in more years than he could count. She fit in his arms as if she'd been designed to his exact specifications. She yielded to his mastery in the most delightful way and her little moans of pleasure were the sexiest he'd ever heard.

Only one thing could pull him from the sublime feel of her kiss...

The sun.

As the very first rays of dawn kissed the eastern sky, Marc knew his moment out of time with Kelly was at an end. He pulled back, regret filling his world.

"I haven't been tempted to stay out this late in many long years, but I'm glad my first vision of dawn in centuries was with you, *ma cherie*."

Kelly's beautiful blue eyes held the glaze of someone dazed with pleasure for a few precious moments more. Then realization of his predicament clouded her expression with worry.

"Get inside, Marc!" Kelly took his hand in her much smaller one and dragged him toward the door to the house. He went willingly, perplexed and charmed that she'd try to protect him.

Her reaction shocked him. She actually seemed to be anxious on his behalf and willing to push him inside, following close after to slam the door on the threatening light. She didn't stop herding him until they were well within the windowless hallway that ringed the inside of the home Atticus had designed.

"That was close." She slammed the door to the hall and leaned against it. Her pulse beat hard in her neck as reaction set in. Marc didn't know what to make of her, but the visible pounding of her blood against her pale skin had him licking his lips, eager for a taste.

He moved close, blinded for a moment by the hunger that grew inside him until it was nearly uncontrollable. Kelly's eyes widened in fear as he advanced on her. His fangs elongated as bloodlust and instinct overrode his saner side.

Marc wasn't sure what he'd have done if Dmitri hadn't chosen that moment to clear his throat. Marc looked up to find Dmitri watching him with narrowed eyes from the other end of the long hall.

A tense minute passed as Dmitri held his gaze, one raised eyebrow speaking volumes. At length, Marc pulled back. This was wrong. He saw that now. In a crisis of passion he'd let his impulses overcome his better sense, but oh, it had been sublime while it had lasted.

Marc drew back, away from Kelly. She trembled in reaction, fear lighting her beautiful eyes. Fear he had put there. Marc felt lower than pond scum.

"*Je suis désolé, ma petite.* I'm sorry." With those last whispered words, he backed away putting even more distance between himself and temptation. It was sunrise. He could feel the sun weakening him already. Lesser bloodletters would soon be down for the day, and the threat to Kelly would ease.

Nodding to Dmitri, Marc left her, realizing with a sinking heart that the only threat to her in this house was himself.

Chapter Five

The next evening, Dmitri cornered Marc in the library. Marc wasn't used to answering to anyone in his own territory—except perhaps his closest and oldest friends—and Dmitri fit that description on both counts. Still, it rankled to have his shortcomings pointed out by another, and Marc suspected Dmitri had sought him out for that reason.

"I'm leaving tomorrow," Dmitri said, taking a seat in one of the leather wing chairs that sat before a wide fireplace.

"So soon?" Marc closed the book he'd been perusing and set it back on the shelf before taking the seat opposite Dmitri before the fire. "I thought you'd be here for a few more weeks at least."

"So did I, but I just received word that the new owner has taken possession of the house above ground. I want to figure out just who she is and why she was interested in buying the place in the first place. It's no show place, that's for certain." Dmitri regarded Marc steadily. "But the question is, do you need me to stay?"

"If you're referring to what you interrupted last night, I assure you that I can handle the situation."

"It didn't look like it to me, if you'll pardon my saying so."

Marc bristled. "I don't care what it looked like. Kelly is in no danger from me. You should go home and look to your own house. And let me know if I can be of any assistance. You know I'm always here to help if you need it."

"That's much appreciated, Marc. And the same goes. Atticus mentioned something about an upstart named Gibson who might issue a challenge?"

The statement was phrased as a question, and Marc was glad to let the subject of Kelly and his lack of control the night before drop, to indulge in talk of the minor vampire who plagued him. Normally, Marc wouldn't have aired the dirty laundry of his territory, but this was Dmitri after all. They'd been friends long enough. They could discuss anything. Well, almost.

"Leonard Gibson is a foul creature, and I regret the day I gave him leave to live in my territory. I should have known he'd be trouble from the moment he came crawling in, seeking my blessing to build a lair nearby."

"Then why did you let him?" Dmitri's tone wasn't judgmental, but Marc had been asking himself the same question for a long time and he didn't like the answer.

"I guess I'd become too complacent. The sad truth is, I didn't care one way or the other at the time. I realize I should have vetted Gibson thoroughly before granting him a foothold in my territory, but hindsight does me no good now."

"So the question becomes, what are you going to do about him?" Dmitri had a way of cutting to the heart of a matter.

"I believe he'll challenge me sooner or later. I don't trust him to fight fair, but after last night... Well, I doubt myself and my control, Dmitri. Frankly, I'm sick of being Master, but Atticus has flatly refused the job, as did Ian, and they're the only two I'd trust with such power of those under my jurisdiction."

"Then you must kill this Gibson before he gets the chance to kill you."

Marc's resolve hardened. "I will." His hands tightened on the arms of the leather-covered wing chair. "As I said, I expect the challenge soon. When it comes, I'll be ready."

"I hope so, my friend. If you need me, all you have to do is call. I will gladly stand second for you."

Marc was touched by the offer. It wasn't something to be taken lightly. A commitment to act as his second in a formal challenge was a very large responsibility. Essentially, Dmitri had just offered to put his life on the line for Marc—something they'd done a few times over the many years they'd been friends, but not recently. It was good to know the bonds of Brotherhood were still strong between them.

"So now we come back to the matter of Kelly."

"I'd rather we didn't. She's driving me crazy, but I can't have her. End of story."

"Perhaps not." Dmitri shot him a glance that spoke of mischief. Marc remembered that look. It had prefaced some wild times in the past and always spelled trouble and pleasure in roughly equal measures.

"What did you have in mind?"

"Well, if you can't have her in the flesh, maybe you could have her in another way."

"Such as?"

Dmitri's grin turned downright devilish. "Are you up for a little dreamwalking?"

Marc wanted to deny the temptation, but he knew he wasn't strong enough. A Master, he had many gifts both physical and psychic but dreamwalking was something Dmitri had perfected to an art over the years. He'd always been fascinated by dreams and slept lighter than any other of their Brotherhood. During the hours of daylight he often amused himself by insinuating himself into mortal dreams, if he could find anyone asleep during the day. Marc knew he found it amusing but Marc also suspected it was a way he could still see the sun—in other people's dreams.

Dmitri had taken Marc along on his dream adventures before. Invariably, he coaxed his mortal dreamers into reliving some vacation on a sunny beach or even a simple Saturday afternoon ballgame in the park. Marc couldn't say he hadn't enjoyed those phantasmical forays into the mortal, sunlit world. Those memories were precious to him to this day.

"You propose invading Kelly's dreams?"

"Come now, it wouldn't be an invasion so much as a coaxing. I saw the way she looked at you. She's attracted, even if she doesn't want to be. I think she could really let go if she believed it was only a dream."

"You'd be there too?"

"But of course, my friend. I'm better at this than you are and we *have* shared women before."

"Kelly's different." Marc forced the words through his teeth. He didn't want to show any vulnerability where the mortal woman was concerned, but Dmitri knew him too well. No doubt he'd already seen how deeply involved Marc's emotions were with the little human.

"She is. Very different. She is a friend of our kind and a good woman. Not at all like the girls we used to bed." Dmitri moved closer, his voice coaxing. "I like her too, Marc. It will be no hardship to bring her pleasure, even if it's just a dream. She'll enjoy it and she'll have no idea that we'll truly be sharing space on the dreamplane. We'll treat her well, Marc. Just like old times. No—*better* than old times."

Marc thought about it. The idea was all too tempting. He'd shared women with both Atticus and Dmitri in the old days. They'd enjoyed finding new ways to pleasure their prey while they drank from them both physically and psychically. They'd been inventive back in their early years as blood brothers.

But they hadn't done anything like that in a long time. Atticus was mated now and would never join in their revelries again. Dmitri was a Master in his own right and they didn't often see each other anymore. This was a rare opportunity to do something both forbidden and entirely appealing. Dmitri could walk in Kelly's dreams easily and Marc could make love to her without her ever knowing it was at least partly real.

He could even bring her a sexual experience she would

likely never pursue in the waking world. Loathe as he was to admit it, he'd seen the way her eyes followed Dmitri. She was intrigued by him and Marc bet she wouldn't be averse to bedding him if she thought it was just a dream.

"All right. I'm in." Marc's bold statement made Dmitri smile. "When do we do it?"

"No time like the present. I'll catch her when she slips into the deepest part of sleep then bring you in. You remember how?"

"Of course. We used to do this often enough. I'll be waiting for your signal."

Dmitri held out his hand for a deal making shake. "Just like old times, *mon frere*?"

"*Oui*. Only better. I think Kelly will surprise us both once we get inside her dreams."

After dawn, Kelly took a breather. All the vampires had gone downstairs for the day and she was left alone in the big house. Surprisingly, she felt lonely when Lissa and the men weren't around.

She had a cup of tea out on the deck as the sun burned off the morning fog, taking time to settle her troubled thoughts. Marc LaTour was on her mind, as usual of late. The man was so frustrating, so handsome, so damned sexy! She had a real problem handling him. She wasn't physically afraid of him. She doubted he'd ever hurt a woman deliberately. But she was afraid for her heart.

He was immortal and she knew the chances of her being the One for him, like Lissa was the One for Atticus were next to nil. That kind of thing only happened in fairy tales. So anything between them could only lead to tragedy. She'd be wiser to stay as far away from Marc as possible, but her traitorous heart wouldn't let her.

She sighed heavily as she went back inside, cleaned what little mess she'd left in the kitchen and headed upstairs to her bedroom. She'd catch a few hours sleep now, then get up in the afternoon to handle whatever business of the Maxwell Winery had to be handled during the day. By nightfall, she'd be back with her friends and once more in danger of the temptation Marc posed with each breath of his sexy body and every flash of his cunning eyes. The combination of muscular male perfection and undeniable wit was her downfall.

Kelly made sure the house was secure, then went upstairs. She changed into her nightgown, and lay down on the plush mattress. Her room here was almost bigger than her entire apartment had been back in the city, and it was certainly decorated with much more style, not to mention very expensive furniture. It was gorgeous and she loved the large, fluffy bed with its down stuffing and silk comforter.

Each of the guest rooms and suites had a color theme. This one was pale lilac and it was fast becoming one of her favorite colors. The attached bath was huge and decorated in a complementary pale baby blue color. She could get used to living like this, if only Marc would go back to his own house.

If he weren't always underfoot, her life would be so much simpler. She was living and working with one of her best friends and Lissa's husband was utterly devoted to his new wife. It was a pleasure to watch them together and see the love Lissa had found. Kelly wanted that. She wanted a man to look at her the way Atticus looked at Lissa, but doubted she'd ever be so blessed.

Kelly drifted into sleep thinking about her friends and their love, clinging to the longing for a love of her own. Maybe that's why the first face that met her in her dreams was Marc's. He was everything she wanted in a man, but he wasn't for her. Immortal and impossible, it could never work between them.

"About time you got here." Marc met her with a lopsided smile. "We've been waiting for hours."

"We?"

Marc moved aside, and she saw Dmitri there, leaning

against a pillar in the weird dreamscape. They were in a forested glade, in the sunlight. This had to be a dream. Neither of the men could take the sun.

Woods were all around them, sparkling with life. Four pillars in the Greek style surrounded a giant platform bed hung with billowing white silk curtains. It was like something out of an old Disney film, only with much naughtier overtones.

Dmitri moved forward to stand beside Marc. "Do you like the décor?" He waved a casual hand toward the trees with a polite arch of one eyebrow.

"It's beautiful. It reminds me of a movie I saw once, but without the *were*wolves." She laughed, liking the ambient sound of the forest around her.

"You want a *were*wolf?" Marc looked scandalized.

"Not a problem." Dmitri waved one hand and a howl sounded through the forest, sending a shiver down her spine.

A moment later, a giant timber wolf stepped into the clearing. Kelly was frozen in place, though her first instinct was to rush over to Marc and cling to him for protection. The wolf began to change and from one moment to the next the wolf was gone and in his place was a man. A very muscular, very handsome, very naked man.

"Who's he?" Marc's low-voiced question was directed at Dmitri, but Kelly heard him.

"The Alpha of the wolf pack that lives near me. He's actually not a bad guy, once you get to know him, but he's not really here. He's just decoration."

"Are you saying he's a *were*wolf?" Kelly turned to Marc, seeking answers.

"Ah, *ma cherie*." Marc stepped up to her and touched her face, stroking her skin with gentle fingers as his gaze captured hers. "There are *were*wolves, *were*cats, *were*hawks. All sorts of predator spirits sharing souls with men and women all over this globe."

"This is too weird."

"You don't like him?" Dmitri asked, reclaiming her attention. "No problem." He waved again and the naked wolfman disappeared.

Chapter Six

"How did you do that? Did you just do that?" She looked from where the wolfman had been to Dmitri and back, but Dmitri only raised that aristocratic eyebrow of his and said something to Marc in French that was too rapid for her to follow.

A moment later, Marc's hands wrapped around her waist from behind and his lips touched the side of her neck. Shivers raced like lightning down her spine at his sudden, surprising, utterly devastating movements. He was warm against her back, his hands spanning her waist with open palms to cover as much skin as possible and suddenly she realized her plain cotton nightgown had turned into something much more sinful.

A silk gown flowed to the ground from just under her breasts. It was open at the front, flaring away from the middle of her chest, leaving her skin bare except for a tiny g-string barely covering the spot between her legs that was becoming wetter by the second. Marc's hands roamed lower, teasing the elastic band at the top of her panties, covering her tummy and making little sparks of excitement burst inside. She melted back against him.

"What's going on? Marc?"

"*Ssh, ma petite.* Let us take care of you." His hand dipped lower, beneath the g-string and into the damp curls at the apex of her thighs. Her hips lifted, inviting him deeper. "Good girl," he breathed at her ear. "I can feel how much you want me.

Almost as much as I want you."

"You were right, Marc, she is a beauty." Dmitri stood in front of her and watched all with those stirring dark eyes of his.

He stepped forward, just inches away from her, and lifted one hand to her shoulder. His touch was warm and knowing as he stroked one finger under the spaghetti strap of the gown.

"Her skin is as fine as silk," he commented to Marc.

"And as warm as sin," Marc agreed from behind her.

The way they talked about her made her feel hotter. It didn't make sense to her. She'd never enjoyed being talked about as if she was an object, and she'd never been in an intimate situation with more than one man in the room. Both things were making her squirm now though, and not in anger, fear or humiliation. No, her reaction was far from any of that. If she was honest, she'd admit she actually kind of liked it.

"We're going to make you feel so good," Dmitri purred as he lowered the strap he'd been fingering to slide down her shoulder.

Marc sank behind her, repositioning his hands to smooth down her legs. But the skirt of the gown was in the way. A tug and a loud rip made her gasp as he tore the skirt off, leaving her clad only in the skimpy top and the tiny g-string.

His palms shaped the globes of her ass, dipping between to search out the thin strip of elastic that was the back of her panties. She felt another tug and then two more at either hip and the g-string was no more.

Marc's fangs scraped along the fleshy part of her ass while Dmitri's hands made short work of what was left of her top. She looked into Dmitri's eyes as he snapped the spaghetti straps as if they were straw, and he stilled.

"You are beautiful, *ma petite*, but I suspect you want the Frenchman, *n'est-ce pas?*" He leaned in with a heart stopping smile and placed a gentle, chaste kiss on her lips.

Dmitri stepped away as Marc rose behind her, licking his way up her spine. She shivered as he stepped away, taking her by the hand and leading her a few steps to the edge of the pillared bed.

He spun her out as if they were waltzing, then drew her back in to him so that they were face to face, chest to chest. Both men wore dark pants and dark silk shirts. As she faced Marc, she wanted the shirt gone. She didn't want anything between her skin and his.

She tugged at the silk of his shirt, and a second later it was gone. It had disappeared like magic. She looked up to meet Marc's laughing eyes.

"It is a dream, after all, *mon amour*. Whatever you wish, you shall have."

The reminder that this was only a dream made her bold. She rose up on tiptoe.

"I want you, Marc." She reached up and kissed him this time, mating her lips to his as her breasts rubbed against his muscular chest. It was heaven. Better than she'd ever expected. But it wasn't enough.

And try as she might to control Marc, even in her dream, he seemed to dominate. His tongue dueled with hers in the most delicious way as his hands roamed her bare body. His pants had disappeared as easily as his shirt and she felt the evidence of his arousal against her skin. He was bigger than she'd imagined and very, very hard.

She liked that.

Marc drew away from the kiss with seeming reluctance, only to look down at her with fire in his eyes. He molded her bare breasts with his hands, coaxing the hard tips to even tighter arousal as he whispered love words in his native language. She wasn't sure exactly what he said, but it sounded divine.

A warm presence at her back startled her until she remembered Dmitri had been in her dream too. His hands ghosted down her waist, one in front, one behind as Marc's head dipped to nuzzle her breasts. Dmitri's fingers invaded her in front and in back, one sliding along her folds and dipping slightly within, the other riding the crack of her ass, tickling and teasing.

"She is wet for us, Marc." Dmitri's voice rumbled over her senses.

His faint accent was sexy and coupled with Marc's mouth warming her nipples, the forbidden naughtiness of having two men touch her at once turned her on as she'd never been before. She'd heard things. She'd even read a few novels where the female lead was treated to this kind of kink, but she'd never dared pursue such a thing for herself. She never would. But this was a dream and everyone knew all bets were off in dreams. You could do anything in a dream. It was the mind's way of working things out and experiencing things it never would in real life.

This dream was her way of working out the fact that she found Marc practically irresistible in real life. She could never have him for real, so the dream was her compensation. She'd thought Dmitri was pretty hot, too, though she hadn't had the same instant attraction to him. But he was close friends with Marc, and she had read those books... That had to be why he was in her dream too.

All thoughts of justification fled when Dmitri's fingers pushed deep inside her—both front and back. She'd never felt anything like *that* before. She squealed as he took her by surprise, and Marc's head rose from her breasts to favor her with a knowing grin.

"Like that? You can have that with us tonight. We'll give you everything you want, *ma petite*. I'll fill your pussy while my old friend takes your ass. Would you like that?" His gaze dared her. "I know we would enjoy it."

Slowly, she nodded. She wanted to give him everything. And she wanted more of this glorious feeling.

"*Bon.* On the bed, Kelly." His order made her jump as Dmitri's fingers retreated.

She hesitated, and Marc pushed her gently backward, onto the bed. He followed her down, coming over her the way she'd been imagining for weeks. She'd thought more and more about how it would feel to be covered by his hard body, overwhelmed by his strength and it was even better than she'd imagined.

When she was flat on her back, Marc held her there, letting her feel the way he fit over her, giving her just a bit of his weight as he held her gaze. There was something in his eyes that made her tremble, but it wasn't in fear.

"You are mine, Kelly. Do you hear? Mine."

She nodded, unable to speak as his head lowered. He kissed her as if it were the first time, beginning with a gentle possession that turned into a sensuous demand. He shifted his legs to one side while his mouth thoroughly ravished hers. His hands went to her breasts, tugging and toying, and driving her higher. Then more hands began blazing a trail of heat and seduction up her legs, one at a time.

Dmitri. She'd almost forgotten about him. She jumped and Marc broke the drugging kiss, looking down her bare body. He only grinned when Dmitri looked up and winked at her. They were working in tandem.

"Have you done this before?" she squeaked out.

Dmitri paused. "Not in a very long time," he finally admitted.

"We've shared women before, *ma petite*, but that was long ago. No woman has stirred either of us to this in a very long time." He leaned in to kiss the swell of her breast. "You are special, Kelly."

Their confession had the opposite effect of what she would have predicted. The thought of the deviltry they'd gotten up to in the past with other women made her hotter.

"You like that, don't you, little one? The fact that you inspire two Masters to a course they have not taken in decades?" Dmitri asked. He was watching her when she looked down to her feet and met his gaze.

She couldn't deny it. For the first time in her life she felt powerful and feminine. Marc wanted her. And more than that, Dmitri did too. She got the feeling they wanted *her* specifically, not just any female body. To her knowledge no man had ever wanted her like that. Most of the men she'd dated—and there hadn't been all that many of them—left her with the impression that they just wanted a girlfriend, and any woman would do.

None had been so focused on her as these two men. Vampires. They were vampires and she had to remember that.

And this was a dream. The idea made her sad, but also gave her freedom. This was her dream, so she supposed she could have anything she wanted. She didn't want to passively accept. If she was going to have this dream ménage, she wanted to be an active participant.

She sat up, Marc moving to the side to allow her room, but he didn't go far.

"I can really have both of you, can't I?" She looked from one handsome face to the other.

"That is why we are here, *petite*." Dmitri agreed readily.

She felt a smile bloom over her face as her thoughts turned lascivious. There was no other word for the way they made her feel. Two strong, naked male bodies, two powerful men with their attention focused solely on her. It really was a dream come true.

She launched herself into Marc's arms, nuzzling his ear. She felt him start in surprise, but the shock didn't last long.

"Make love to me, Marc. I've been waiting for so long."

"Your wish is my command." Marc let her push him to his back on the bed as she came over him.

She didn't want to wait any longer. She wanted him now. And Dmitri.

"You too," she whispered, looking over her shoulder at the dark-eyed Russian.

Fire leapt in his gaze as he watched her climb over Marc,

straddling his erection. She turned her attention to Marc, showering his face with kisses as he fondled her breasts.

"I've wanted you for so long, Marc."

She drew back, holding his gaze as she slid down onto him, driving his cock right up into her with one long, pleasurable glide of her hips. He felt even better than she'd imagined, but she had to move. She began a slow, sexy rhythm, climbing higher as her breathing increased.

He wasn't unaffected. Marc's pupils dilated, and his breath came faster. Sweat broke out on his brow and his teeth... She was startled to see fangs emerge from his mouth. She hadn't seen him like that since the awful night she and Lissa had been attacked, and he'd come to their rescue. There was no fear this time, however. This time, she knew his fangs were stirred by passion, not anger. She knew they were meant for her this time, and she felt no fear.

She felt other fangs nibbling along her shoulder, then up to her neck as Dmitri pushed against her back, asking her without words to lean forward. Marc's hands went to her ass, kneading, fondling, stretching.

Dmitri settled behind her and she felt warm oil of some kind that had appeared out of the nothingness of her dream. It drizzled between her cheeks as Dmitri's fingers helped it find its way within her. A few moments later, his cock followed. It was slippery with the same warm oil, but still it was a challenge to accept.

Her body eased under his knowing ministrations, and he claimed her ass as fully as Marc filled her pussy. Having both of them inside her at once was enthralling. It was utterly fulfilling and incredibly arousing. It was the naughtiest thing she'd ever done, by far, and it stirred her senses.

Of course, looking down and seeing Marc beneath her was arousing in itself. His smile when he felt Dmitri slide fully home within her was only fuel to the fire that already raged within her body. She moaned as the men began to move in concert as if they'd done this many times before.

And they had. She was sure of it. They'd told her so. But they'd also said no woman had made them want this in decades. Oddly, that made her feel special and almost...cherished.

The look in Marc's eyes only added to that feeling. He was careful with her. He regulated the thrusts of both Masters, coordinating her pleasure as her passion rose higher and higher. She'd never felt this way before with any man, never had such a scintillating dream. Ever.

She cried out as a climax hit her. Blindsided her in fact, and still the men thrust within her, lifting her higher. As a new, even higher peak approached, she felt Dmitri pressing against her back, pushing her down. Marc's head came up and nestled in her neck as Dmitri nuzzled the other side.

As an even bigger climax approached, she felt both men's fangs against her throat, one on each side. They struck simultaneously, launching her into the greatest pleasure she'd ever known.

The bites didn't hurt. They stung for a flash and then carnal heat suffused her being, rocking her world and making her scream. She felt them come inside her, exploding with warmth and groans of masculine satisfaction that rumbled against the tender skin of her throat as they continued to feed.

She felt like a goddess, a giver of life. She wanted to make them feel good and sated. She wanted them to feel the love in her heart. Or rather—she wanted Marc to feel the love she held for him alone, the willingness to follow anywhere he led, even into a ménage with his good friend, Dmitri.

She liked Dmitri, but she loved Marc. It was both the most fulfilling and the most frightening realization she'd ever had.

"I love you, Marc," she whispered as oblivion claimed her. It was only a dream, so she could say what was in her heart without fear of consequences. For this one moment out of time, in the privacy of her mind, she could speak freely, knowing she could never say it in the real world.

She felt his arms tighten around her as she drifted away, satisfied as she'd never been, her body and soul humming with the glow of ultimate satisfaction.

Chapter Seven

Marc heard her words and they shocked him out of the dreamstate. He woke abruptly in his room below ground, filled with the weakness that struck him during the daylight hours, but he remembered everything about the shared dream.

Kelly had said she loved him.

He hadn't dared hope she was harboring feelings for him, but now that he'd heard the heartbreaking words from her lips—even if just in a dream—he grew afraid for the first time in many long years. He didn't want the love of a mortal woman. He really didn't want to become involved with a creature that would grow old and die, and leave him alone again. He'd done it in the past, and each time he'd lost another piece of his heart. He'd steered clear of emotional commitments for decades and though Kelly called to him as no other had in a long time, he would steer clear of her as well.

If he could.

Marc was honest enough with himself to know the attraction between them might be too hard to fight, but he'd do his best. He'd fulfilled a fantasy. He'd trespassed in her dream and taken her like a savage with Dmitri's help. That should hold him for a while. From this moment on, he would avoid being alone with her as much as possible. It would be better for both of them.

Marc was resolved, but somewhere in the back of his mind he wondered how long he could hold out. Kelly called to him in a way no woman ever had. He'd do his damndest to stay away, but he feared he was too weak to accomplish that goal for long. Still, he had to try. For her sake, and his own.

Dmitri went back to his territory that night, and Marc did his best to avoid Kelly. He enlisted Ian's aid in keeping tabs on the woman, preferring to man the electronic monitors that spied on her when she didn't know it.

He bedeviled himself watching her working alone in the large office while Atticus and Lissa were off playing lover's games. Ian was a constant presence, annoying but faithful, doing the job Marc had tasked him with to protect Kelly. A silent shadow, Ian's stealthy presence acted as a check on Marc's nearly uncontrollable impulses. Everything in him wanted to go to her and take her in the flesh, but he was a civilized being—for the most part.

He could at least be civilized about this. He was a guest in Atticus's home. He would abide by Atticus's rules. And he would go to any length to protect Kelly from the gruesome fate Lissa had foreseen, even if that meant cutting himself off from Kelly completely.

He limited the time spent in Kelly's presence. He noted the strange look in her eyes the few times they came face to face. It was both accusatory and hurt, a combination that cut him to his core. Each time he thought of it, he realized the wisest course of action was the one he was on—whether she understood his sudden withdrawal or not.

After a time, she got used to the new détente. Life rumbled along as usual, with Kelly ably managing the vineyard offices for Atticus and even taking a few messages for Marc when people called the vineyard seeking him.

And so it was no great surprise when she delivered a message to him just after he rose for the evening. Atticus had sought him out for a private moment in his study and Kelly tracked them there, tenacious in her duty to deliver the message.

"A man named Leonard Gibson is trying to reach you. He asked his private secretary to set up a meeting at your earliest convenience."

Atticus looked over at Marc and raised one telling eyebrow. "Looks like he's decided to face you head on."

"Damn!"

Kelly was a little surprised by the vehemence of Marc's tone. It was the first time she'd ever heard him use any sort of vulgar language and it made her realize that this Leonard Gibson had to be something of a thorn in his side. If his tone hadn't conveyed it, the look on his face would have confirmed her guess. Something was definitely up.

"What are you going to tell him?" Atticus asked.

"I don't suppose you're willing to take my offer?" Marc challenged in return.

Atticus held up both hands in denial. "I told you already, I don't want to be Master. I'm enjoying my new wife too much to enter politics. Even for you, old friend. I'm sorry."

Kelly's eyebrows rose in surprise at learning that Marc had been ready to hand over his position of power to Atticus. It had to have something to do with the phone message, but she was too polite to come right out and ask. Instead she listened, shamelessly eavesdropping on the men.

She had missed Marc. Ever since he'd kissed her the night before she'd had that scandalous dream, he'd avoided her. She'd missed his handsome face and charming grin. She'd missed the way he teased her and most of all, she missed his kiss—that one fateful night had ruined her for any other man. The memory of those stolen moments haunted her dreams and her waking moments, but Marc had drawn away.

In retrospect, it was probably for the best, but it still hurt. She was glad he'd taken the initiative and backed off. When sanity returned, she knew there was no future in a relationship with a vampire. In fact, she wasn't altogether certain that he hadn't just wanted her blood. She wasn't sure if there really *was* a difference between sex and blood for a vampire. She wasn't sure if she hadn't been reading too much into his attention. Maybe all he'd wanted was a good time, and she'd fallen for him like the sap that she was.

Better not to get any more involved than they already were. She could be professional, and he'd been a gentleman the few times she'd seen him since that interlude on the veranda. It was good they'd both had time to come to their senses. Still, she couldn't help but admire the way he looked, the way he talked, the way he moved. He was a handsome devil, but he was no good for her and it was time she woke up and smelled the coffee.

She refocused on the ongoing conversation, alarmed by the varying expressions of disgust, resignation and fury on their faces. Something was seriously wrong if even Atticus was upset. He was usually the most even-tempered of men since his marriage to Lissa, but he was visibly upset.

Marc paced, turmoil following his every step to permeate the room.

"Then it'll be death," he said, turning to face Atticus.

Kelly gasped, and the two men seemed to finally realize she was in the room and had heard everything.

"Whose death?" The words tumbled from her lips, all thoughts of restraint banished by the air of desperation in the room.

"Nothing to be concerned with, *ma belle*," Marc assured her, but she noticed he wasn't giving any details. For all she knew, they could be talking about his death.

Suddenly she knew she didn't want to see him dead. No matter what had happened between them, she didn't wish him ill. Quite the contrary, she thought with shock. She'd come to respect and like him. More than like, if she were being honest with herself. In a perverse way, she missed their little confrontations and found herself oddly disappointed—even lonely—that he wasn't making a nuisance of himself anymore.

"Like hell," Kelly's voice rose. "You can't just say something like that in front of me, then pat my head like a toy poodle and tell me to be on my way."

"*Ma petite*, I can assure you, I do not think of you as a poodle. Where do you get such notions? I'm sorry. I didn't mean to dismiss your question. I only wish to spare you worry. It's not my death we were discussing, but Leonard Gibson's. If he presses his challenge, we will battle to the death and he is far less experienced than I. His death will be quick and as painless as I can make it, but I'll have to kill him if he challenges me."

"That's totally barbaric." Kelly was appalled.

"It's the way of our kind," Marc spoke in soothing tones, moving closer to her. He stepped right up to her, his arms coming around her loosely, naturally. She didn't even make a token objection to his nearness. Instead, she burrowed closer, tucking her head under his chin. She rested her cheek against his beating heart, like she was made to go there. She didn't question why she felt this overwhelming need to be close to him, and apparently neither did he. The distance that had been between them was no more.

Atticus seemed surprised for the short moment she met his gaze before she closed her eyes, but it didn't really register. All that mattered was Marc. She inhaled his warm, exotic scent, ignoring everything but being in his arms again. Being home, at last.

"I'll be right outside." Atticus cleared his throat and excused himself.

She'd forgotten he was even in the room. A moment later, Atticus was gone, leaving the two of them alone, though she only noted his departure peripherally as Marc held her close.

"I don't like the idea of a fight to the death, Marc. You may be a royal pain in the ass, but I don't want to see you hurt."

"Royal, I am not. But you're not the first to call me a pain in the ass, so on that score you might be right. I can assure you, I've fought many challenges over the centuries, and I've held on to this position for some time. That I still hold it should be proof enough that I can prevail against almost any challenger." He pulled back to tip her chin up with one hand. "Do not worry, *ma petite*. Though it touches my heart that you care for my welfare." He chuckled as a gentle smile stretched his lips. "I thought you hated me."

She reached up to cup his cheek. "I don't hate you, Marc, but you do frighten me."

"I could never hurt you, *ma belle*. It's not in me to cause you any kind of harm. I would sooner greet the dawn than cause you pain."

"Why?" she whispered. "Why me?"

Marc's eyes narrowed. "I don't know. All I know is that you fire my senses more than any woman has in more than five hundred years. When I smell the delicate scent of your skin, I want to lick you all over. When I see your beautiful face, I want to kiss you senseless. And when I hear your laughter, I want to be the one bringing you joy."

"Then why have you been avoiding me?"

"Precisely for those reasons, *ma cherie*. You are far too tempting, and I do not trust myself around you."

His voice trailed off as he tilted her head, angling his head down so she could see his kiss coming a mile away. He was giving her a chance to move away, a last chance for escape, but she didn't take it. Instead she raised her beautiful, stubborn chin and met him halfway, participating fully in the kiss, not merely accepting it, but demanding it.

Chapter Eight

The thought of her open acceptance sent his senses reeling, almost as much as her delicate flavor. She was the finest wine, softly scented and full of delight as he stroked her lips open with his tongue. His sharp canines lengthened almost to their full extent before he could reign in his uncontrollable response to her. As it was, he nicked her soft lip, sending just a microscopic trace of her essence into their kiss, bringing his hard body to instant attention and to an even higher state of arousal.

It wasn't enough for him to really get a taste of her. More a tease to his enhanced senses. A tantalizing taste of what could be. He wanted more. His body ached for more.

It seemed he had walked around half-aroused since the moment he'd caught sight of the lovely Kelly. That was unusual in itself. Centuries had passed since a woman could so completely captivate his senses and even longer since he couldn't control his masculine responses to a lush female form. The dream had only made it worse. He knew her darkest desires now and had an idea of what she was like in passion. The memory of how she had responded tormented him every waking moment.

He plunged his tongue inside, savoring the taste of her, and knew he must have more. Licking and tasting, he drew away from her delectable mouth, down over her chin to nuzzle his sharp teeth against her neck. He was almost there. He salivated at the thought of the rare vintage pulsing through her veins and how he suspected it would soothe the hungry ache deep in his soul.

"I've got to have you," he whispered, drawing back, preparing to strike.

A hard shove against his chest caught him off balance.

Unprepared as he was for her attack, she actually succeeded in moving him a few inches away from the tantalizing skin of her neck. He looked down into her blazing eyes, surprised by the light of battle in them when only a moment ago he could have sworn she was as deeply under his spell as he was under hers.

"I am not on the menu, LaTour. If that's all you want from me, you can find a blood donor somewhere else." She pushed against his chest, and he was so surprised by her sudden reversal and the tears gathering in her beautiful eyes, he let her go.

How could he explain that sustenance was the furthest thing from his mind when he thought of tasting her essence? He realized taking her blood into his body would be more than a simple act of feeding. This one woman had a power over him that no woman in over six centuries could claim. This one woman was not just another warm body flowing with life.

This one woman represented something much greater.

He didn't dare hope that she could be the One for him, but she was definitely something special. It was time he made her aware of that little fact. It was time for some real honesty between them. Time for him to lay his cards on the table. Before she could flee the room completely, he was there, in front of her, blocking her way.

"What I desire from you goes beyond sustenance, Kelly, so get that thought right out of your head. If all I wanted was a meal, any warm body would do. For that matter, I could have clouded your mind and you would have bared your neck to me eagerly." He pulled her almost roughly into his arms. "But I don't want that from you. I want you to come to me freely, of your own will."

"Is that some kind of vampire mojo? Do you need me to invite you in so you can have total control over me? Because if it's something like that, you can think again, mister. I am my own woman. I won't subjugate myself to you or any other man."

"Who said I want to subjugate you, *ma petite*?" His hold tightened as he stared into her eyes, using just a tiny hint of his influence to coerce her answer. He didn't want to use his powers on her, but this was too important to let go. If she'd been hurt in the past, he needed to know about it. "Where did you get that idea?"

It wasn't easy, but she was just susceptible enough to his mental push to comply. Her eyes went hard and cold, and he nearly growled.

"Who hurt you, *bebe*?" he whispered, desperate to erase the harsh look on her soft features. She shook her head. "Not me," she said finally, haltingly. "One of my friends. Her husband beats her, I just know it, but she won't say a thing against him. She won't leave him or even try to get out of her marriage. She's completely consumed by him. Under his total control. I won't ever let that happen to me."

The relief that shuddered through him took Marc by surprise. He wasn't happy she had to witness one of her friends in an unhealthy relationship, but he was glad she hadn't suffered at the hands of some other man. He hated to think what he might have been driven to do if a man who'd hurt her still lived. One thing he knew for certain, such a man would not live for long, and he wouldn't enjoy his last moments. Marc would make sure of that.

"I don't want to control you, Kelly. I want you to be my partner. My equal."

"Me, the equal of a six hundred year old vampire? Yeah, right. I'm as far out of your league as it's possible to get, Marc." She tried to pull out of his arms, but he wasn't letting her go.

"I think not." He caressed her back, his hands making small circles. "I think you're perfectly capable of playing in my league, as you put it. In fact, I think you outclass me by a mile. I'm the one who must work to be worthy of you, not the other way around. Won't you give me the chance?"

"Why? Why me?"

She'd asked him that before, but he still didn't have a good reason he could articulate. He only knew in his soul that it was so.

"I know not," he whispered, drawing her close. "I only know that I need you as I have needed no other woman in a very long time. I tried to stay away, but it's impossible. I want your blood, but I also want your body. I want to make love to you until the dawn parts us. I want to drown in your essence and fill you with mine. It's as basic and as complicated as that."

"And what about when you tire of me?" Her voice was small, almost smothered against his shoulder. "I don't want a broken heart, Marc, and you could easily tear mine to shreds."

He kissed her temple lovingly. "I doubt I could tire of you within your lifetime, *cherie*. Suppose I promise to stay with you as long as you want me? That would give you the control over how long our relationship lasts, no?"

She moved back just the tiniest bit to look into his eyes. "You would do that? You would yield part of your control to me?" She seemed stunned by the idea as he nodded. "But how can you know that you'd want me beyond the next week or two? We could be totally incompatible and yet you'd promise to be with me for as long as I want? It doesn't make any sense, Marc."

He pressed her small hand to his heart. "But yet, it is how I feel. I've only known you a short time, but my heart feels as if it's known you forever. It's been waiting forever, just for you."

She backed off, and he let her go this time. "You're scaring me, Marc. You're beginning to sound the way Atticus does about Lissa."

His head shot up. "I do, don't I?" He mused on that idea for a moment. "But yet, I am still unsure as to whether you could be the One, *cherie*. To be honest, I doubt I will ever find my one and only, but I do admit to feeling drawn to you as to no other woman before."

"How does a vampire know when he's found his mate?"

"I've heard tales, but Atticus told me that when he made love to Lissa for the first time, they joined more than just bodies. They joined minds and souls. She was in his thoughts as he was in hers." Marc was filled with awe at the very idea. "It must be heaven itself."

"So if we had sex and it was just sex, then it would prove we're not destined to be mates, right?"

Marc looked back to her, regret in his heart. "That's true. You either are my only one, or you're not." They both thought about that for a moment. It was a weighty concept.

"Okay," she finally said.

His eyes jumped to hers. "What exactly are you agreeing to, Kelly?"

She met his gaze with resignation, a bit of daring and a lot of uncertainty. It was an odd mix, but he felt something similar down deep in his heart, so he understood. This was a monumental moment. He could feel it.

"I can see how much this means to you and to be honest, I'm curious myself. I'm agreeing to have sex with you. Once." She was emphatic on that point. "If it proves to be more than just sex, we can take it from there, but I'm not agreeing to anything more until that question is settled."

Marc's blood heated as he stepped closer to her. "You do realize that when my kind makes love, we take the blood of our partners, don't you? We need both physical and psychic sustenance and psi energies are strongest at the moment of climax. I will want to drink of your essence as I make you come for me."

She seemed nearly mesmerized by his words and the hot

look of his eyes. Mutely, she nodded. Memories of her cries of delight in their shared dream haunted him. He wanted to hear that again, for real this time.

"Then meet me in the burgundy bed chamber at midnight. I'll hurry to take care of my other tasks for this evening beforehand so I can spend the rest of the night devoted to your pleasure. If you don't appear, I'll know that you've changed your mind." He wanted to crow in triumph at the acceptance written on her features, but made an effort to control his emotions. It wouldn't do to gloat. Or jump for joy, either. That would be highly undignified, even if he did feel giddy inside.

"I'll be there," she whispered. "I don't renege on promises."

"Neither do I, *ma cherie*, and I promise that I will show you more pleasure this night than you have ever felt before. There are some advantages to having lived over six hundred years, and I plan to show you them all, one by one, starting tonight." He lifted her hand and kissed the back and then her palm with a lingering touch before letting go and leaving the room. He had a lot to do before he could make good on his promise, but he reveled in the fact that before this night was through, she would be his.

Atticus met him in the hall and waited for Marc to follow him into the nearby library. When the door shut behind them, Atticus turned to face Marc. He knew it was only right to let his old friend have a say in what happened in his house, but Marc would not be denied. He would make love to Kelly this night, regardless of what Atticus had to say.

"My mate won't like this, but I can see how much you need to settle the questions in your mind. I think we will have no peace in this house until you've had her. I ask only that you not hurt her."

"I would never." Marc was insulted, though surprised by Atticus's consent. Kelly had been a point of contention between them. He wasn't asking him not to take Kelly, but only not to hurt her.

"I don't think you would hurt her physically, Marc, but it's clear her heart is involved in this...whatever *this* is between you two." Atticus threw his hands up in the air. "Even I can see you could hurt her badly with just a harsh word. She's been moping around this house since you backed off teasing her. Lissa worries for her friend. She believes Kelly might be in love with you."

The thought of it sent a thrill through his being, but Marc also felt the weight of responsibility as he'd never felt it before. He felt hopeful and joyous, but also reverent, wanting to cherish the idea that Kelly might feel affection for him. And he'd done little to earn it.

"I'll keep your words in mind, but Atticus, you have to know I cannot ignore this any longer. I've tried—" He pounded one fist into his other hand in frustration. "I've tried to stay away from her...to no avail. Better to settle the question, I think, before the impulse to take her becomes completely uncontainable."

Atticus looked at him with grave eyes. "Just remember the vision, Marc. I won't be listening at the door, but I will be attentive."

"Thanks for that, at least." Marc grimaced at his friend. "I mean only to make love to her, not harm her emotionally or physically. That vision will not come to fruition this night. That I can promise you."

Atticus regarded him for a long moment before nodding. "All right then. I'll keep Lissa occupied so she doesn't worry. Enjoy your evening, Master LaTour." Atticus winked, bowed slightly and left Marc shaking his head at his friend's temerity.

Chapter Nine

Minutes before midnight, Kelly sat in front of her vanity mirror, staring almost blankly at her pale reflection. She was downright scared of what the next hours would bring. Could she go through with it? Could she find the courage to meet the devastatingly handsome—not to mention persuasive—Master vampire in the burgundy bedroom? She wasn't sure, even after bathing, primping and perfuming herself for him.

She wanted him. That wasn't the problem. She wanted to know the feel of him, the length and breadth of his possession. More than that, she wanted to know the man inside. The man who had roamed the Earth for more years than she could grasp. She wanted to let the wild side of herself free to glory in his carnality. Every time she looked at him, her temperature spiked with desire, but she did her best to repress those responses. She feared the heartbreak he could deal her so easily.

Just this once, she wanted to tempt fate, to play with fire, to dare enter the dragon's lair and steal one small moment to treasure. One night.

Steeling herself, she rose and headed down the hall from her room to the burgundy guest room. This wing of the house was uninhabited except for her. It had been set up for the few mortal guests Atticus and Lissa sometimes entertained. Ostensibly the couple had the master suite in another wing of the mansion. In reality, they spent little time there. It had been sun-proofed just in case they found themselves above ground when dawn came, but they preferred the hidden, subterranean love nest Lissa had confided they'd created in one of the extensive cellars.

Lissa told her how Atticus and the other vampires felt safest when they knew they could sleep safe from the sun— preferably below ground in a cellar or cave during the day. That Marc would choose one of the sun-proofed guest rooms for their assignation was proof of his desire. It was a significant gesture that he put himself at considerable risk to be with her. It was also a silent vote of trust. That alone was a staggering thought.

She paused for a moment before the massive doors to the opulent guest room. Grasping the knob, she turned it lightly. Before she knew it, she stood on the other side of the solid door, holding the handle behind her back as the door clicked shut. She leaned against it. Marc was already there.

He stood by the huge bed, lifting a decanter of the deep red wine he favored, pouring out two glasses. He smiled with a light of fierce satisfaction in his ancient eyes as he moved closer, holding one fragile stem out to her. She took it and sipped automatically, barely noticing the fine vintage as Marc stared at her over the rim of his own sparkling crystal glass.

"I'm glad you came." He toasted her before taking another long sip.

"I don't know what I'm doing here," Kelly admitted nervously, "but I want this. I want you. For tonight."

Marc growled low in his throat as he took her glass and placed it with his own on a small table by the door. Without further comment, he slid one strong arm around her waist and pulled her close to his hard body. He bent over her, nearly sweeping her completely off her feet as his mouth drifted down to nip, kiss and lick the sensitive skin under her ear, over her beating pulse.

Kelly gave in completely at the first touch of his wet tongue. The sharp feel of his lengthening teeth surprised her at first and sent shockwaves of excitement down her spine. It felt even better than the dream. Her legs could no longer support her. Marc's strong arms carried her as if she weighed nothing. He deposited her on the bed with the gentlest of caresses as he removed her frilly white nightgown and let it drift to the floor.

He worshiped every inch of skin he revealed, never rushing, never really giving her a chance to catch her breath or object. He simply steamrolled over her sensibilities, doing things to her body she'd never allowed another man to do. Of course, she thought, he'd lived for centuries. He'd probably done things— sexual things—she'd never even dreamed. Of course, that dream ménage had been nothing short of shocking in the light of day. She'd bet he'd done that and more—for real—with other women.

The thought of him teaching her some of the forbidden things he knew sent her excitement level up another notch.

Marc couldn't get enough of the taste of her. She smelled like heaven and tasted divine. As he revealed her soft, pale body, he marveled at her flawless skin and her warm, womanly shape. He loved women of all shapes and sizes, but this one seemed as if she had been made just for him. She had everything he liked—large breasts with pouting nipples, a slightly rounded, womanly tummy, curvy hips and an ass that just wouldn't quit. She was built like the women of his time, not the stick thin models of this age, and he was enjoying every moment of discovery. He'd seen her in the dream, of course, but the reality was much better, much clearer and distinct. The dream had been intense, but it could not begin to compare with the real thing.

He lay her back on the large bed and spread her legs, thoroughly enjoying the view as he leaned down and inhaled the fresh scent of her. When he licked her skin, he felt her jump. He growled in satisfaction, knowing exactly what he wanted to do to her this first time they would join. From her innocent yet eager responses, he'd bet good money that no man had ever gone down on her before. It made him feel good to know that he was the first to bring her this special treat.

He licked lower, stroking with his tongue, letting her feel just the tips of his fangs against her super-sensitive skin. She moaned as he drew his tongue down and into her, pushing within where he would soon invade with his hard cock. He couldn't get over how soft she was and how good she tasted. She was the rarest of vintages, the finest of champagnes, light, airy and crisp on his tongue. She made his senses swim. He focused on his goal, tonguing her with single-minded intensity until she trembled with need.

When she cried out and shuddered with pleasure, he was almost unprepared for the flood of feeling that washed over his senses. Her delicious psi energies empowered him with a rush of sensation. He felt pride that he could bring her to climax with such small attentions. She would reach orgasm many, many times this night, he vowed.

"Feel good, *mon coeur*?" he asked, his breath fanning out over her most sensitive skin as she came down from the first little peak.

She nodded, humming her agreement as he enjoyed the sight of her flushed cheeks and elevated pulse. She was surprisingly innocent for a modern woman, and he found it completely enchanting. There were many things he could teach her about pleasure. It would be a joy to show her, but first things first.

First, he needed to know what it felt like to be inside her. He'd wanted to feel her warmth around him since almost the first moment he'd seen her, and he doubted he could put it off much longer without losing what little was left of his sanity. The dream had only made him more needy, not less. He needed to know the reality of what she felt like around him. Just as he needed to know if she could be the One for whom he'd been waiting all of his long, lonely life.

Frankly, he doubted it. He couldn't be that lucky. She was

perfect for him in almost every way, but he'd grown used to walking his path alone, he didn't quite believe that he'd ever find the woman who could walk that path with him.

Still, making love to her would at least settle the question, and he needed some relief before he exploded in his pants. With a grunt, he pulled away to divest himself of his clothing. He undressed with little finesse, throwing his clothes to the floor behind him. In moments, he lay beside her again, naked, hard and wanting. But not for long.

She was soft and dewy after her climax, but he had much more to show her. He moved his hands downward, toward her waist. Pausing to play with her nipples, he squeezed hard enough to bring her full attention back to him.

"You're a beautiful woman, *cherie.*" He lowered his face to kiss his way to her lips. "The most beautiful I have seen in my many years." His voice whispered across her skin.

She laughed softly, a mere puff of air as his skilled hands continued their way down through her neatly trimmed curls, zeroing in on the little nubbin standing at attention for him before finding their way inside her tight channel. She gasped as he tunneled into her, his fingers slippery in the slickness of her arousal. He smiled against her neck.

"I'm no beauty," she insisted in denial of his words.

He would prove her wrong if he had to spend all night doing it. Frankly, he looked forward to it. Kelly squirmed as he began to slide his fingers rhythmically inside her. He lifted his head to meet her eyes.

"I beg to differ, *ma petite.* To me, you are the most beautiful woman in the universe. Especially when you come for me." He drove her up that cliff again, using his hands and all his skills to enflame her senses. His fangs grew longer and sharper as the need to feast on her blood rose in him. His cock rose too and it needed relief as much, if not more, than he needed to taste her essence. "I must have you, *cherie.* I must have you now."

With a swift movement, he was over her, his fingers slowly

slipping from her core. She made a sound of protest that turned to a purr as he brought his fingers to his mouth, licking at the fluid of her desire. He closed his eyes savoring her unique and almost drugging taste. He held out his hand to her. He'd leave it to her how far she would go. Would she be a vixen, willing to tease but go only so far? Would she be bold, sucking his fingers like a professional? Or would she be shy, hesitant or even unwilling to get down and dirty with him?

He almost relished the idea that she would be reluctantly led into his sometimes nasty predilections in making love. There was no doubt he liked to push the envelope sexually. He had indulged in almost every perversion at least once. His tastes would probably be considered kinky, though not too extreme, except for the blood sucking, of course. Still, he'd never hurt or violated anyone. His partners had all been willing and willingly given him anything he'd wanted.

He would show Kelly the joys of following where he led, and she would love every minute of it. This he vowed.

But he wouldn't push too far, too fast. He'd break her in slowly, teaching her a little at a time until she was as eager for his cock in any orifice, or in any way, as he was to give it to her. This small first test was just the beginning.

With satisfaction, he felt her hot, little tongue peep out to lick at his fingers, coated in her come. She seemed shy but willing, a combination that fired his already overheated blood.

"I can't wait, *mon coeur*. I must join with you."

"I want you inside me, Marc. I need you inside me."

She was breathless as he fulfilled her wish, entering slowly but steadily. She was tighter than a woman of her years could be expected to be in this day and age. He wondered idly for a moment at the stupidity of mortal males that they couldn't see the diamond shining so brightly in his arms. At the same time, he was glad she'd had few lovers. It made what they shared together more special than it already was. Though he couldn't remember a time in the past few hundred years—in his entire lifespan as a matter of fact—when he had ever needed one specific woman more than he needed this one, pale little human who whimpered so nicely under him at the moment.

His dick slid, hot and heavy, into her wet core. He loved the feel of her. He loved the smell of her, and he loved the taste of her excitement. He knew he would love the taste of her blood even more. That could wait while he got her used to his cock, sliding in, then pulling back slightly, spreading her lubrication and easing his way further inside her.

She whimpered as he seated himself fully within her, but he could tell she wasn't in distress of any kind. Unless one counted dying of pleasure as distress. She was eager for him. He could feel the emotions rushing from her in waves that battered at him, filling him with urgency and the need to possess this one small woman beyond anything he'd ever experienced.

He began to move within her, stretching her tight sheath. Her body responded to him, inviting and encouraging as he moved more strongly within her.

"Faster!" she panted, nearing the edge sooner than he'd expected. To tell the truth, he was glad. Being inside her was more exciting than anything he'd experienced, and he wasn't sure how much longer he could hold out himself. This was going to be fast, but oh, so good.

He moved faster and she grasped his shoulders, wrapping her shapely legs around his waist. He loved the feel of her soft skin, urging him on.

"God! Please, Marc!" She was begging, the sound music to his ears.

Only one thing would make this moment more perfect. She was feeding his psychic need, but he needed her blood too.

Marc leaned down, letting his sharp teeth graze the spot on her neck he wanted. He could feel the pulse of her lifeblood just under her delicate skin. He wanted it. He wanted her. He wanted to taste her essence and make her come.

Moving faster within her, he pierced her skin with his sharp fangs, letting her feel only a tiny sting. Just enough to let her know what was happening. He didn't want her memory of this historic moment clouded by pain. He wanted this amazing woman to remember every moment, to remember him always with a smile on her lips as she thought about the incredible climax they were about to share.

The first drops of her blood hit his tongue and exploded through his senses, making him desperate for more. He pounded into her, tunneling deep, his mouth drawing the essence of her into his own body. He would fill her with his seed, she would fill him with her blood, and together they would find bliss unlike any either of them had ever experienced.

Her orgasm started almost the moment he'd pierced her flesh. She contracted around him, the climax building stronger and more powerful until she cried out, bringing him along with her. Her blood flowed into his mouth as he erupted into her welcoming body, each finding a home within their destined mate.

He realized that startling truth, beyond a shadow of a doubt, as they climaxed together for the first time. He felt everything she was feeling within his own mind, almost as if he were living it, looking through her eyes, feeling with her emotions. He knew it was the same for her. He could tell by the dazed look of the eyes that met his when he finally sealed the wounds on her neck and lifted his head.

She felt what he felt. They were sharing their minds and emotions fully. They were one. She was his One.

Chapter Ten

"You're my mate," Marc said reverently, stroking the mussed hair back from her cheek. "I can hardly believe it. You are my one and only. *Mon amour.*"

"I can feel what you're feeling. Know what you're thinking." He could see she was completely stunned. "And don't you dare laugh at me."

He chuckled, holding her tight, still tightly lodged within her body and her mind. He didn't want to leave. Ever.

"I'm not laughing at you, *mon coeur*, I'm simply giddy. I have searched for you for over six hundred years, and now you are mine. I honestly didn't think this day would ever come to pass." He leaned in and kissed her soundly, lifting to look into her eyes for a moment, then moving in for a deeper kiss as he grew hard within her once more. "*Je t'aime, mon amour.* I love you, Kelly."

"How can you love me?" She seemed utterly confused. Charmingly so, he thought. "You barely know me."

"How can I not?" He stroked her beloved face. "I am in your mind, *ma petite*, in your very soul. I love you. Of that, there is no doubt. Look into my mind, my memories, my soul, and see if you can deny that you love me too. It is fate. You are my destined mate, and there is nothing else I can do but love you. Even if the fates had not decreed it, I would still love the beautiful little hellion you are under that conservative facade. You are perfect for me, Kelly. You need only look within my heart to see it."

She tried to do as he asked, but her senses were in a jumble. Between his thoughts and emotions mirroring back on her inexperienced mind, and his cock, hard and rocking within her, she was more than a little overwhelmed. She focused on the physical. At least that she understood. Cock in pussy, orgasm soon to follow.

At least with Marc's huge cock in her greedy pussy. The man had more sexual skill in his little toe than all of her past lovers combined. Not that there'd been many. She'd bet he'd had hundreds, maybe thousands of women over his centuries of feeding off female blood and lust.

"They are as nothing when compared with you, *mon amour.*" He sucked on her skin as he rode her, deep and slow.

"Get out of my head." She tried to sound tough, but it came out sounding charmingly grumpy. At least that's what he thought. Damn, now she was doing it too. She'd lifted that thought right from his mind.

"Legend says it's natural for mates to share their thoughts, their blood and their bodies. Now that I've found you, I need never feed from another again. Your blood and our passion will sustain me for the rest of my days."

Marc rolled, letting her sit astride him. It was like the dream, but different.

"Did you like our dream, *mon ange?*" His voice purred, temptation itself, and in that moment she realized the dream had been much more.

"It was real?" She didn't quite understand what she was reading from his mind.

"No, my love, it was only a dream, but we shared it. We three."

"Three? Then...Dmitri was really there?" She was shocked nearly speechless.

"He has special skill in dreamwalking. He brought us both to your dream and the rest, as they say, is history. It was beautiful, wasn't it?" She gasped as he lifted beneath her, his cock reminding her of the sensations they'd shared in the dream. "Do you want Dmitri, my love? Do you miss him behind you?"

"No!" she shouted as he pulsed within her once more, but she knew he could read her thoughts. She didn't want Dmitri. She wanted only Marc, though the experience—now that she knew they had actually shared that scandalous dream with her, impossible as that seemed—would be one she'd remember all her life.

"You make me happy, *mon amour*." He lifted up to tease her breast with his tongue. His fangs followed, trailing over her tender skin. "Now ride me, my angel, and take us both to the stars."

She felt his desire, mirroring her own as he licked at her skin, making small love bites that didn't penetrate but sent her senses reeling all the same. When he finally bit down, she was moving on him rapidly, her own climax so near, she could taste it. He was close too, and feeling his emotions mixed with her own was both distracting and electrifying. She wanted to savor the sensation, but it was too intense.

She couldn't concentrate on anything as Marc's cock exploded, sending them both to the stars as he'd wanted. She'd never been pushed so high by an orgasm, never had it feel so perfect, so special, so...right.

He held her as she trembled, tears wetting her eyes and drifting down into her hair. Soothing her with his soft lips, he nuzzled her face, licking the tears away and holding her close. Cherishing her.

"Don't cry, little one. I'm here. I'll always be here for you now. For as long as we live." His whispered words reassured her, and at the same time struck terror into her mind.

"But how long will that be, Marc? Will you want me to

become like you? Will I have to become a vampire?" Her mind was in chaos. She didn't know what to think.

"Sweetheart, I would not force your decision. If you don't want to make the transition, I'll end my days when yours end." His eyes pled with her as her tears increased. "But that won't be for many, many years. We can worry about it when the time comes. For now, let's just be glad we've found each other. I won't ask you to take my blood. It must be your decision."

"But you want it." She could feel that from his mind.

He shook his head slowly. "I can't deny the truth of that. I'd like nothing more than to spend eternity in your arms, sharing the night with you, seeing the world change and evolve around us, but I want your happiness first and foremost. If that thought terrifies you—and I know at this moment it does—then I'll abide by whatever decision you make. I love you. I want to share whatever time is left to us in this realm with you."

He kissed her so sweetly, she cried even harder. He shushed her gently, rocking her in his arms as he lay back against the cool burgundy sheets. He held her long into the night as her mind whirled. She was simply overcome. Too much, too soon. She didn't know what to think, or feel, or do. She only knew that being in his arms felt more right than anything she'd ever felt before.

He was her rock, her comfort, her port in the storm of her emotions, and she loved him for it. Come to think of it, she loved him. Period.

"I'm glad you realize it." His soft voice drifted out of the darkness as he kissed her temple with gentle lips. She jumped. He was reading her mind again. "I love you too, *mon coeur*, my heart."

She turned into his arms, the storm of emotion flooding her once more. Her voice was a desperate whisper against his hard-muscled chest when she could finally manage the few words she knew in her heart and soul that he needed so desperately to hear.

"I love you, Marc."

Early the next evening, just after sunset, Atticus and Lissa drank a toast to Marc and Kelly. It was impossible to hide their relationship now. Marc was proud to have Kelly at his side and if she was still a little uncomfortable, it was to be expected. He'd pulled back mentally, giving her space to grow used to their connection.

He liked her shyness in front of their friends as much as he liked her boldness when they made love. They'd spent the rest of the night and the following day together. Marc had slept in the burgundy room, protected from the sun by the heavy shades and Kelly's love. She had left him for a while, but even in his sleep he sensed her in the house, eating, answering email and generally puttering around, doing her job.

She returned to him just before he woke fully for the evening and he greeted her with a kiss he would have liked to take farther, but Atticus and Lissa were waiting. Atticus had left word he wanted to see Marc before Atticus and Lissa left for a business outing just after sunset.

When Marc and Kelly came downstairs together, there had been no hiding their new status from Atticus and Lissa. Lissa had run forward to claim Kelly in a laughing hug of congratulations. Atticus had clapped Marc on the back with similar enthusiasm, giving hearty congratulations to them both.

Marc had waited his whole life to find Kelly and was proud to have their friends bear witness to their love. If he'd been wearing a suit, he would have bust a button his chest swelled with so much pride.

After drinking a toast to the newly mated pair, Atticus and Lissa took their leave and headed for the local business owner's dinner meeting. They didn't participate often, but as the owners of one of the largest and most successful wineries in Northern California, it was prudent to put in an appearance at mortal events from time to time.

"If Leonard comes for you before we return, send word." Atticus was deadly serious, admonishing his long-time friend before he left. He looked significantly in Kelly's direction, but Marc knew his mate could do little to alter the flow of events that would unfold. He wanted her kept as far as possible out of any possible confrontation. Marc grudgingly agreed to call Atticus if needed, though he much preferred to handle Leonard quietly without a great deal of fanfare.

"Ian is near." Marc knew that's all he had to say to reassure Atticus that Kelly would be looked after if Marc had to deal with Gibson this night. Ian was the most gifted at stealth among them. Even Marc couldn't always pinpoint where his most talented enforcer was when he was trying to blend into the background.

Almost before the tail lights of his host's car were out of sight, another luxury vehicle appeared at the gate. Marc sighed as he pushed the button to let Leonard Gibson in and within moments, his gaudy foreign-make limousine was winding its way up the long and twisting drive.

He'd hear what Leonard had to say, then send him on his way, if possible. If not, he'd finish him once and for all.

The car was an affectation, and a silly one at that. Vampires could easily transport themselves by shapeshifting into something that could run or even fly. Even the less gifted usually mastered the ability to shift by the end of their first century. Leonard had at least three centuries under his belt, but he still felt the need for showy, human trappings. It was just one of the man's many weaknesses.

Marc knew Leonard would never make a good Master. He was too wrapped up in himself and had too little regard for the welfare of those around him. It was the Master's job to keep the peace and the balance between the vampires in his region and the humans they lived alongside.

Marc was part enforcer, part judge and jury, and part lawmaker. His judgment alone stood between humanity and those like him, who held such vast power. It was important the Master have the good of both groups firmly in mind at all times. As Marc well knew, Leonard was too self-absorbed to think of anyone but himself.

Marc kissed his new mate soundly, sending her off to finish the paperwork she took care of for Atticus. He told her he had some things to take care of by himself and that he'd meet her shortly, but in reality he left the big house and went to meet the challenge out of her sight. He was glad that he'd kept his mind separate from hers in order to spare her confusion. He and Leonard would fight—if they must—beyond the first outbuilding where some of the wine vats were located.

After the connection he'd made with Kelly the previous night, it went against the grain to shield his thoughts from his mate, but it had to be done. Above all, he had to protect her from the harsh reality of his existence. At least, whenever he possibly could.

Chapter Eleven

"I don't want to fight you, Leonard." Marc sighed as the other man sneered.

"I don't want to fight you either, Marc. I want to kill you."

Shaking his head as he removed his jacket and folded it neatly, Marc knew there was no way to avoid this. He knew Ian was out there somewhere, watching over Kelly should the unthinkable happen and some twist of fate let this sniveling wimp win. In all likelihood though, Marc would see Leonard Gibson dead before the hour was through. It couldn't be too soon as far as Marc was concerned.

Leonard's people stayed with the limo, and Ian remained out of sight. Marc didn't know where his friend was, but he trusted Ian to be where he needed him most.

The challenge went as Marc expected it would. Leonard did all the posturing and proclaiming of any of the challengers he'd faced in the past, but like them, he went down quickly. Marc fought a clean fight, as he always did, but he should have known Leonard was enough of a snake to fight dirty.

There were few things in this world that could kill a vampire. A stake to the heart, full sun, the rare catastrophic injury that led to complete blood loss...and silver. Silver was agonizingly painful and took its time killing. It was a substance his kind steered clear of at all costs, but Marc should have foreseen that if Leonard didn't win their challenge, he'd have some way to get even.

He saw it in Leonard's eyes first, but by then it was too late to avoid the deathblow—a mere scratch in reality, but executed with devious zeal. Leonard clutched a silver claw whose hollowed out tips were loaded with pulverized silver dust. He raked it across Marc's chest and it burned everywhere it touched. Leonard fell dead with Marc's next blow, but he'd already killed Marc. Damnably slow and excruciatingly painful.

As Leonard's body turned to dust with the extinguishing of his life force, Marc fell to his knees, clutching his chest. He was only dimly aware of Leonard's people climbing back into the limo and driving away.

Marc's skin began to blister as the silver worked its way inside. The only thing that could save him now was blood and alcohol. Perversely, he lay in the middle of a vineyard with the deep red fermented blessing only a few yards distant in one of the outbuildings, but he had no strength to get there.

He felt himself losing the ability to reason or to think beyond the incredible pain. The doorway in his mind he'd been careful to keep shut opened wide. He felt the gasp of shock from his mate and he regretted the pain he caused her, even as he slid into a semi-conscious state on the grass next to Leonard's ashes. He'd be joining him soon, he knew.

"I love you, *mon coeur.*"

The thought whispered from his mind to his mate's in his last moments of coherence. It was all he could say but there was a wealth of feeling behind those simple words. He had many regrets, but most of all he regretted leaving her so soon. He'd only just found her, and now she would have to go on alone.

"I'm sorry."

Kelly gasped as she was hit by a wave of pain. Atticus and Lissa had just arrived home and were speaking with her in the hall when her world began to spin.

She vaguely felt herself being caught in her employer's

strong arms. She saw his worried face floating above her, but her mind was focused on the pain of her mate.

"Marc!" she screamed, clawing at Atticus to let her go, knowing that just a few hundred yards distant, her mate was breathing his last.

Atticus must have let her go because the next thing she knew, she was running across a field toward Marc's gasping body. Kneeling at his side, she uncovered the festering claw marks, at a loss as to what to do for him.

"Silver," Atticus hissed, placing his mate behind him. They'd apparently followed close behind her in her mad dash from the house to the field. "We have to get him inside to the vats." Lissa tried to move next to her friend, but her husband barred her way. "You can't touch him. The silver could kill you."

Worried eyes went from Marc's convulsing body to Kelly's tortured eyes. "Someone has to help him."

Atticus nodded solemnly. "I know."

Kelly took it all in with brutal clarity. Atticus was willing to risk his own life for his friend, but he wanted his mate far from the danger. Apparently she was the only one to whom silver wasn't a poison, human as she was. Making a quick decision, she found the strength somewhere deep within herself to hoist Marc partway off the ground, scooping her arms under his broad shoulders. She couldn't lift him, but she could drag him. She began moving while Atticus watched from a distance, knowing she had to do as much as she could. She didn't want her friend Lissa to feel this same excruciating pain of the heart at the potential danger to her own mate.

She struggled to drag Marc, turning back to gauge the remaining distance to the building. She was close, but her strength was flagging. Suddenly, she felt her load lighten. She looked back to find Atticus, his hands wrapped in as many layers of cloth as he could manage to help fend off the spreading silver dust, lifting Marc's feet so he didn't drag. It made it easier to carry him, sharing his weight without the friction of the thick grass against his lower body.

Atticus hissed with pain when stray particles of silver found the skin of his arms, but he was okay. They made good time to the building and brought Marc inside. Atticus dropped Marc's feet in front of one of the large vats and went to pull the covers aside.

"What now? What do I do?" Kelly was losing it. Marc was slipping away from her, she could feel it.

"Get him in the vat."

"You want me to drown him in red wine?" She was fast becoming hysterical.

Atticus lifted Marc's feet again, hissing when his hands came away blistered from the silver dust, but he lifted and pulled, getting Marc's lower half into the vat.

"The burgundy will counteract the silver. It's the only way." Atticus reached to help wrestle Marc's torso in, but had to stop. The pain was overwhelming. "You have to do it. Get him in there now or we'll lose him forever!" he shouted as he opened another vat and immersed his hands and arms up to the shoulder, sighing as the deadly silver was nullified by the rich red wine.

Kelly heaved and shoved until Marc flopped fully into the huge vat of burgundy.

Almost immediately, the wine started to bubble.

"What's happening?" She was terrified.

"Don't worry. It's reacting with the silver and his blood. The silver is poison to us because of the special substances in our blood and tissues. He had a lot of silver in his wounds. It may take a while to counteract." Atticus pulled his hands out of the other vat and let the wine drip off his skin as he walked over to watch the progress of his friend.

Kelly looked at his hands and arms carefully. She'd seen how blistered they'd become with just a small touch of the silver dust. They were nearly healed, but his skin still looked angry and irritated.

"If he comes out of this alive, he'll need blood the moment he rises from the vat."

Atticus spoke in a low voice at her side. "He won't be reasonable. The beast within will be in control. He'll be mad with pain. He could, and probably will be dangerous."

She knew what he wasn't saying. Marc could kill her. She understood the reality of that with one part of her mind while the larger part of her heart shouted that she'd do anything if it meant he would live.

"I'd give my life for his." Her voice was a mere whisper. She turned her solemn gaze up to Atticus. "Tell him that if..." She didn't finish the thought. She didn't have to. They both knew the next moments could be her last. "Tell him I love him."

Chapter Twelve

After a full half hour, the bubbles faded inside the vat. Kelly peered down anxiously, looking for any sign of life. Atticus had insisted that Lissa go to the house. Ian had emerged from the shadows, looking much worse for wear after being subdued by a dozen of Gibson's goons, to escort her. Atticus asked him to make sure his wife stayed inside the mansion. Whatever happened next, it was better to keep the number of people involved to a minimum.

Kelly screamed, caught off guard when Marc rose suddenly from the vat with a great whoosh of force as wine spilled all around. His skin was red from both the wine and his injuries, his eyes mad, flickering red in their depths, and she knew he was not himself. It broke her heart to see him like this...so close to the edge of utter madness.

With a peace in her heart she didn't expect, Kelly gave in when he grabbed her, hauling her close to his wet body and tearing into the strong pulse at her neck. The pain was nothing when compared to the pain of seeing Marc in such a state. She'd give anything to restore him—up to and including her life.

He drank greedily and without any finesse, his main objective to feed quickly and strongly from any available human. It didn't matter who or how. It didn't matter in his unreasoning mind if he killed. The idea of killing his prey didn't even register, he was so far gone.

The sweetness of her blood strengthened him like nothing he could have imagined. Somewhere in the back of his mind, he had the thought that this human was special in some way, but the agonizing pain overrode any real rational thought. He drank and drank, feeling himself gaining strength as the moments wore on. His pain started to ebb around the time he felt her heart flutter, her breath gasping weakly against his neck, and her body going completely limp in his arms. He drew back, a furrowed brow the only sign that his sanity was returning.

He frowned down at her, then looked around. He was standing in a vat of burgundy, his torso burning with pain and the most beautiful woman he'd ever seen, dying in his arms. Another was there too. Atticus, he remembered suddenly, as the other man strode forward.

"Marc?" Atticus's voice was tentative, searching for his friend within the monster he'd just seen.

"Atticus. What happened? Who is she?"

Atticus strode more confidently up to his friend, looking down at the woman Marc seemed disinclined to release.

"She is your mate."

"*Dieu!* Kelly!" It all came back in a rush as Marc checked her for signs of life. She was barely hanging on. He sensed it was only a matter of moments before she left him forever, and he knew he would die then himself. There was no way he could carry on without her, especially knowing that he'd killed her in his blind, horrible pain. He had been the monster from Lissa's vision. He'd been the one they needed to protect Kelly from all along. The knowledge left a bitter taste in his mouth.

"There's only one thing to do." Atticus eyed his friend gravely.

Marc nodded. "I wanted to give her time to get used to the idea. I didn't want to force her to this, but I have no choice." He caressed her pale cheek, taking a moment to shapeshift one of his long fingers into a claw sharp enough to make a clean cut across his wrist. He coaxed her mouth to the open vein. It was important that this first blood exchange be as thorough as possible. He wanted her to wake strong and...immortal, like him.

Kelly woke in her bedroom, Marc's warm, naked body wrapped around her equally bare form. She felt achy and a little odd. For just a moment, she didn't quite remember what had happened, then it came back to her in a rush.

Something inside her told her the sun was setting though she'd never been internally aware of such things before. She felt decidedly different, but was almost afraid to ask herself why. She knew Marc was awake even before he spoke. He didn't move a muscle, yet she was aware of him, in her mind, in her heart, in her very soul.

"I love you, Kelly. You must believe that."

She thought about the desperation she heard in his voice for a moment, not quite understanding, but willing to take him as seriously as he sounded. His arms imprisoned her from behind and would not let her turn to look at him. She let it go for now. She felt the desperation in his embrace as well.

"I believe it." Her voice was sure, but still weak. She cleared her throat and tried again. "I don't understand it, but I believe you."

He sighed, his breath rushing out against the nape of her neck. She felt his tension ease as he loosened his hold so she could turn around to face him. His eyes were sad and full of regret, but above all, she could see the love shining in them. Love for her.

"I'm so glad you're alive." She cupped his stubbly cheek with one hand. He turned slightly to place a tender kiss in her palm.

"You saved me, *mon amour*. Your love saved me."

"But what happened after...?" She trailed off, trying to remember, but all she could recall was his glowing, mad eyes and then profound darkness.

171

He soothed her, stroking her back gently. "I'm sorry, my love. I'm so sorry."

"For what?" She was starting to really wonder now. He was acting strangely—even for him.

"For attacking you when I was out of my mind. For taking away your choice. For bringing you over without your knowledge." He appeared to brace himself for her reaction, but she was stunned.

"You made me like you?"

"It was the only way to save your life. In my madness, I nearly killed you. It was the only way to keep you alive."

"I would have died?" Intellectually, she'd known she was very likely trading her own life for his. Atticus had told her how out of his mind Marc would be when he came out of the vat, but to hear him say it so starkly still shocked her. She'd been prepared to die to save Marc, but the question remained, was she willing to live as a vampire?

Marc had given her the choice...before. Now the choice was taken out of her hands. Whether to live with Marc as a mortal and die together at the end of her natural span of years, or to allow him to change her into an immortal that needed blood and lust to live was the choice she'd been faced with. She honestly didn't know how she would have solved that little conundrum had the choice not been taken from her by fate.

She could see that Marc was agonizing over her reaction. She also knew that he could read most, if not all of her thoughts. He would know the truth of her feelings, no matter what she tried to tell him, so it was worth thinking through and reasoning out.

In an odd sort of way, she was glad the decision had been made for her. She didn't want to give him up, and she didn't want to be the cause of his premature death if she'd chosen to remain mortal. She didn't doubt for one moment that he'd meant what he'd said about living out her lifespan, then choosing death when she died of old age. She couldn't bear the thought of that.

Yet, she found, suddenly all of that didn't matter. If he was to be believed, she was immortal. She would live forever, barring unforeseen circumstances, and she could share that time with him. Her spirits perked up. This was going to be okay. So, she'd have to drink blood. The thought still repulsed her, but then, so did liver, asparagus and caviar, but she'd eaten them all at one time or another. She could do what she had to do to survive. Even if it meant biting some poor guy on the neck every once in a while.

Marc growled. "The only man you will ever bite is me, *mon amour*, so don't even entertain the thought of drinking another's blood."

"I only have to bite you?" She snuggled closer to him. "Suddenly the idea has possibilities."

She gave him a devilish smile, which he returned full blast. He took her breath away when he smiled like that.

His mate was even more precious than he'd known. Not many women would have forgiven him so easily. Not that he wanted any other woman ever again. She was it for him. She was his one and only. His mate, for all time.

He was the happiest of men. His joy bubbled over and spilled into her, his smile touching both souls, joined as they were.

"I love you, my mate."

His lips found hers in a torrent of love, joy and need. He kissed his way down her throat, pausing at her pulse, knowing that this, her first feeding, would be special for both of them. He placed her on the bed, ridding them of the covers with one hard tug. They billowed out behind them to the floor, unnoticed.

"You will drink from me as I join with you, body and blood. Don't be afraid, Kelly. This is as it was meant to be between us."

She nodded, swallowing hard. Her eyes were enormous in her beloved face, her fear of what was to come shadowed only by her desire. Which was the stronger of the two was yet to be seen.

"I don't know if I can do this."

"I believe in you, *cherie*. You will do what you must so that we both may live and thrive. Never forget that I love you. You are the other half of my soul."

She smiled softly. "When you say it like that, I can't deny you a thing, Marc. You're downright dangerous."

"Never to you. Never again." His eyes were serious, his lips curving in invitation as he moved over her. "I will protect you from all harm for the rest of our nights. I will love you, honor you and give you sustenance as you sustain me."

He rubbed against her, his hardness sliding into its home between her legs, though not within her just yet. He felt her slick heat against his aroused skin and grinned.

"I want you inside me, Marc." She tugged at his shoulders, but he didn't move.

"You're so impatient, my little love. All in good time."

"I'm going to die here, if you don't get a move on!"

"You will never die, *mon amour*. Not now. Not ever. You will stay here with me, and when it is time for us to move on to the next realm, we will do so together. Do you understand?"

He couldn't help the fear that shot through him. She felt it too, he knew, echoing his emotions through their link, but he couldn't control it. When he'd come to his senses with her life draining away in his arms, he'd known a panic the likes of which he never cared to feel again. She would not leave him. She could not.

She must have understood his desperation because she tugged him closer, kissing his face with tender touches. He allowed himself to be pulled down into her warm embrace.

"I'm here, Marc. I'm not going to leave you. Not ever. I love you."

To hell with waiting. He'd love her slow the next time, but

right now, he had to join with her. He had to be inside her, body, mind and blood. His passion flared, and he knew she felt it.

He felt the resulting echo of her joy and passion as her body rose to meet his. With one long, hard thrust, he shoved home, finding his place inside her tight body.

He groaned as he thrust within her, knowing she welcomed him in every way. He could feel her mind opening to him and soon he'd take her blood into his body as she would his. He could hardly hold himself in check, just thinking about it.

Slowly, he began to move in and out of her tight pussy.

"Do you feel the need building? Do your teeth ache with the need to expand into fangs?"

He knew she was feeling the ache of her first fangs, and he had to guide her through this first small change. He moved deeper into her mind as well as her body, bringing rhythm to them both as he gave her a gentle, mental nudge toward the change of which she was so afraid. He witnessed the surprise in her mind as her canine teeth elongated into the sharp, piercing fangs that would allow her to feed from him.

"Marc?" She was uncertain, he knew, but willing to follow where he led. God, how he loved her.

"I'm with you, love. It's okay." He lowered his head, nuzzling her. "Lick my neck just below the ear," he coached in an excited whisper, "find the pulse with your tongue."

He nearly came as she followed his instructions, but held himself ruthlessly in check. This first time they would come together as they fed together. As it was meant to be.

He licked her in return, showing her without words how to zero in on the pulsing throb that meant sustenance to their kind. He groaned as she teethed him, teasing him as only a vampire lover could. He hadn't made love to many fanged women in his time, but he'd been with enough to think eagerly of the ways they could play together as she became more comfortable with her new strength and abilities.

They had a lot to look forward to.

"Bite me, Marc!"

Her plea rang through his heart, surprising him into action. She was ready.

He bit down, through her delectable skin and into her pulsing essence. Her taste flooded his mouth at the same moment he felt her first hard bite. His face buried in her throat as hers was in his, he could only groan against her skin as she took her first tentative sips from his body.

She moaned in pleasure, and he knew all would be well when she sucked harder at his pulse, demanding more. Her fears were still in the back of her mind, but the hunger for her mate was stronger at the moment. He pulsed within her, and she took all he could give and demanded more. He was nearly out of control. She was precious, his mate, and perfect for him.

He stroked into her as her essence flowed into his body, reviving his cells as his blood restored her in return. The psi energy of their mating was strong. It pulsed in them both, feeding their need for blood and lust at the same time—the way only mates could do.

It couldn't last forever. Marc neared his climax even as she began to shiver and shake around him. Her mouth stayed on his throat even as she screamed in their shared minds, her orgasm overtaking her and dragging him over the edge into the blissful oblivion of her body.

He groaned, his body seizing as pleasure washed over him. He knew she was flying every bit as high as he was, deep as he was in her mind, her body, her soul. He rejoiced in the joining that was as complete as they could make it. Never would he be alone again.

After long moments of bliss, they slowly floated back to earth. She kissed his neck, sucking lightly as he licked her wounds closed with a few final, nuzzling nips. She followed his example, healing him with her tongue, using her new powers without really thinking about them, having learned from his mind how to wield a few of the lesser powers of her new form.

"Are you okay?" He knew she was dealing well from the merging of their minds, but he wanted to hear her say it.

She nodded, nuzzling his jaw. She was soft in his arms, and very distracting, but he wouldn't be distracted. This was too important.

"*Mon amour?*"

She made a humming sound of satisfaction deep in her throat that threatened to make him hard again. He fought against it until he was sure she was okay with all that had transpired. He drew away, taking some of his weight off her and was slightly amused when she refused to let him go far. He took it as a good sign.

"Kelly? My heart?"

She lifted one sleepy eyelid to look at him. "Can't you see I'm basking here?"

He grinned. "That good, eh?"

"Don't get a swelled head. I'll admit the opening round was fantastic, but I have yet to learn if that was just a fluke."

He chuckled at her words. It had been centuries since a lover had teased him so brazenly. Never had he been with a woman he'd taken into his heart and his very soul. She was so special to him, it hurt, but in the best possible way.

"I can assure you, that was no fluke."

"Oh, yeah?" She arched an eyebrow. "Prove it."

He growled and pushed his newly awakened cock back into her. "Never dare me, *ma petite*. You'll find I'm always up to a challenge."

"*Mmm*, sounds like a good quality in a man."

"Not just a man," he panted just a bit as he started to stroke his way inside her, "your mate."

"Is that the same as husband?"

He slowed, looking down into her eyes. He knew how important it was to her. He hadn't wanted to push her, but yes, he did want her to accept him as her mate and her husband according to the traditions in which she'd been raised.

"If you want it to be. I was going to wait for you to get used to the idea of me before I sprang the question."

"Popped."

"What?"

"Popped the question. That's the proper phrase."

"You can correct my English at a time like this?" He stroked deep to emphasize his point.

She nodded against his shoulder, kissing any skin she could reach. "I was a school teacher before I started working for Lissa and Atticus. Correct use of language is important."

"I had no idea I was joining my life to such a stickler." Satisfaction purred through his voice as he picked up the pace, moving deep within her, though still in a leisurely way. "You'll be able to teach our young."

She pulled back, staring at him with hope burning in her eyes.

"We can have children? I mean, I thought—"

He sorted through the confusion of her thoughts. "Ah, I see. You thought our kind could not reproduce in the traditional way. It is rare, I'll admit, but possible between a truly mated pair. I suspect Atticus and Lissa may have the first announcement, but we will not be far behind. I want to have a child with you, Kelly, if you want it too."

She pushed at his shoulders again. "Then you damn well better pop the question, buster. I will not have our baby without a ring on my finger."

He laughed with the pleasure. "You're an old-fashioned woman, I see. That's good, for I am an old-fashioned man. I've made you mine in the way of my kind, but you're right, we should observe the traditions of humans. You will marry me."

"Stop."

Chapter Thirteen

His smug tone grated on her nerves. She found the strength to push him off her, immediately missing the feel of his hardness inside her, but needing to set something straight. He seemed surprised that she would use her new strength against him. The hurt look on his face almost stopped her, but dammit, she was going to have a real proposal, not some half-assed order to marry him.

"What's wrong?"

"I want a real proposal, Marc. I won't be ordered to marry you like some faithful dog."

His tension eased, but he was puzzled, she could tell. She was getting better at reading his thoughts, though it still freaked her out a little bit.

"What do you wish of me, *ma petite*? I will do anything for you."

She liked the sound of that. She smiled as she sat up on the bed.

"Get on your knees."

"Now that sounds interesting." His devilish smile lit the room, and she chuckled.

"Hold that thought. I want a traditional proposal."

"Ah, I see. And are most 'traditional proposals' carried out in the nude?"

"Among nudists, I suppose they are, but this will do for us.

I want a moment. A question and an answer. Is that too much to ask?"

He kissed her playfully on the nose before going down on one knee next to the bed. He took her hand in his, kissing it as he looked up into her shining eyes.

"You could never ask too much of me, my love. But now, I believe, I have something to ask of you."

She sighed as she watched him. He was a beautiful, powerful man. How did she get so lucky to have a man like this want her forever?

"Will you marry me, Kelly?"

Even though she knew it was coming—had demanded it, in fact—the question still took her breath away. Tears formed behind her eyes as she looked down at him, holding her hand so gently, with a hopeful light in his compelling dark eyes. She could feel the love shimmering in the air and in the space that joined their two souls. He loved her. She knew it soul deep, as much as she loved him.

Nothing would ever tear them apart.

"Yes." Happy tears ran down her cheeks. "I love you so much, Marc."

Her whisper set him free and he rose, standing at the side of the bed before her, gloriously nude and fully aroused. He was so beautiful it made her eyes hurt. She loved him more than life, more than anything.

"Show me," he whispered, cupping her nape under her hair and drawing her head close to his straining erection. He must've been listening to her thoughts because all she could think of as he stood before her was tasting him.

She moved forward without further urging, though he kept his hand at the back of her neck to guide her exactly where he wanted her. She let him lead, since her experience in this area was minimal and she wanted to know exactly what he liked.

She took him into her mouth, relishing the salty, primal taste of him. He groaned, and she felt her female power, daring to look up at him from under heavy eyelids. His taste was like a drug, his mesmerizing eyes focused on her, hot, smoldering and intense. She felt empowered that she could give him such pleasure. She felt it through their connection and reveled in her ability to please him as he'd pleased her.

"Suck harder, *ma petite*. Use your teeth." His words hissed out between his own lengthening fangs and the thought of it enticed her.

Vampires seemed to enjoy the slight rasp of their lover's fangs in a way that she imagined would frighten off most human males. With an inner smile, she felt her teeth grow just enough to make her oral explorations of his hard cock...interesting. She scraped gently downward and licked his tight balls.

"*Merde!* I'm going to come in your mouth if you don't stop."

She didn't heed the warning. She wanted to taste him fully, to know she'd given him pleasure. She focused on that thought so he could read it through their linked minds. His balls drew up and his cock tightened before he spurted down her throat.

She loved the flavor of him, so unlike the few mortal males she'd been with in this way. The feel of his emotions washing over her heightened the experience, his lust driving her own higher and feeding her senses. She swallowed every bit, licking her lips as he trembled in the aftermath.

When he calmed enough, he sank to the floor and drew her close. He was on level with her breasts and he paused a moment to salute them with his tongue before dragging her head down to his for a salty, wondrous kiss.

"You amaze me, *mon coeur*."

"I amaze myself sometimes." She tilted her head, smiling at him. "I'm glad you liked it."

"Liked it? Such terms are too insipid to describe how it felt, but it's your turn. Get on your knees, *ma petite*."

She eyed him suspiciously, but did as he asked, moving to balance on all fours in the middle of the huge bed. He positioned himself behind her, entering her aching channel in one deep lunge that stole her breath. He began to move, driving her higher and higher with each impossibly deep stroke. One devious hand reached beneath her to tease her folds and the nub hidden within, and while she was gasping, he brought his other hand down in a hard smack against her fleshy ass.

She jumped and squealed, totally unprepared for the loud sound or sharp feel of his hand. None of her prior lovers had ever spanked her, but that didn't mean she hadn't thought about it. That Marc would pick that particular fantasy out of her mind thrilled her. She could tell from the pure male satisfaction purring through their linked minds that he had enjoyed it every bit as much as she did.

"Have you been a bad girl?"

She smiled devilishly as she turned her head to look at him over her shoulder. He was so magnificent, he made her want things she'd never dared dream of before.

"I think I've been a very bad girl."

He slapped her ass with a reproving look. "How do you address me?"

She drew a blank, so he tried a different tack after giving her another swat.

"What is my title?"

Understanding dawned as she smiled again. "I've been a very bad girl...Master."

He growled in satisfaction as he moved more forcefully within her. He pounded into her deep, hard and fast, while raining hard, exciting smacks down on her delectable ass. She wouldn't last long, he knew from their linked minds, and he planned to come with her when she exploded, but he needed one more affirmation first.

"You once said you call no man 'master'. Did you lie to me?"

She gasped as she neared her peak. "Only you, my love. Only you, my Master."

He let go then, jetting hard into her as she came around him with a scream of delight. Her ass was a lovely shade of pink he would remember always.

Long moments later, they drifted in the afterglow. He stroked her hair as she snuggled at his side.

"You've never been spanked before, have you, *ma petite*?"

She shook her head. "I thought you'd lifted that fantasy from my mind. You mean you didn't know?"

He shrugged. "It was a lucky guess. So far you've been my perfect match in every way. No doubt you will like all the things I choose to do with, and *to* you."

"I can't wait." Her voice was teasing, but her eyes were shy as she tucked her head into the curve of his neck.

"We have lifetimes of discovery ahead of us. First, we'll get married and make our relationship legal in the eyes of your friends. Then we can work on the rest...for eternity."

Phantom Desires

Dedication

To the folks on my chat group who make each day so much fun.

To my family, who support me no matter what crazy thing I choose to do.

And to my editor, Beth, for her help and persistent good humor.

Chapter One

She woke, bleary-eyed, in that state where the mind is half-conscious but the body still believes it is asleep. She blinked several times, but sleep was winning. In the darkness, she thought she saw a man sitting in the antique chair at the side of her bed, watching her. He was utterly relaxed, and something about his stillness was confident and supremely masculine. Those impressions lasted even as her body won the fight with her semi-conscious brain, and she dropped back to sleep.

The next morning, the image of the man's shape stayed with her. A dark outline of a man that frightened her almost beyond reason. It had seemed so real. Not like a dream image at all.

She was a capable, steady career woman not given to fits of imagination. Yet, she could have sworn she'd seen a man sitting in her bedroom, watching her sleep in the dark of the night. Was he a phantom? Some sort of spirit left by the former owners of the old Wyoming farmhouse into which she had just moved? Or merely a stray figment of her imagination?

Carly shook her head and tried to ignore the shivers coursing down her spine at the memory of the slightly sinister apparition. The house needed a lot of work, and there was only her to do it. She pushed back the strange memory in the cool light of day and went to work unpacking, moving furniture into place and cleaning house.

The phone rang unexpectedly on Wednesday afternoon while she was polishing the wood in the foyer of the old house. Carly usually worked nights and spent part of the days working on her fixer-upper house. Her friends knew her schedule and knew when to call, so most likely it was one of them. She picked up the receiver and smiled when she heard the voice on the other end of the line. It was Jena.

"Are you ready to come home yet?" her friend asked only half jokingly.

"Not yet, Jen. I'm actually really enjoying myself. This old house has character and the town is kind of nice. It's good to get away from the hustle and bustle of California."

Jena sighed. "Well, I guess you did need less stress in your life, but I hate that you're so far away. We miss you at our monthly get-togethers."

Jena was a doctor and the mother hen of their group. She worried about all of them—the old college study group that had evolved into lifelong friends. Three of them were married now. The others had chosen various careers to which they were devoted. Jena was a physician, Sally a detective and Carly had her own software business.

"Oh, come on. Christy hardly ever shows up at our dinners anymore and Lissa and Kelly only come for drinks now that they've got hunky husbands to get back to."

"Exactly! Which is why we single girls can't afford to lose touch."

"I promise we won't lose touch, Jen. Besides, you know you have an open invitation to come here and see my new place. There's plenty of room and the local guys—from what I've seen—all fall into the big, brawny stereotype. Lots of ranchers out this way and real live cowboys."

"Be still my fluttering heart." Jena could be the queen of sarcasm at times, but Carly loved her all the same. "What about you coming home to visit us once in a while?"

"Jena, I've been gone less than a week!"

They both had a good laugh and caught up on the doings of their mutual friends before Jena got paged—which happened too often to Carly's way of thinking. The stresses of city life had truly gotten to Carly, which was why she'd sought this radical change in lifestyle and pace. So far it was working. Her stress level was lower, as was her blood pressure. She hadn't even told Jena about the new medication her doctor in town had prescribed. Jena would have had a cow. But the change in lifestyle was already making a dent, and she had a new doctor monitoring her health, which was already looking better.

She hung up the phone and started in on more restoration work. She could've hired a crew to do it, but she preferred to do it herself. She had wanted a hands-on project—which pretty much described the entire house—to give her something to do that was both relaxing and rewarding. She'd cleaned most of the house and was now working from front to back, restoring what she could along the way. If she found anything beyond her skill level, she'd call in an expert, but for now she was content to do what she could on her own.

On Friday night, after sleeping undisturbed for a week, a vivid dream once again assailed her. She was in a bedroom filled with lit candles, the spicy aroma of scented wax wafting sensually throughout the room. A strange man leaned over her naked body, caressing her with his eyes, followed by his strong, masculine hands.

"*Bella*, your skin is like warm satin." His words whispered over her, thick with an accent she couldn't place.

The stranger was handsome. Perhaps the most handsome man she had ever seen, but she knew this more from impressions than any real vision of his face. It was nighttime in the dream and shadows from the tiny flickering flames played about his angular features like a lover's touch.

He had a foreign air about him, from the cut of his shadowy hair to the thickness of his accented whisper. He watched her with a fiery hunger, and he was one with the darkness. Strangely, he seemed to know her, though she'd never seen him before in her life. She would have remembered him. Of that she was sure.

"Carmelita Valandro, you are a siren sent to tempt me." His whispers worked their way down her spine as his breath licked over her skin. He knew her full name. Nobody called her that anymore. How did he know?

"Your body is ripe and womanly, made to take mine." He praised her as his fingers delved between her legs, touching, torturing with pleasure. His lips moved down her body with leisurely deliberation, his teeth dragging at her skin, making her shiver with excitement. Slowly he repositioned her limbs, settling like a master between her legs, gazing his fill at her swollen folds as his hands drew nearer to her core, spreading her open for his touch.

His fingers were blunt tipped, long and thick. One speared into her, drawing a cry from her lips in the dream. She was ready for him and the feeling of his possession was like nothing she'd ever felt before. He knew her body and just how to play it. Like a master violinist with a Stradivarius.

He added another finger, twisting his hand like a corkscrew, using the blunt tips to arouse places within her she hadn't known existed. She whimpered in the dream, wanting more. He chuckled—a dark sound in the haze of the dreamplane.

"So responsive." His voice dripped with approval and made her even hotter. "I'm going to enjoy fucking you, Carmelita."

His harsh words made her jump. Dirty talk had never been this exciting, but this stranger made her want...so much.

"I will fuck you until you scream, little one. Then I will drink of you and fill you with my seed."

She could picture it as his fingers danced within her, stoking an intense fire in her body. She wanted it. She wanted to be possessed—fucked, as he so crudely put it—by this man, this shadow in the night.

"But first I want to taste you. I bet you're as sweet as cream and twice as addictive." His face loomed closer out of the darkness. A devilish smile graced his masculine lips and a sparkle twinkled in his dark eyes as he removed his fingers. She wanted to protest, but he moved closer, stilling her with his strong hands.

Leaning forward into the V of her legs, he gave her the most intimate kiss of all. His hot tongue slid inside her, a warm, wet invasion. Nothing had ever felt so good before. She convulsed in the dream and in reality with a gasping cry.

Shocked to wakefulness by a burst of pleasure so intense she'd never experienced anything like it in real life, Carly remembered the moment his tongue had touched her. The shock of it still coursed through her. It was familiar, yet as foreign as he was.

The feel of that unprecedented dream haunted her all day as she went about her chores, shopping, cleaning and putting the old farmhouse to rights. It puzzled her, excited her and heated her blood. But it made no sense.

Carly had been fondled by men before. She'd dated more than a few men in her life, but she had never once felt the instant flame of response her dream man had elicited. The echoes of the dream made her feel empty and that bothered her. Those few moments of dreamtime made her ache with longing for something she doubted she would ever find in the real world.

And it was just pitiful that the most exciting her love life had been lately were some vivid dreams. She was fast approaching spinsterhood, with no social life to speak of, but a very healthy bank balance due to her own hard work. She'd needed a change and moving out here to the middle of nowhere was the first step.

She could write the custom code for her computer software

anywhere, so why not the wilds of Wyoming? She had a contract with one of the colleges near Laramie and a sturdy SUV to get her there when it snowed. She'd bought the old farmhouse on a whim, but it suited her.

She had her work and lots of quiet and open spaces in which to do it. She had her friends too. Earlier this year, she'd gone to Lissa's wedding in California. Her old college friend had found a hunk of a man who owned a vineyard and together they seemed happier than anyone had a right to be. The old study group had stayed close all these years and she spoke on the phone with Kelly and Lissa often, now that Kelly had gone to work for Lissa and her new husband at their vineyard.

Work kept Carly busy, even on this isolated job. Once a week or so, she would meet with staff at the college. She also had to go down to the campus more frequently to test, observe and fix any glitches that came up. It was a challenging job and one she enjoyed.

Up until a few months ago, she would have been overseeing several of these installations at once. Now she was delegating the other installations and overseeing just this one, which was the most complex her little company had on the table.

Professor Dmitri Belakov watched the small woman race from her car. The sky had darkened sufficiently but still held that just-after-sunset glow he loved. Dmitri had checked the installation schedule and knew tonight the young computer programmer would be performing a key part of the installation process that would take her most of the night. It was his perfect opportunity.

First, he would teach his evening course in history, then casually drop by the administration building where his office was located. It was also where the sexy woman would be working, probably until dawn. He would meet her then.

She would never know he had been watching her in her new home for weeks, biding his time for the opportunity to meet her legitimately and put her under his spell. If such a thing was possible. This woman seemed to be immune from his more subtle abilities to an almost alarming degree. She had even caught him as he watched her sleep that first night. It was all he could do to overpower her strong mind and lull her back into a dreamless sleep.

She also had the disturbing ability to see him in her dreams. Several times, he had found his consciousness seduced into her dream. Each time, he was able to extricate himself only after some difficulty, leaving her none the wiser.

Except that one time.

In that particularly hot dream they had shared, he'd pushed her too far. He had wanted so badly to taste her—even if it was only in a dream. He'd brought her to a screaming orgasm with surprisingly little effort. The wave of pleasure had jolted her out of the dream before he could pull back and mask his presence. She had seen him that night, without a doubt.

But she was so sweet. He wanted to taste her in truth and perhaps he would, but first he had to work on seducing her mind.

Her strong mind and their close proximity made it imperative that he meet her in person and bring her under his power, but it had to be done in a subtle way. She had to be convinced that he was nothing special, no cause for alarm, so they could both live peacefully side-by-side in the wilderness.

Dmitri needed the solitude and peace of the open land as much as he surmised she did. He'd done some investigation into her background and learned of the high-powered lifestyle that had finally driven her out of the city and into the open places. He could commiserate with that feeling, but he needed the privacy of the open land for his very survival. Without the secrecy of his existence, all would be lost, and he could not let this one mortal woman endanger him.

She would come under his power tonight or she would die.

Chapter Two

The coffee was strong and black, just the way she liked it. Carly gulped down another mouthful as she set the high-powered computer in front of her to its task. The program would take almost an hour to load and install. She would have to sit and watch, to be sure it all took place as it was supposed to. Not a very exciting part of her job, but essential nonetheless.

She was settling back to watch the screen when she felt a presence at her side. Looking up, she jumped a bit. The most handsome man she had ever seen was standing above her, his gaze inscrutable as it passed over her form like a caress. He looked vaguely familiar, his handsome face teasing her memory for a moment until she dismissed the odd thought as foolishness.

"Uh, Professor Belakov?" The department chair had warned her that his colleague might stop by to check on her progress. In answer, he rolled a chair out from the neighboring workstation and sat altogether too close for comfort.

"Call me Dmitri."

His accent rolled over her, bathing her senses in warmth. She clenched her thighs together under the desk, feeling the wetness gathering there. All from just three words! What would happen, she wondered with an inward chuckle, if he uttered a longer sentence? Would she come on the spot? Gah! How embarrassing. But this guy was too good to be true. He was like a walking, talking erotic dream.

"Dmitri." She tested how the exotic name rolled off her tongue and found she liked the taste of it. "I'm Carly. As you can probably see, the installation is proceeding according to plan. So far, so good."

"Excellent." He turned his gaze from the slowly scrolling screen to rest fully on her. "I was told you were the best in your field when I researched this project."

She liked the sound of that. Even more, she liked the sound of his voice, his slight accent, his warmth. She could listen to him for hours. And yes, she decided he probably could make her come with just his voice alone. His voice sounded somehow familiar, but she couldn't place it. He too, seemed familiar to her, but the memory was elusive. Like a dream. She shook her head at her own foolishness, trying to focus on the matter at hand.

"That's a lovely thing to say." She fumbled, realizing he was waiting for some response from her.

"It's no more than the truth."

His eyes seemed to sparkle in the low light of the office. She kept the lights down when she worked late so as to minimize the glare from the computer screens, but now it was serving a double purpose. The low light made the atmosphere more intimate between them, causing her to shift in her seat. Her stomach fluttered, as did regions farther down.

The computer beeped, requiring a few keystrokes from her, which she put in almost by rote. She noted his gaze following her fingers as they flew over the keyboard. Usually when people watched her work they made her nervous, but this man had an entirely unexpected effect on her. This man fired her long-dormant libido. He made her want things she had never wanted this badly before. He made her want to throw caution to the wind.

She finished entering the last string of commands and turned back to him. He was such a disturbingly masculine presence at her side she needed to make him leave so she could think.

"I'll be at this a few more hours. It should probably finish the loading sequence somewhere around three in the morning."

"So late?" His voice warmed with concern. "I don't like the idea of you walking around campus alone at such an hour."

She shrugged, trying not to show how much his concern warmed her inside. She had been alone so long. Nobody had ever really worried about her keeping odd hours. No one since her foster parents, and they were long gone.

"It can't be helped. But I'll be careful. I can call campus security to escort me to my car if I feel the need."

"That will not do." He made a slight *tsking* sound as he shook his head gravely from side to side. "I'll tell you what. I need to mark a huge stack of essays. I can do that while you work here and when you're done, I'll walk you out myself."

"Oh, I wouldn't want to put you to any trouble."

"No trouble at all." He stood with some finality, his body language making her realize he would not take no for an answer. And what a body. He was muscular and hard in all the right places.

"I insist," he continued. "Perhaps you will join me for a cup of coffee at the all-night diner in town? I suffer from insomnia and find it difficult to sleep at night."

His self-effacing little shrug touched her heart. For such a strong man to admit to any sort of weakness was somehow very endearing. How could she turn down such a simple request, especially when her more adventurous side was yelling at her to take him up on his offer. She took a steadying breath and nodded, liking the immediate light that came into his eyes.

"That would be nice. I could probably use a bit of time to unwind after this is done. It's always the most boring, but nerve-wracking part of the job." She chuckled and he followed suit, the slight upturn of his lips lighting up his whole face. She thought just maybe a full out smile from him might very well kill her. He was that potent.

Dmitri surprised her by taking her hand. Bowing slightly, he kissed the back of it in an old-world gesture that would have seemed silly coming from any other man, but Dmitri Belakov had the right kind of dashing charm to carry it off. She nearly swooned when his lips parted, and his tongue brushed ever so lightly against her knuckles, dipping into the crease between her ring and middle fingers for a sensuous lick.

Her breath caught, and her eyes shot up to his. The amusement in his gaze lit a fire in her blood, daring her to laugh back and she did, surprising herself. The man was magic. He had to be. She had never responded to any man this intensely or this fast. Ever.

"Call me if you finish before three. Otherwise, I'll come check on you at that time."

She found she had no breath to answer him, merely nodding as he offered her a slight smile and left the room. She had been right, she realized. His smile was completely devastating.

At three in the morning, Dmitri returned to check on the small woman who was busily typing away. She was so intent on her work she didn't sense him at first, though that was hardly surprising. Most mortals would be unable to sense his presence at the best of times but he had come to realize this woman was much more sensitive than most mortals. She had sensed him in her dreams, pulled him into her phantom desires and was aware of him on a level most mortals would never plumb.

He liked that. Perhaps a bit too much.

She would, in all likelihood, die at his hands, but he would give her a fair hearing at least, before deciding her fate.

"Carly."

She gasped and jumped in her seat. Her gaze turned to him in the darkened room. "You frightened me."

"I apologize. I came to see if you were almost ready for that coffee."

She bit her lip, turning back to the glowing screen. He found himself staring at her perfect, white teeth as they worried the plump, pink lower lip. How he wanted to be the one biting her.

"Uh, I should be done here in about ten more minutes. The last module is being a bit stubborn." She turned back to her work, dismissing him from her mind as the computer problem took his place in her thoughts. He did not like being so summarily dismissed. The thought jarred him.

Usually, he was more than happy to leave his human prey with no recollection of his presence. In fact, it was important that he be able to exert control over their weaker minds in order to contain the secret of his existence. It was imperative to his survival and one of the most important rules he had set when he had taken over this territory some three hundred years before. He was Master of this region now, as he would be well into the future, barring some unfortunate circumstance. Only his death would cause him to relinquish leadership of the vampires in this region. He loved this wide-open country too much.

There were not many of his kind here, but enough that he had to exert his power and authority now and again. He led them with equanimity and fairness. None had ever complained about his leadership, though he ruled with absolute control and his word was law. Luckily for his people, he was a fair-minded man with more inclination to let them live as they would with only a few simple guidelines and laws they could not break. Breaking one of his laws, they all knew, would be cause for immediate and deadly punishment. Adhering to his few, well-reasoned mandates, however, allowed them all to live harmoniously in the shadow of the mountains where so many *were*creatures resided. There was an uneasy truce maintained between his kind and the *were*tribes and he wanted it kept that way.

Chief among his laws was secrecy. If it could be helped, no mortal should ever be left with a memory of their kind.

Vampires needed to feed from mortals, but he taught even the youngest of his people to cover their tracks. No memories remained with the mortals of their encounters with his kind, unless they were memories of exquisite sexual pleasure with an unknown, faceless partner.

He would love to give Carly those kinds of memories, in truth. He would fuck her over and over while he feasted on her blood, but manipulating her memories might prove more difficult than with the average woman. Her mind was enticingly complex for a mortal, with hints of something...other...he could not identify. It was there and then it was gone when he had invaded her dreams. It intrigued him, as did the woman.

She was bright—brilliant in fact—and had a confidence in her intellect that was very attractive. At the same time, she seemed wholly unsure of her attractiveness as a female. She had a voluptuous body, though her manner indicated she was still untried in many ways, her eyes going shy whenever he looked at her breasts with interest. That intrigued him as well.

More than that, she had a purity about her, a kindness that manifested itself in the small ways she interacted with those around her. He'd watched her closely over the past weeks. She was thoughtful, respectful of her elders and those for whom she worked, and honest in her dealings. Those were rare traits, he knew, among mortals of this generation. She was unique and uniquely arousing.

She turned him on as no woman had done for centuries. All he had to do was look at her for his body to go hard and wanting. All he had to do was think about her for his fangs to drop, seeking her essence.

Before he realized the passage of time, she was turning back to him, a brilliant smile on her face. She seemed genuinely happy about the victory she had just won over a stubborn computer program.

"All done."

He found himself smiling back and noted the hitch in her

breathing. His eyes strayed to her pounding pulse then down to the swell of her breasts. She was so aware of him, he knew it would be easy to take her now, but he needed more information. He needed to know if she was a threat to him, and if so, he needed to decide her fate. Live or die? He did not want to rush to judgment on this one.

"Shall we see about that coffee?"

She nodded, collected herself and stood. With a few economical moves, she shut down the computer system, then grabbed her coat. He took it from her before she could put it on and held it open. He wanted to get his arms around her, the sooner the better, but he was cautioning himself to slowness. He had to get her used to his touch first. Gentleness wasn't something he was used to giving, but he instinctively knew it was what this particular female needed.

She turned her back to him and allowed him to help her into the coat. When he didn't let go, she started nervously, like a frightened doe, but he held her close, her back to his front, his arms wrapped around her over the bulky shearling coat.

"You are a beautiful woman, Carly."

He nuzzled her soft hair, seeking the scent of her skin where her shoulder joined her neck. He felt her shiver and smelled her rapidly rising arousal. Good, he thought, she is as responsive in the flesh as she was in her dreams.

"Um, thank you." She seemed frozen in place, curious but frightened. He liked that she did not run from him. If she had run, he knew his predatory instincts would have come to the fore and he would have chased her down. This was so much better in the long run. He needed her to come to him willingly. Keeping that goal foremost in his mind, he let her go and stepped back, breaking the spell.

The all-night diner was surprisingly busy, but they were able to snag a corner booth that was relatively quiet. Dmitri was the perfect gentleman, encouraging her to order whatever she liked though he stuck with plain black coffee. She noticed he didn't drink much of his coffee, just a few sips. When she questioned him on it, he said he didn't want the caffeine keeping him awake. She wondered why he hadn't just ordered decaf, but let the question slide as he neatly changed the subject and started asking questions about the new software system she was installing.

Before she knew it, three in the morning was only a memory and it was getting closer to dawn. Dmitri drew her attention to the slight pinkening of the sky and she gasped. They had talked for more than two hours though it seemed like only minutes. She was that comfortable with him.

With a few parting words and a somewhat awkward—at least on her part—peck on the cheek, he let her go. She climbed into her car and set out for her little farm, about twenty minutes away by car. As she crested a hill, the sun greeted her and the beauty of the dawn stole her breath. It was a beautiful day to be alive.

Chapter Three

Dmitri made it home from their rendezvous with only moments to spare. He could fly quite fast when there was need, but he had cut this just a little too close for comfort. Still, he reasoned, any time spent with the enchanting Carly was time well spent. She had thoroughly captivated him as they had sat in the diner, talking about anything and everything.

His mental abilities allowed him to probe a little beneath her complex surface, learning more about the thought processes that went into her answers to the many, many different questions he had posed to her. Though she hadn't realized it, she was being carefully studied, analyzed and judged. He had decided rather quickly to let her live at least a bit longer while he probed deeper into the amazing effect this surprising mortal woman was having on his mind and body.

All she had to do was smile, and he was ready to fuck her. Hard.

He knew he could make her want it. He had read her attraction to him in the subtle shifts of her body, the alluring scent of her arousal. It was heady stuff. He hadn't wanted sex with a mortal in a very long time, but this one woman was making him want sex with her, and her blood, in the worst way.

And he would have her. Both her luscious body and her sweet, life-giving blood. She would feed all his desires, his hungers and his needs. Then he would decide her fate. For now, he would invade her dreams once more and begin the process of seduction. While she slept in the farmhouse two stories above his own dwelling, he would seduce her senses and bring them both an echo of the pleasure they would find together.

He spread her out before him in their shared dream, her whimpering cries of pleasure music to his ears as he licked through her folds and delved his tongue within, mimicking the motion he wanted to make with his cock. She writhed beneath him, her legs churning as pleasure threatened to overtake her.

"Come for me, little one." He whispered against her wet, silken flesh as his fangs came down, his excitement growing. With a growl he nipped at her little clit, fighting against his baser nature to treat her gently, his teeth teasing, not hurting. He never wanted to hurt this small woman, giving herself so freely to him in the realm of dreams. He vowed silently that she would give herself just as freely in the flesh.

He couldn't wait much longer to claim her in truth. The short time he had already spent studying her only made him want more.

She spasmed against his mouth, crying out her release as he rode her through the storm, licking softly. This time, the climax didn't startle her out of the dream. He knew she was greedy for him now and the pleasure he could give. She stayed in the dream, wanting more. Wanting him. It made him feel like a king.

At length she quieted, and he knew it was only a matter of moments before she was once again writhing in his arms. He worked toward that goal, stretching out over her, suddenly naked in the way of dreams. He rubbed up and down, his body against hers, his hardness against her softness, his hunger against her welcoming warmth and wetness. She was almost there.

Lowering his head, he brushed his closed lips against hers, pulling back, making sure he held her eyes as he smiled, letting her see his fangs. The moment of truth. Or close to it, at least. If she thought about it at all, she would put his appearance up to her imagination in the harsh light of day. Dmitri wanted her to think about what she had seen in the dream. There was no question in his mind. She would be remembering this dream when she woke up. He willed it so.

He'd done his best to mask his identity in their past shared dreams but no more. He wanted her to think of him and wonder until he could see her again the next night.

Then he would challenge her. He would confront her perceptions of reality and dreams. He would claim her for his own. At least for one night. Maybe two. Maybe a decade. Time meant little to him, a Master of his kind.

She gasped as she saw him fully on the dreamplane, her hand coming up between them. He thought she meant to push him away, but she would find him impossible to move. Instead, she surprised him, her soft eyes turning curious as she traced delicately with one finger over the sharp point of one deadly fang.

The motion cut her and a drop of her precious blood welled up onto her skin. She drew back, but he grasped her hand and brought her bloody finger to his mouth, licking to taste her.

Her eyes darkened with desire, shaking him to his core as he sucked her finger in deep. He laved the little digit, coaxing more of her essence into his suddenly starved senses.

Too bad this was only a dream. He longed to know what she tasted like for real. Soon, he counseled himself. Soon.

He pulled back, allowing her to pull her finger free with a slight suctioning pop. He parted his lips, letting her see what was coming as he lowered his mouth to her soft throat. She fired his blood as she made no move to stop him, uttered no words of fear. She wanted this. If only in her dreams.

As he moved down to her beautiful throat, he moved his cock to the hot, wet opening that was so ready for him. As his fangs plunged into her jugular, his cock thrust home inside her.

A hot, wet glide of possession that fired his senses as her blood bathed his tongue in the most delicious flavor imaginable.

Too bad it was *only* imaginary. He would have her in the flesh. Soon. This phantom taste of her only whetted his appetite for more.

Her blood pulsed into his mouth on the dreamplane as his cock pumped into her hot pussy. In and out, harder and stronger, his desire flamed higher than before.

"Please," she begged in a gasping whisper as she strained beneath him.

He could read the desire, the need in her voice. She was desperate to come. He felt her beginning to contract around him, her cries speaking nothing of fear, only of ecstasy.

"Harder, Dmitri! Harder!" She gasped next to his ear, sending him higher into the throes of his own desperate desire.

He pushed her to her limits and then beyond, his mind intimately twined with hers in the realm of the dream. Her heart pulsed in time with his thrusts, hot and hard, fast and strong. He knew she was seconds away from exploding, as was he.

With a groan, he sucked deep on her delicate throat. In a surge of ecstasy, he exploded hot within her tight depths, feeling her release squeeze him with velvet gloves while he came and came, longer and stronger than anything he'd ever known. Even in dreams.

Their coming together was magical and sublime. He found himself already thinking of when they could do this again. He wanted more of her body, more of her blood. More of her.

With a polite lick of his tongue, he closed the wounds on her neck, pulling away as they both floated back to Earth in the dream. He made sure he had her full attention before speaking, not allowing his fangs to retract. She needed to see all of him, even if she would only think it was part of her imagination the next day. When he knew he had her focused on him, he dipped his head close, holding her gaze.

"You will remember this, Carly. You are mine now. All

mine."

Carly woke that afternoon, her mind hazy from more odd dreams, her body still humming from a dream orgasm that was better than any real one she'd ever had. She remembered every moment of the strange, hot, incredibly erotic dream. Suddenly her phantom lover had a face, and it was Dmitri Belakov's!

She scoffed at her own imagination. Why, she had dreamed he was a vampire, of all things. How ridiculous.

The man was definitely sexy and had gotten under her skin in a big way, but he was no vampire. Vampires didn't exist. It was just his sexy foreign name and slight accent that put her in mind of those old horror movies she had loved as a kid.

Still, he certainly made one sexy hunk of a vampire in her dream. She couldn't remember ever achieving such complete sexual satisfaction from a dream before. One thing she knew— Dmitri Belakov was potent if just the memory of him in her imagination could make her come like a freight train.

She had work to finish on campus that night and as she showered and dressed, she couldn't get the memory of that incredible climax out of her mind. How on earth was she going to face the man when in her mind he had been making love to her half the day and sucking her blood? There was no way he could know the content of her erotic dreams, but *she* knew, and the memory would claim her the moment she saw his handsome face.

"Well, this is going to be an interesting night at work," she said to her reflection as she got ready. She was still shaking her head as she made her way out the front door of her little farmhouse.

Down below in the secret dwelling, Dmitri laughed. She had no idea.

Chapter Four

Carly sensed Dmitri's presence an hour after she settled in for the night in front of the bank of computers. She had more loading to do, then a bit of testing and it would be all done. She was always happy when a project completed successfully, but she would miss the campus. If she were honest with herself, she would admit she'd miss more than just the campus. She'd miss the man. Dmitri intrigued her more than was probably good for her, but she just couldn't help herself.

Carly yawned as she faced the screen, suddenly aware of Dmitri at her back. He moved so silently she hadn't heard him come into the room though the whole building was pretty much closed for the night.

"Didn't sleep well?" he asked, a sexy smile on his lips.

She smiled and shook her head. "I had some odd dreams."

He swiveled her chair around to face him.

"Some dreams," he purred, his eyes lit from within, "are more than just dreams."

"What do you mean?"

"How did it feel when you came in my arms last night, Carly? Did you like the way I licked your pussy and fucked you with my tongue? I can assure you, it will feel even better in the flesh."

Carly gasped as his fingertips traced down her arm, over her soft knit shirt. Even with the fabric between her skin and his, she could feel the electricity of his touch. "What are you talking about?"

"I'm talking about last night in our dream. I shared it with you, Carly. I've never come so hard or so good as I have these past nights in your arms. In your dreams."

"That's not possible!" She drew back from him in alarm, but his strong hands on the arms of her chair held her in place.

"Oh, I assure you, it's more than just possible. It's real. As am I."

Dmitri felt his fangs aching...dropping...and he knew she would see everything. It was time. He smiled. She gasped.

"Oh my God. You're...you're..."

"Vampire." His voice vibrated through the room, and he knew she was affected. He detected a slight trembling of her lithe body.

"You're crazy! There's no such thing."

"I beg to differ." His smile widened as she brought her fingers up, as she had in the dream, to test the sharpness of his feeding teeth.

Like in the dream, she felt the sharpness of his tooth but pulled back before it could pierce her skin. He found himself disappointed. How he wanted to taste her.

"You're not kidding, are you? This isn't some kind of elaborate joke?"

Her voice was soft with wonder and a touch of fear. All in all, she was taking this better than he would have credited. It had been decades since he'd had to reveal himself to any mortal and such revelations usually did not go so well.

"I'm afraid not. I am, as they say, the real deal."

"Are you going to kill me?" She asked it straight out, with a courage he admired.

He shook his head. "I had given it some thought, but you are too interesting to destroy, Carly. Too intelligent." He stroked her soft hair away from her face. "Too beautiful."

"Then what are you going to do with me? Why show yourself?"

He stepped back, releasing her chair completely. He paced away a short distance, his eyes following her movements as she straightened her sleeves unnecessarily.

"Now we come to the crux of the matter." He sighed. "I have been watching you for some time. Since you moved into the farmstead, in fact."

"The farm? Why?"

His gaze pinned her. "Because I live there as well." He paused but she made no comment. "Under your home, several stories down into the earth is a replica of the farmstead. I have been living there in peace and safety for over a century. For all that time, the same family owned the land and house above and we peacefully co-existed until old Jacob died. He had no family to leave the place to in his will, so it was sold."

"To me." Her voice was a surprisingly calm whisper.

"To you," he agreed with a nod. "Now I am faced with the problem of a mortal inhabiting the space above me who has no idea of my existence and no loyalty to the agreement I had with Jacob's ancestors, binding on all subsequent generations. That agreement is, in effect, null and void now that their line is ended."

"So you want to make a new agreement with me?"

He smiled. "I thought so at first." He moved closer to her once again.

"But?" she prompted.

"But I recently became dissatisfied with the old arrangement. I want to broker a new deal with you, Carly. A much more intimate deal." His hands framed her face, tilting her head up to his. "I want you, Carly. In my bed at night and safeguarding my rest during the day."

"Does this also include...um...my blood?"

His smile turned carnal. "Indeed. I want to taste you, Carly.

I want to drink you and take your essence into myself. But I won't hurt you. I will only bring you pleasure, like I've been doing in our shared dreams, only much, much better."

"Oh, God." She was overwhelmed by him...by everything.

"I can see I've given you a great deal to think about." He stood and headed for the door. "Finish your work here and I'll see you home." He turned to look at her, his dark eyes pinning her in place. "I'll give you a bit of time to decide, Carly, but I can't wait long. I want you more than any woman I've ever met and believe me, that is saying something. Call my name, and I will come when you're ready to leave."

How she got through the final installation and testing, she never knew. Around four in the morning, the job was finally done. True, it had taken her quite a bit longer than she had originally estimated but with such chaotic thoughts racing through her mind what else could she expect? It wasn't every day she was propositioned by an honest-to-goodness vampire.

Holy shit! That thought and several others raced through her mind every few moments despite her best efforts to stay focused on the project. She had to finish it tonight. It was important she settle her work before tackling the much larger personal problem she had just inherited by buying a cursed farm.

How was she to know there was a vampire living under her house? Shouldn't the real estate agent have disclosed something as serious as that? She laughed inwardly at the thought, knowing the old man who had owned the house before her had taken the secret to his grave as his ancestors had before him.

They had lived with the vampire, apparently with no ill effect. All the people she had spoken to about old Jacob had loved him. He had been a happy old man, always ready with a kind word or a helping hand, or so everyone claimed. No way could he have been some kind of evil servant of the undead.

Right?

But Dmitri wanted more from her than peaceful coexistence. He wanted her blood and her body. He wanted her to be his mistress, she realized with some shock. Here she'd been hoping since she was a little girl to find some good man and become his wife. Apparently fate had something different in mind for her. She was to be the mistress of a vampire. Either that...or what? She realized with a shiver that Dmitri hadn't given her an alternative.

When she could delay no longer, she called his name softly. In moments he was there, his dark gaze boring into her, watching her every move as if he could see into her mind. And perhaps he could, she thought with a gasp.

"Can you read my mind?"

He chuckled. "Actually, not well. Most mortals have surface thoughts that are easy to pick up, but your mind is more complex, Carly. Beautifully complex."

"Well, thank heaven for that," she muttered but still, she could tell from his amused expression, he had heard every word.

"Come." He picked up her coat from the chair and held it open for her.

She allowed him to help her as he had the night before and, as before, he did not release her right away. He held her close, wrapped in the coat and his strong arms while his mouth teased the skin behind her ear and down to where the pulse beat strong in her neck.

She felt his sharp teeth scrape over her flesh. It sent shivers down her spine but whether of fear or arousal was anyone's call. She knew what he was now and it gave every one of his motions a whole new meaning.

He released her and stepped back, holding the door for her. When they got to her car, he simply held out his hand for the keys before taking the wheel and guiding them safely, if a bit speedily, home. Apparently the undead liked to drive fast.

When he pulled into her barn as if he lived there, she recalled with a start that he did. If he was to be believed, there was structure under her house where he slept during the hours of sunlight. She wondered if it would be some kind of creepy crypt.

He held her door and tugged her small hand into his. He guided them toward the opposite end of the large barn, passing her collection of odd automobiles as they went.

"I meant to tell you I really liked the Aston Martin," he said as they passed the car in question. "I've always loved those cars and the '66 Mustang is gorgeous. Will you let me drive them sometime?"

She chuckled at his obvious enthusiasm. "Vampires like vintage cars?"

"Everything about me is vintage."

She laughed along with him as he led her to one of the few remaining horse stalls. Inside, he tugged on a nondescript piece of wood and revealed an ingenious trapdoor that she never would have noticed in a million years.

"This is one of the entrances to my home. There are a few tunnels running deep under the property so you'll understand my caution about any plans you might have been making to dig anywhere near the house."

"Yeah, hidden tunnels would be kind of hard to explain to a construction crew, but not to worry. I have no plans to dig anything, except maybe a few pansies and tulip bulbs."

"That should be safe enough," he agreed with a sharp-toothed smile as he led her down a dark, winding spiral staircase.

He took a flashlight from his pocket and gave it to her. Apparently he could see in the dark but had brought the light for her. It was a thoughtful gesture that seemed oddly kind considering the dire situation.

When they had walked a distance down a relatively straight

and surprisingly well-appointed tunnel, he unlocked a massive steel door, inputting several combinations of numbers and at least two keys before it swung open with hardly a sound. He motioned her to precede him and with a wave of his hand, lit several candles to illuminate the spacious room.

"Take a look around." He swept his hand out in a welcoming gesture.

They were in her living room. Well, not her living room, but a replica of the room in her house above ground that was the same size, shape and position to the front door. She moved forward, noting the lovely, antique furniture. In pristine condition, it was the elaborate décor of a bygone era. It was beautiful.

The doors from the living room led off in the same configuration as her home above, though the rooms were used for different purposes. Her kitchen, for example, was a very masculine study complete with wingchairs, a beautiful writing desk and an elaborate computer station. As she explored further, she found a spacious bath with waterworks probably shared from the house above.

She avoided the door that would lead to the master bedroom, but Dmitri was behind her every step of the way. He cornered her in the room next door, a room he used as a library, though it had comfortable chairs and a sofa near the door.

"So what is your answer to my proposal, Carly?"

She faced him squarely, her heart in her throat. "Do I really have any choice?"

He shook his head slowly. "No. Neither of us has any choice in this at all, I fear." He moved closer, taking her in his arms, gently but securely. "Fate has decided for us, my sweet. You are mine."

Chapter Five

"I'm not a promiscuous woman, Dmitri."

"I know." He smiled gently. "I value your discretion and the fact that I will be the only man to know your beautiful body from this moment forward. You will be mine completely, Carly. Don't expect me to be able to share you or let you go."

He brought his lips down to hers, probing inside with his hot tongue, unable to wait, but she was with him every step of the way. A little hesitant at first, she was soon grabbing at his clothes, pushing the jacket from his shoulders with eager hands. She wanted more of him. For real this time.

He took her to the sofa, tucking her under his large frame as he tore at her clothing. The coat had been dropped in the living room, thankfully, but the button down shirt and jeans she wore were definitely in his way. Buttons popped and scattered as he tore the shirt open, literally ripping it from her body. Her jeans were harder to deal with but he dispatched them just as easily with his great strength. The lace of her bra was gone with the snap of his fingers as was the little scrap of lace between her succulent thighs.

When she was naked, he sat back and looked his fill. She was gorgeous, as he knew she would be. Generous breasts and a womanly, hourglass figure nearly had him drooling. She had the body of a 1940s pinup girl. His own personal wet dream come true. Lifting her in his arms, he took her into his bedroom, where he had dreamed of having her for many long nights.

"This is the room from the dream." She seemed to recognize the opulent four-poster bed and the tapestry wall hangings as he deposited her on the plush goose down mattress.

"This is my bedroom, Carly, where I have brought you and taken you many times already in our dreams. This time, it's for real." He smiled, allowing her to glimpse his fangs as he spread her legs as wide as they could go, securing them to the posts of the bed with silk cords.

He'd known all along she would be his and had prepared accordingly. He tied her arms with the soft silk ropes he'd placed at all four corners of his bed, just for her. There were other surprises and supplies in the nightstand next to his bed. They'd get to them all...eventually.

"Why are you tying me? Are you going to hurt me?" He didn't like the fear that had entered her eyes.

"No, love," he dipped his hand down between her thighs, testing the amazing wetness that waited for him there. She was already excited, ready for him. "This is for my pleasure. And yours as well. I've dreamed of you tied to my bed. Now that you're here, I can't wait to make the fantasy into reality. Humor me." He licked the inside of her knee, settling between her legs as he let her get a full view of his fangs.

"Are you going to bite me...there?" True fear shadowed her words.

"Not tonight, sweet, but in time, you might come to beg me for it. Still, for our first time, we will try things the traditional way."

"Tied up and spread eagle is traditional?" Nervous humor sparked in her eyes and he marveled at this special, brave, beautiful woman who was tied to his bed—where she belonged.

"It's about as traditional as I get, I'm afraid." He silenced anything she might have said by the simple expedient of diving down to plunder her pussy with his tongue.

Just like in their dreams, he fucked her with his tongue,

his sharp teeth combing through the folds of her pussy delicately. He was careful not to injure her tender skin. He would die before he hurt her. The slick feel of her tantalized him. She tasted so good. Like ambrosia. The nectar of the gods. Just as he'd known she would.

He sipped at her, using his lips to tease her engorged clit, sucking on it, then laving it with his tongue. When she gave up more of her moisture, he licked through it, lapping at her opening eagerly, then pushing up into her the way he would soon push into her with his cock.

Setting up a fierce rhythm, he brought her to a quick climax, sucking on her clit at the end to send her up to the stars. After long, shivering moments, he watched her come back down to find herself spread and tied to his bed, ready for more. He was so hard, he couldn't wait. He needed her. Now.

Climbing over her, he rocked his cock in the folds of her pussy as she creamed again and again for him. Dmitri kissed her lips, bringing her back up to the precious peak they would tumble off together this time. She squirmed beneath him, panting, nearly begging for his possession.

"Dmitri, please!" Her voice was ragged, on edge as she whispered brokenly.

"What do you want, sweetheart? Do you want my cock?" He teased her clit with the head of his cock, pushing against her in rhythmic bursts that made her squeal. "Say it and it's yours, Carly. Say you want me."

"I want you, Dmitri!" The words were torn from her body as she strained toward him, but still he wasn't satisfied.

"What do you want?" He held out for the words, wanting her to succumb to his sexual power of her own accord.

"I want your cock. In me. Now, Dmitri!" He felt her capitulation, her surrender in the subtle shift of her psychic energies. She was more than ready for him, and she had given into his demands. It was time for her reward. A reward for both of them actually.

He adjusted his position, pushing down and in, joining their bodies in reality for the first time. It was a tight fit, and he had to move more slowly than he expected, but it was heaven brought down to Earth. She moaned in his ear, lost in the passion flaming between them as he seated himself all the way within her. He held her gaze, noting the dazed dilation of her pupils with pride. She was perfect for him. She had been made for him.

He bent to her neck, starting his slow slide in and out of her hot core, waiting for the precise moment to join them completely. He didn't often fuck while feeding anymore, though he had indulged countless times since becoming immortal several centuries before. In the early years, he had enjoyed the wicked sex as much as the feeding, and he always got more energy from the blood of a climaxing woman. His kind fed on two levels—the physical and the sexual. Both were needed to sustain life.

Often these days, he brought his prey to a sexual peak with the power of his mind and the stimulus of his bite without actually fucking them all. The fun had gone out of it after several centuries and thousands of different cunts. Only one pussy would do for him now, and he suspected as he drove home within Carly's tight hole, he had finally found it.

The bite would tell him what he needed to know. If they connected body and soul when he took her blood, she was the One. Impossibly, after all this time, he might have actually found the one woman in all the world and all the years that could sustain him through eternity. With her at his side, he would need no other. They would feed each other fully for the rest of their immortal lives.

But Carly wasn't immortal. Still, he could turn her, if she was the One, and if she agreed. He cared for her too much already to take such a decision from her.

"Dmitri!" She was nearing another peak, her breath coming hard as he pushed her higher with every stroke. He covered her completely, his body over hers, his head nestling near the crook of her neck, drawing ever closer to his goal. He licked the sensitive skin of her throat and she shivered.

"I'm going to take you now, Carly. I'm going to drink of you while I fuck you."

"Do it. God! Just do it, Dmitri. I need..."

She clearly didn't understand what she needed so desperately, but she soon would. That he vowed.

Dmitri groaned with satisfaction at her eagerness. It was time to find out one way or the other. He needed to taste her essence. With a growl of pure animal lust, he reached down with his sharp teeth and bit decisively into her pulse.

Sweet, hot warmth blossomed into his mouth, feeding him with the richest, most fulfilling taste he had ever known. A moment later, new sensations registered. Things he had never felt before. Her mind was open to him, as his was to her. He was feeling their lovemaking from her perspective and knew what she wanted as soon as she thought it.

Sucking deeply of her life essence, he moved one hand down to pinch her clit hard, forcing the orgasm that she wanted so desperately. He came with her, pulsing long, hot and hard into her depths, greedily drinking deep while filling her womb.

The question was answered. Amazingly, she was the One.

They were joined now in body...and in mind. Given time, they would be able to share their thoughts completely, but for now, the first sensations of two minds touching, blending into One, was the most sublime thing he had ever experienced. He felt her pleasure, her confusion, her fear as if it was his own, and he reveled in the fact that she seemed cautious but curious about the information now flooding her mind directly from his.

Immersing himself in the flow of energy, of memory, of life, he let it wash over him like the inevitable tide, cleansing his soul and renewing him in ways he could only imagine until this moment. This was the moment he had lived so very long for. This was the moment of unification with the perfect soul meant only for him. She brought her light to his darkness, and his vast knowledge would now be hers as well. They would carry on as One for as long as fate allowed.

Nearly drowning in the wild sensations, he became aware of her escalating fear, and it sent a ringing claxon through the connection they now shared. He backed off, even though it went against every dominant instinct in his body. He pulled back mentally though they were still joined physically, and she began to breathe easier, though her confusion remained.

"What was that?" She was out of breath, her eyes wide with an edge of fear that nearly broke his heart.

"It was the confirmation of my dearest wish. We are One, my dear. You are mine." He couldn't help himself, leaning down to place a sweet kiss on her lips.

"One? What does that mean?"

"Look into my mind, Carly. Our mind. They are no longer separate, a pathway has been opened between us, never to be closed again."

For just a moment he eased his control of the place in their minds—the beautiful, wondrous place—where they were joined. He had enough experience and skill to be able to tighten the connection or let it loose, flowing wild, as it had been formed between them. But he didn't think she would be able to handle the information flow at full throttle yet. She was new to this and didn't have the skills necessary to be able to regulate what came into her mind and what went out. He could easily overwhelm her at this critical stage and that was the last thing he wanted to do. It was up to him, as the more experienced partner, to protect her.

She would learn rapidly from his memories, but first she had to grow accustomed to the lines of self being blurred, yet still distinct. They were two bodies, two brains, but when they chose, they would be able to share One mind. With time would come skill and the ability to judge when and how to use their unification to the best advantage.

But he had to get her used to the idea first. From the initial wave of information that had cascaded from her mind into his, he knew she had no background or experience with psychic abilities of her own. Still he had seen some information that intrigued him about one of her friends. One of her college friends had a touch of foresight, but that's all he'd had time to learn before it became necessary to limit the connection.

He felt the tentative push of her mind in his, warming him from the inside out. It was a miracle. It was a wonder. It was the best thing that had happened to him in all his long years. A tear formed at the corner of his eye as their gazes met and held.

"Dmitri?"

"I'm here, my love."

"Oh, God. I can hear you in my mind!"

"That is just one byproduct of the way we are joined." He leaned down to kiss her, unable to stop the giddy feeling racing through his heart. "You are a wonder to me, Carly."

"I feel that." Her voice was breathy and full of awe. "But I don't understand how. I don't understand any of this."

"I know." He made soothing sounds as he nuzzled her cheek, her neck, her tender flesh. "It's all right. We'll take this slow. For now, I can regulate the connection."

He demonstrated by pulling farther back mentally. The information exchange slowed to a trickle as he constricted the connection between them. He would never close it completely. In fact, he didn't think that was even possible, but he would never try. He never wanted to lose this feeling of belonging. It was something he hadn't felt in far too long. Perhaps he had never felt this way. He could not remember a time when anything had ever felt this good or this right.

"Is that better, my love?"

She was breathing easier. "Yes. What did you do?"

"I have been immortal a long time. Over the years, I have learned how to control many things about my mind and the minds of others."

"You're controlling my mind?"

"No! Never that. I would not do that to you, Carly. What we have is special...sacred. We are One."

"You keep saying that, but I still don't understand!"

He rolled away, reaching to untie her. Scooping her into his arms, he soothed her with long strokes of his hands over her skin.

"I know you don't and for that I'm sorry. I'm not handling this well. I just..." he searched for words, "...I just never truly expected I would find my One. And now here you are..." He looked deep into her eyes, mesmerized by the very idea of her.

"I feel what you're feeling, Dmitri. You're overwhelmed by awe and nearly shattered by the most profound joy I've ever experienced. This is so strange."

He chuckled. "As I can feel your fear and confusion. I'm sorry for that, Carly. Perhaps I can find a way to explain without overwhelming you again with the sharing of our thoughts."

"That would be good. That was a head-rush, you know? I was seeing things from...your memories? It was so weird!"

"I know. I saw things from your mind as well. In the future we'll be able to share our thoughts completely, but I realize it's something you'll have to get used to. Luckily, you can learn a lot of the skills you'll need directly from my mind. That will lessen the learning curve substantially, I should think."

"Um...I don't know if I'm ready for that."

"I know. Don't worry. We'll take this one step at a time. In fact, it will be a delight to explore this new union slowly..." He lowered her to the bed once more, coming over her with intent. "And thoroughly."

She smiled tentatively and made room for him between her legs.

They made love many times that night, only parting when the sun rose. He showed her the secret entrance from her pantry to his den and saw her off at the landing with a quick, hard fuck against the wall before she left for the house above to do her daily work.

The next night, Dmitri didn't wait for Carly to come to him. The moment the sun set, he rose, touching her mind.

"Where are you, my love?"

He felt her shock and knew she'd jumped. He felt the fear and didn't like the way her heart raced. She was afraid of him. No—not of him, but of sharing their minds. He sought her out in the house above his lair, finding her in the library, polishing the wooden shelving. There was a fire burning in the hearth, two old-fashioned leather wingchairs facing it at a welcoming angle.

"I did not mean to startle you, Carly. It is natural for mates to touch each other's minds. I thought you understood. We are One now. Our bodies, our hearts, our minds."

"All the time?"

Dmitri felt the fear that pervaded her mind. It wasn't anything sinister. He doubted she was some kind of covert agent bent on mayhem, but she had a fear of intimacy. Not physical intimacy—he'd cured her of that at least—but emotional intimacy. He backed off, leaving only a thin trail between their minds.

"Is that better?"

She sagged in relief. "Yes, thank you. But—"

"What, my love? You can tell me anything."

"That's just it. I don't want to hurt you, but I need a little space." He drew away, feeling like he'd been punched in the gut by her rejection. "Not physically," she raced to reassure him, already pouring warmth down the small line in their minds that still connected them. He began to relax. "But mentally, I need room, Dmitri. This is all so new and so...shocking. It's hard to take in. Can you give me a little time to get used to the idea?"

"I am immortal, my love. The one thing I have to give is time." He leaned down to kiss her. "I will keep our thoughts separate as much as I can, but in the heat of passion, there will be slipups. It is inevitable. But I don't think you'll mind. At such moments, I think we'll both only be thinking about one thing and by sharing our thoughts, we can bring each other more pleasure than mere mortals can ever hope to share."

"Okay," her voice was breathy, and he knew she was seeing the images that leaked over from his mind to hers. Erotic images of them bound together in lust.

"For example..." He invaded her personal space, moving forward as she moved back, herding her in just the direction he wanted her to go. She stopped when the backs of her legs hit the front of one of the wing chairs. "Right now, I'm sensing our thoughts are running along the same lines."

"Really?"

She let out a squeak that would have been humorous in other circumstances. But neither of them was laughing as Dmitri pushed her farther, stalking her in the small space. She flopped backward, landing in the chair. He didn't give her any time to recover, boxing her in with his arms, imprisoning her as he leaned over, one hand braced on each arm of the chair.

"I know what you're thinking. It's what I'm thinking too."

She gasped. "What's that?"

"That you want me to fuck you in this chair." He ran his hands over the leather arms of the chair. "I love these old chairs, you know. So many intriguing possibilities."

Chapter Six

The look he gave her almost melted her bones. Dmitri had to be the sexiest man she'd ever seen, hands down. All he had to do was look at her, and she got wet. She was hot and sticky now, ready for him, yearning for him.

"Take these off." He pushed at the edges of her clothes, and she hurried to comply with his gruffly voiced command. She loved that tone of voice, that edge of dominance. It pushed her buttons and sent her to another level altogether.

She shimmied in the chair awkwardly, but he didn't give ground. His arms boxed her in, her body touching his when she lifted away to wiggle out of her jeans and panties. The top went next, and he helped her with it, tugging it over her head. She was left in just her bra.

Her mouth went dry when he dropped to his knees between her spread legs, leaning forward and reaching around her back with his big, warm hands. He was inches from her, tempting, titillating. She wanted those strong hands on her body, but first he had to deal with the diabolical clasp of her bra.

He got it on the third try, making her want to laugh, but the situation was too heated, too significant. She felt him in her mind, a presence she'd never felt before that somehow seemed right and good, if a little scary. His hands shook as he skimmed the bra straps down over her bare arms, and the mental hold he maintained on the pathway between their minds grew shaky as well. She could feel him losing control and rather than fear, it instilled excitement in her very bones. She made this powerful man tremble. It was a heady sort of feeling.

Carly had never been much of a *femme fatale*. On the contrary, she'd been a bit of a geek and while she was reasonably pretty, she wasn't the kind of woman to inspire the kind of feelings she was receiving from Dmitri. It was new in her experience and it was something she cherished, for she knew he wouldn't give this part of himself to any other woman. Only her.

She felt the same way about him, but all the changes— coming so fast and furious—were overwhelming. She wanted to take things slow and give her mind a chance to catch up with her emotions, which already seemed to be fully committed to him.

She was a goner. She knew it, and she knew he knew it. But he'd given her the space she requested and that, more than anything, endeared him to her.

He drew back and tossed her last garment away. She could feel the flames from the fire flickering and heating her skin but it was Dmitri's eyes that warmed her soul, and his touch that set fire to her body.

He leaned back, looking his fill at her bare body as he shrugged out of his shirt. His hard muscled body wasn't what one would normally expect of a university professor, but then, Dmitri Belakov was no ordinary professor. He was all male animal in his prime, his body honed, his intellect sparking in his dark, dangerous, daring gaze.

He looked deep into her eyes as he lowered his trousers, baring himself. There was no need to wait. From the look of him, he was more than ready to take her and Carly knew she was more than ready to be taken. She wanted nothing more, but still he held back.

"I like this." One broad tipped finger traced down from her shoulder to the tip of her breast, then lower, skating over her slight belly and down through her curls to circle the slick opening spread before him. "You're very wet, my dear."

She heard the approval in his voice. He pushed inward all at once, sliding right up into her as far as he could with his finger. Turning his hand, he began a torturous little movement with just the tip of his finger against a secret, hidden spot inside her.

"You like that." It wasn't a question. Dmitri owned her pleasure. He knew just what to do and where to touch to make her squirm.

The action of his fingertip inside her was making her crazy. Her head thrashed from side to side against the back of the old leather chair as her body moved forward, seeking more, pushing herself farther onto his hand. She wanted more than just his finger, and she wanted it now.

"Give it to me. Please, Dmitri! Please!"

He removed his hand, and her eyes shot open at the loss even as a faint objection sounded from her throat. But he only laughed.

"Oh, I'll give you all you can take and more, but you must behave, little girl."

The wicked intent she heard in his voice made her squirm on the soft leather of the chair.

"What do you want me to do?" She would do anything he asked, and he damned well knew it, still there was something forbidden about the way he was looking at her. Something naughty and exciting.

"Put your hands on the arms of the chair." He waited until she complied before continuing. "Grip the ends of the arms with your hands and keep them there. No matter what." He moved closer, sliding his hands down from her knees to her ankles then lifting them one by one. "Good thing you're a flexible little girl." He sent her a wicked smile as he pushed her legs back and over the arms of the chair—over her own arms as well, pinning her. "Slide your ass forward to the edge of the chair." She shimmied closer to him in the odd position, exposing herself utterly.

Dmitri sat back to admire his handiwork and she could feel herself creaming for him. All it took was a look from him and she was ready.

"Dmitri..." She heard the pleading tone in her own voice but was powerless to stop it. She wanted him so badly. She *needed* him.

He chuckled, kneeling between her spread legs. "*Ssh, bebe,* I'm enjoying the view." He sank down so his head was on level with her pussy. She could feel his warm breath waft across her most sensitive skin, making her shiver. Dmitri leaned forward and she felt sharp fangs drift across her inner thigh.

Then his tongue lapped out, sliding through her folds searching for and finding the hard nubbin that cried for him. Circling, swirling, licking and making her pant with desire, he tortured her in the most delicious way.

"You taste divine. Like a goddess. My own personal goddess come to Earth to torment me. To fulfill me." Dmitri licked his way up her body as he rose on his haunches until he reached her breasts. His body pressed her back into the chair but any discomfort in her odd position was negated by the waves of rapture pushing her to do whatever he asked.

She cried out when his mouth closed around one nipple. He sucked and pulled with his talented lips and tongue before switching to the other side. One of his hands went to her pussy, two fingers sliding in deep and beginning a pulsing rhythm as his other hand went to her free breast, tugging at the nipple while his mouth teased the other one.

Then he struck. Fangs scratched at her breast, making her scream. The edge of pain turned her on more than she would have expected and she felt her womb ripple in climax as his fingers continued to tease and his tongue lapped at the small marks his teeth had made around her nipple.

"Dmitri!" She trembled in his arms as he pushed her deep into the chair, his hand in her cunt imprisoned between their straining bodies.

"I love to hear you cry my name, my love." His voice was a breathless whisper as he lifted his head away from her breast and trailed kisses up her chest until he could nuzzle into her neck. "You come so sweetly for me, Carly. Are you ready to come for me again, sweet?"

"Anything, Dmitri. Anything for you." She wanted to feel him inside her. She wanted his possession, his cock in her pussy. She wanted to feel him come apart in her arms and fill her with his come.

"I know what you need, my mate. I will always know." He drew back just far enough to look into her eyes as he withdrew his fingers from her wet pussy. His gaze held hers as he pushed forward with his hips—at the perfect level with her in the chair and him kneeling before it. These old chairs had possibilities indeed.

He pressed inside and stilled, just at the entrance, the wide knob of his hard cock spreading her opening, so close and yet so far from the hard, fast, filling possession she craved. She tried to move down onto him, but he stilled her. Her eyes flashed to his.

"So impatient, my love." The deviltry in his gaze wasn't lost on her but she really couldn't appreciate his teasing ways at the moment. No, at that very moment she wanted nothing more than his cock fully inside her.

He could hold her off physically. There was no question of that. But would he be able to hold off a mental assault? She could already feel the pathway between them widening as he lost control little by little. She felt his need, ruthlessly kept in check while he toyed with her. She felt his matching desire, his redundant restlessness, the urge to move, to conquer, to take. And she wanted to be taken.

Daring greatly, she sought the knowledge to whisper into his mind.

"Come to me, Dmitri. You know you want it as much as I do. Don't make me suffer."

His eyes widened. *"I thought you wanted more time to get used to this, vixen."*

"I do. Just..." She stroked her hands over his hard shoulders as he eased his hold. She used him for leverage as she pushed herself onto his cock. *"...not right now, Dmitri. Now I want everything you have to give. I want it all. With you."*

He growled and took charge. She loved the way he mastered her body, the way he powered into her, making her clench around him with the slightest variation in tempo or pressure. He hit something deep within that made her insides respond like never before.

And he watched. When she looked at him again, she saw his gaze was focused on the place where they were joined. She looked, struck by the sight of the longest, thickest cock she'd ever seen making itself at home inside her. It was a raunchy sight, a naughty vision and she understood why he watched. She felt his need for possession as deeply as she felt her own need to be possessed by this man. This vampire. This immortal lover who had so easily ruined her for anyone else.

As she watched, his motion increased, as did the power of his strokes. She gripped his forearms and their eyes met and held.

"Soon, beloved. Very soon." He moved closer, his teeth already lengthened to sexy, sharp points.

"Drink, Dmitri. Do it now, please!" she pled with him for the pleasure-pain of the bite that only days before had scared her spitless. Now she craved it as much as she craved him.

He lost all control then. As his fangs pierced her flesh, the trickle in her mind became a flood and their thoughts merged, twining together as closely as their bodies. She absorbed a little more of him as he did her while their bodies reached for a climax higher than any that had come before. He drank even as he filled her both physically and mentally, and she loved every last minute of it.

She screamed at last. A harsh, guttural sound of a female

beast utterly devastated by her mate. He groaned as he came, licking at her flesh, sucking at her blood as his warm essence filled her womb with heat, pleasure and the manifestation of their love.

Long moments later as her breath steadied and Dmitri regained control by small degrees, she sighed and gazed into his fascinating eyes. She'd learned more about him this time—seen memories of his past that she didn't fully understand, but she thought she might in time. He'd been around far longer than she'd originally thought. Some of the things she saw in his mind were centuries old.

"You're a mysterious man, Dmitri Belakov."

"To you, I am an open book, my love. Ask me anything. I will keep no secrets from you. Ever. This I pledge."

"Do you really love me?" A demon of doubt made her ask. She'd never had a man say the words, but she felt Dmitri's love with each new encounter. Still, she wanted to hear it out loud.

"How can you doubt it?" He stroked her hair away from her face. "I love you, Carmelita Valandro. More than life. More than anything. You are my mate, and I want you to be my wife."

"You do?" Shock warred with the warm feeling in the pit of her stomach.

Dmitri's smile held the world. "I do." She heard the echo of those words like the vow they implied.

"I do too," she whispered. "Dmitri, I love you so much."

He kissed her then, the kiss holding the wonder of their shared love. It was sweet. It was tender. But it was also wild and unfettered, like the love flowing between them.

She didn't know how long they'd been caught up in each other when a piercing animal howl sounded through the room, making her jump.

"What was that?"

Dmitri shifted away to peer out the nearby window. The howl had sounded very close. Right outside the window, in fact.

His mouth firmed into a thin line, and his brows drew together in annoyance.

"What?" she prompted again.

"Probably an emissary from the local wolf pack. Get dressed and meet me outside. You might as well get to know the neighbors. And they need to know about you."

He left before she could even stand. "Wolves?" she said to the empty room. What in the world was going on?

She arrived on the porch shortly after Dmitri. He'd apparently made a quick stop in her guest bathroom. She could tell by the bright canary yellow bath towel in his hand.

"Shift." He threw the towel at the wolf. "And put this on. There's a lady present."

Unbelievably, the creature shimmered and...changed...paws turning to hands and feet as a man's form appeared where before there had been only the wolf. And the man was gorgeous. Brown hair liberally streaked with gold, expressive eyes and a chiseled face, he was model pretty but muscled like a linebacker.

Carly watched from the porch, her emotions ranging from fear to awe as she watched the wolf shift shape into man. He bent down to retrieve the towel, then wrapped it around his hips at a jaunty angle, but not before giving her a good look at a most impressive bit of anatomy. The man was built.

"So I noted through the window. Can't say I've ever known you to be one to play with your food, Belakov." The stranger pierced her with a challenging, sexy, lopsided grin. She could see his curiosity but also the careful way he acted around Dmitri. This man—wolf—whatever—was wary. He didn't get too close, but he also wouldn't allow any show of fear. He was cautious.

Considering he'd just come to call on the resident vampire, Carly figured that was a wise stance.

Dmitri held out a hand to her, and she walked down the steps. She did her best to keep the tremble in her stomach from translating to her legs. She surmised it wouldn't do to show fear in front of either of these men.

"Jason, this is my mate, Carly."

Rather than some expression of disbelief or a knowing smile, the half-naked man's response was surprising. He came forward and sank to one knee directly in front of Carly, shocking her.

"Be welcome, Carly. My pack extends to you the same agreement we have with your mate."

He took her free hand, kissed the back of it, ending with an audacious lick as he winked up at her. She got the sense this man was seldom serious for long.

"Knock it off, Moore. She's mine." Dmitri tucked her under one arm, drawing her away from the wolf-man's hold on her hand. Luckily, he let go, leaving her firmly under Dmitri's wing, so to speak. All in all, she felt far safer with her vampire lover than this jokester wolf-man.

"Congratulations to you both." Jason rose to his feet. "I hear it's not often a vamp as old as you meets his One. I think I understand why you were so preoccupied that I was able to prowl right up to the house without you hearing me." He gave her a bad boy smile, and she knew from his tone he was teasing her mate. "Of course, I saw through the window what had you so enthralled. Can't say I blame you, poor devil."

Carly gasped, realizing he'd seen them—

It didn't bear thinking about. If she did, she'd just die of embarrassment. Already she could feel a flush of heat rising to her cheeks, and she couldn't look the man in the eye, focusing instead on his feet.

"Go easy on my mortal bride, Jason," Dmitri's voice rumbled with power. "She's had a hard time adjusting. She's not used to my ways, much less your animal nature. In fact, until you shifted just now, she didn't even know about your kind."

"No shit?" Jason's curious gaze felt like a laser sight

focused on her, but she refused to meet it. "But I thought you guys shared a brain or something when you found your mates?"

"We do, but she's having a hard time adjusting to that as well." Carly could hear the frustration in Dmitri's voice and it was the first time she got an inkling that he was less than satisfied with her desire to take things slow.

She looked up at him, sorry that she was so afraid, but he tightened his arm reassuringly, smiling down at her. She felt the love through their small connection and warmed to it, allowing him to open the connection just a tiny bit more. She figured if they did it in small increments it wouldn't be so jarring as that first flood of overwhelming information had been.

"Well, ma'am. I'm Alpha of your friendly neighborhood wolf pack." He made a little bow as Carly looked at him, embarrassment forgotten now. "Jason Moore, at your service."

"Carly Valandro," she replied politely.

"Soon to be Belakov. As soon as we can arrange it." Dmitri tugged her closer and she felt warmed by his words and his embrace. Carly Belakov. She liked the sound of it.

"I just came by to advise you we intend to hold a howl over in the woods by the far pasture at full moon. Some of the party might spill over into the pastureland, but I'll do my best to keep my people in line. Just wanted to let you know we'll be there, as per our agreement."

Dmitri seemed to relax just a fraction. "That's fine. Though it's Carly who legally owns the land now. You should really ask her." He let her go a little, so she could stand more freely on her own. She got the sense that it was somehow important that she be seen as a person in her own right rather than a mere extension of him. She followed his lead. After all, he knew these...um...people, better than she did.

"Ma'am?" Jason smiled at her and she nearly forgot the question.

"If I didn't know you were already mine, I'd be jealous." Dmitri's voice purred through her mind, but luckily she didn't

jump this time. Could it be she was starting to get used to his silent commentary?

"What is he?"

"Werewolf."

"They actually exist? And here I thought vampires were bad enough."

"Bad? Get rid of the puppy, and I'll take great pleasure in showing you just how bad I can be."

"Is that a promise?"

"Send him on his way, and I'll make it worth your while."

"As you can see, the pasture isn't being used, so I have no objection. But thank you for asking. I think I would have been a little alarmed if I saw something and you hadn't told me you were going to be out there."

"As would anyone, I reckon." Jason winked at her, seeming more relaxed now that she'd agreed. "If you'd like to drop in at the party at the pack house as my guests after the hunt, you're both more than welcome."

"Thank you, Alpha." Dmitri took over the conversation again, and Carly was glad. She wasn't quite sure what Jason meant by a hunt, but she had some wild ideas, considering he could turn into a wolf. "We'd be honored to drop in for a few minutes. It will give your pack a chance to meet Carly, since she will be Mistress here."

Jason bowed in a very formal way for a man dressed in only a canary yellow towel, but he was so handsome, he could make even that silly towel look like *haute couture*.

"I'll see you at full moon, then. It was a pleasure meeting you, ma'am."

"Likewise."

Carly had barely spoken when the man shifted form again, leaving the yellow towel in a puddle as he landed on four paws, a tawny wolf with gleaming eyes. He barked once, then dashed away faster than anything she'd ever seen.

Dmitri retrieved the towel and ushered her back into the house. She wanted to know all about *were*wolves. But then, there was so much she wanted to know about. She knew the easiest—most tempting—way of getting the information was also the scariest. She could have all the knowledge Dmitri possessed if she would just agree to sharing their minds fully.

She just wasn't sure she could do it. Not yet. Dmitri was such a powerful personality, she was too afraid of losing herself.

"When is the full moon?" she asked when he led her into the kitchen.

"A couple of days from now. He usually gives me some warning when his pack intends to frolic anywhere near." Dmitri opened a few of the cupboards, taking down glasses and a bottle of wine. "I brought this up from my wine cellar. Tonight is a celebration." He poured the wine, giving her a glass of the deep red liquid. "Of course, every night with you is a celebration. But tonight you have taken one step further into the world in which I live. You've met and been accepted by the local Alpha. That—whether you realized it or not—was a big step."

"Why?"

"Let's just say, as a general rule, our kinds don't mix much. Because I live way out here, I've had to have more contact with the *were* community than most immortals. Bloodletters, they call us, since most of my kind object rather strongly to the term, 'vampire'. Personally, it's never bothered me, but if you meet others—and you will—you would do best to remember that."

"Don't call them vampires. Check." She raised her glass to his with a teasing smile, but she was fascinated by what he was telling her. "So bloodletters and *were*wolves don't get along?"

"It's not that we don't get along. It's more that we prefer to give each other a wide berth. And there are more than just wolves out there, Carly. Jason is Alpha of the dominant wolf pack, but there are other clans and tribes of *were*folk in this region as well. By comparison, our presence is small. There are many more *weres* in the open places. My kind tend to prefer cities because of the availability of human prey, while the *weres* prefer open space in which to run."

"It makes sense." But she didn't like hearing human beings called *prey.*

"To us," he toasted. They touched glasses and drank, the excellent vintage warming its way down her throat. It was delicious. Curiosity made her look at the bottle's label.

"I've never had a bottle this old."

"You've never had a lover this old," he joked, pointing to himself. "But like fine wine, I promise, most things do get better with age." She laughed, and he moved closer.

"I didn't know you could drink wine." She grew breathless as he invaded her personal space in the most delicious way.

"It is my last tie to the sun. It is one of the only things we can ingest besides blood. It is a delicacy. Like you, my love." He traced down her neck with the fingers of his free hand. "Like the wine, you heal me, Carly. You make me whole."

"That's the most beautiful thing anyone's ever said to me."

"You have a beautiful soul, Carly. I've gotten a glimpse within, and I can say that with certainty. I only hope..." he sat next to her, "...that when the time comes and you see as deeply within my heart, you can forgive me my past. It hasn't been very pretty."

She felt the very real trepidation in him at the idea of her seeing his past through his memories. In an odd sort of way, that made her feel better about the whole idea. She hadn't thought of it from his point of view. She'd been more focused on herself—how he'd be seeing all her memories—both good and bad. But it went both ways. She would see his long past, and she was sure he probably had several lifetimes worth of experiences waiting for her to view. The idea was tantalizing. The things he'd probably seen in his past and experienced firsthand would be like seeing history unfold.

But it was selfish to think only of what she would gain in knowledge, she realized almost immediately. The things she would see were things he had lived and done, people he had known, now lost to him and lifestyles long gone by the wayside. It would be bittersweet to relive those memories with him and wrong of her to look forward to putting him through it.

"I'm sorry, Dmitri." She covered his hand with hers. "I've been selfish. I've only been thinking about myself."

"No, my love. Don't think that. We both have reservations about taking such a huge step, I'm sure."

"You're being kind, but I can feel how badly you want to share my mind. It hurts you."

"It's a delicious sort of hurt, I can assure you. You have no idea how wonderful it is to know that you're in the world and we will be One. I'm enjoying savoring the moment."

She climbed onto his lap. "But wouldn't you rather get right to it?"

Chapter Seven

Dmitri knew the moment her intentions changed from serious conversation about their predicament to something much more...sinful.

"I like the way your mind works. It'll be my pleasure to learn it—and you—slowly...steadily...satisfyingly." He licked his way from her jaw to her neck, nuzzling under her long hair. Her skin tasted divine and smelled like heaven. His own, private paradise.

"Mmm. I think we're on the same page now." She tried to stretch back on the couch, but he stopped her with a gentle tug on her shoulders. Without words, he coaxed her to stand, making short work of her clothing and his own.

"Offer yourself to me, Carly. Push your breasts together and lift them up in your hands like an offering."

A thrum began in her blood with his stark words as she followed his instructions. She'd never been so bold with a lover before. She'd never had a man who was so commanding, so dominant, so delicious. She'd do just about anything for him...or to him...at his direction.

And he knew it. The knowledge was there in his eyes every time he looked at her in passion. It turned her on and made her wet with anticipation. Never failed.

She lifted her bare breasts up for him and was rewarded when his head dropped—as did his fangs. She felt them scraping along the tender skin, not hurting, but enticing, exciting. She loved the way he treated her body. Strong when the moment called for it, he was also gentle when it counted most. He knew just how to touch her to make her scream with pleasure and writhe in delight.

He licked over her breasts, his fangs teasing the delicate skin before his tongue closed around first one nipple, then the other, swirling and circling and making them even tighter. He feasted on her tender skin for long moments while her excitement level rose. Her knees were close to buckling when he finally drew back.

Almost negligently, he threw a decorative pillow from the couch to his feet. She followed its progress, her mouth going dry in anticipation. She wasn't to be disappointed.

"Kneel," came the simple, powerful order. She did as she was told.

The cock he presented her was hard, long and ready for action. She wanted it inside her, but first, she wanted a taste. She wanted to make him writhe as he'd done to her. She wanted to show him how much she appreciated his demands and all that he gave when he made love to her. It was a subtle give and take that brought them both to the ultimate pleasure and it was her turn to give. More than that, it was her pleasure, though she'd never really enjoyed giving head in the past.

With Dmitri, everything was new and exciting. He made things that she hadn't experienced, or hadn't really liked before, better than they'd ever been. He made her want to do anything and everything—for him.

"Suck it down, Carly."

He fisted her hair in one hand, watching her progress as she leaned forward, her eyes straining upward to watch him as she took him into her mouth. She loved the look of nearly painful satisfaction on his face as he watched. She loved that she could bring this pleasure to him. She just plain loved *him*.

"Take it deep, darling. Suck hard now." He coached her with grunting words as he pushed into her mouth, never giving her more than she could handle, but pushing her limits with each new thrust. She felt his excitement, and it drove her wild too.

"Enough!" He was trembling when he suddenly pulled free.

With impressive strength, he lifted her to her feet and positioned her in front of the couch. He bent her forward, facing the couch, but not on it, much to her surprise. She could see her reflection in the dark window, her gaze rising to capture the rough look of possession on Dmitri's beloved face as he looked down at her bare bottom.

He kicked her legs apart with gentle shoves of his bare feet against hers, but she got the idea. She leaned forward, resting her arms on the back of the couch, standing in front of it, bent at the waist, her ass up in the air. They hadn't done it this way yet and the added mirror of the window in front of her was an enticing touch.

She watched the expression on his face as he moved up behind her. He dragged a footstool over by one leg, kneeling on it. The level was just right. His hands went to her ass, spreading and lifting, delving between, seeking the slick wetness of her.

Two fingers thrust up inside her, and she yelped in surprise but soon got the rhythm. She smiled when he raised his eyes to their reflection in the nighttime glass.

"Okay, baby?" he asked.

She nodded, smiling while his fingers created a lovely friction inside her.

"It's going to be hard and fast, Carly."

"Do it, Dmitri. Do me hard." She didn't know where the words came from but she was glad of her bold reply when she saw the fire leap in his eyes reflected in the window.

His fingers left her core, replaced by that devilishly hard cock. He was thick and long, filling her completely. She moaned when he'd gained full entrance and sank back against him as he started to rock.

One of his hands rested on her ass, squeezing as he powered into her. The other came up and smacked her ass cheek with a crack that sounded through the room, though it didn't really hurt that much. It shocked her, but by the time his hand rose to do it again, she quivered in anticipation of the small pain that she now knew would bring so much pleasure.

"You like that, my vixen." He sounded pleased and she suddenly got an image in her mind. Like the Lord of the Manor fucking the scullery maid in the sitting room where anyone could walk in at any moment. The element of danger in the fantasy appealed to her more wicked senses.

She knew the fantasy image had to have come from the place where they joined in their minds. She also knew, though she had no way of understanding exactly how she knew it, that the image was not memory, but pure fantasy. So he wanted to play games, did he?

The thought of it was appealing. She'd never done such a thing with any of her other lovers, but they'd been men utterly lacking in imagination. Dmitri, it seemed, had imagination to spare and she didn't mind it one bit. She'd play along.

"My lord, someone might hear if you keep spanking me."

"Let them hear." He smacked her again, and she could see the wide grin on his face in their reflection. "If I want to fuck you with half the staff in here, you'll let them hear and let them watch. They might learn something. Now be quiet and move with me, girl."

"Yes, my lord." She did as he said, both of them rising to the occasion, spurred on by the naughty fantasy he communicated into her mind. "You'd like them to watch, my lord?"

"Aye." He sounded so authentic when his accent slipped into old patterns of speech, and she realized with a start it was because he was the real deal. He'd lived in those times. He'd spoken that way.

And now he was hers.

His fantasy shifted as his thought patterns merged with hers. They were no longer lord and scullery maid. They were Dmitri and Carly, two modern day people with very different lives who were joined now for eternity. They both had much to learn about each other and she got the sense from his thoughts that he would enjoy it as much as she would.

"Do you like to be watched, Carly?" He dropped down over her back to whisper in her ear, his gaze holding hers in the reflective surface of the window.

"I—I don't know. I've never done that before."

"The *weres* do it all the time. They fuck like bunnies out where anyone can see them. Usually with most of the pack looking on, critiquing the young ones, the older ones showing off for their audience. Maybe we should join them one night, out in the woods. Would you like that?"

"I don't know, Dmitri." But the idea of it made her hot. He pounded more fiercely within her, driving them both higher as their crisis neared.

"We'll save that for another time then."

He drew back, standing behind her, his big hands roaming over her backside. One delved down between her legs in front to toy with her clit while the other zeroed in on the crevice between her spread cheeks. His fingers were still slippery from when he'd had them up her pussy, and one slid easily within the tight rosette that had never been invaded by a man.

She gasped in shock...and rising excitement.

"Never done that before either?" He must have picked the thought from her mind. Lord knew she was beyond speech at this point. She was so close! A second finger joined that first one, thrusting shallowly into her ass, making her squirm and want to scream. "We'll have to explore that, Carly. Soon. I can make it so good..." He trailed off as his breathing hitched into high gear. He thrust into her in short, hard digs, his fingers driving her wild.

And then she exploded. She felt him following her in both

mind and body. His climax reflected her own, added to it and multiplied it, reflecting back to him and doing the same until they were in a spiral of bliss, an upward climbing pyramid of pleasure. She wanted it never to end, but as all good things, eventually they reached the pinnacle and began the languorous slide back to themselves, far below. But they were together. As it should be. Now and forevermore.

She understood in that moment, they were truly One.

Chapter Eight

They were drowsing in bed after a protracted bout of lovemaking when Carly's phone rang. They'd finally made it to her bedroom after a stop in the shower, where he took her up against the wall. By the time he was done with her, she was nearly asleep on her feet, purring with satisfaction. Dmitri smiled at the memory.

He sat up, leaning back against the headboard to look at the bedside clock. It was about eleven at night—too late for a casual call, but still within the realms of possibility for good friends. Dmitri saw the caller ID and was jolted to full wakefulness. He listened unabashedly to the conversation as Carly spoke with a woman who could be no one other than an old friend. When she hung up a few minutes later, Dmitri thought of delving into her mind to take the information he sought, but he'd promised her he wouldn't do that.

"Do you care to tell me why you are receiving calls from another Master's mate?"

"Master? You mean Marc is..." He could see her quick mind puzzling through his words. "Holy shit! Marc is a vampire?"

"As is his mate, I believe, though newly made. It was the talk of the Masters when he took a mortal as wife. I even sent them a gift." Dmitri chuckled at her look of utter shock. She truly hadn't known.

"Kelly is a friend. We went to college together. A group of us formed a study group and we've been friends ever since."

Realization dawned on her expressive face. "So that's why she never joins us for dinner anymore. She only shows up for drinks and only drinks wine. She used to love those fruity drinks with umbrellas, but we figured it was her new husband's tastes rubbing off on her."

"In a manner of speaking." Dmitri laughed as he drew her into his arms.

"But then, why does Lissa do the same? Oh my God!" She turned wide eyes to him. "Don't tell me Atticus Maxwell is a vampire too?"

Dmitri nearly laughed out loud at her surprise, but he was taken aback at the same time. Why would two women—three now, counting Carly—be vampire mates and close friends? It seemed to defy the odds.

"Atticus is one of Marc's oldest friends. And I mean that in the truest sense. Marc is Master of his region, but Atticus is his right hand man. I've known them both for many years and have called them friends for almost as long. I've even met your friends, Lissa and Kelly, when I was staying at Atticus's winery a few weeks back. They are lovely women."

"You've met them? And they're both..."

"Both have been turned by their mates, and they are true mates. They share minds as we can."

He felt how overwhelmed she was by the news that two of her best friends had become immortal. He soothed her as best he could, all the while planning to contact Marc and Atticus to compare notes. His old friends would no doubt have much to say about a third mate being found among such a tightly knit group of women.

"So if they're vampires, does that mean you'll want me..." she trailed off and he felt her discomfort.

"I would like it if someday you decided to share immortality with me, Carly, but I wouldn't ask you to give up the sun lightly. We have time before decisions of that magnitude have to be made. Years, even. So don't worry about it now. We can go on as we are for quite some time."

He knew his words didn't make her feel that much better, but they did take the edge off her panic. The turmoil of her thoughts, however, wouldn't be conquered so easily.

They rolled along at status quo for a while, Dmitri sleeping the day away below ground while Carly inhabited the house above. She enjoyed a few hours of sunlight each day while she continued to put her house to rights. Dmitri would join her each evening after the sun went down and they'd do various things.

Sometimes he'd help her with the restoration work. Sometimes they'd just sit and talk. They always made love. Usually several times a night and always at those times, the passageway between their minds opened wide for those heart-stopping moments of rapture.

A few nights after the *were*wolf had shown up at her door, the moon went full. She heard howls in the distance even before the sun went down as she stood on the porch, rubbing her arms against a chilly wind, looking toward the far pasture. She couldn't see anyone or anything out there, but she heard them. And it sounded like more were arriving as the sun set in the western sky.

Dmitri's arms came around her, instantly warming her. She hadn't jumped this time. She was getting used to him sneaking up on her as soon as the sun left the horizon. She melted back into him with a sigh.

"What else is there besides wolves?"

"Oh, there are shifters of many kinds. Wolves, big cats, even bears. Most of the larger predators have their shifter equivalents. Even some birds of prey. Hawks, eagles and the larger owls."

"It must be amazing to fly."

"It is."

She turned in his arms, startled by the knowing in his

voice. "Can you shift shape?"

A sexy smile played about his lips as he nodded. "I can. It is something we learn with time, but it is not the same magic the shifters use. From what I've heard, they can only take on the form of the animal spirit that shares their soul. We use an altogether different sort of magic. It is hard to master, so only the oldest of us have the skill."

"What do you turn into?" She was fascinated by the idea.

"Just about anything I want. I can replicate the same animal forms as the *weres*—wolf, panther, the larger birds—but because my change is entirely magical, I can also become creatures of legend."

"Like a dragon?"

"That's one of my favorites." His eyes sparkled. "I can also do partial shifts. My hands into claws, for example."

He held out one hand in front of her and let it change. Gleaming, dark claws slid out from the tips of his fingers making her jump. Then the claw turned back into his hand, and she breathed easier once more.

"That's...startling."

"Isn't it?" he murmured, rocking her back against him. The cool night air washed around them, cocooning them in its inky darkness.

"What do you use that sort of skill for?" She almost dreaded his answer.

"Combat," came the terse reply. "Every once in a while, a man is called upon to fight. Masters are challenged and the only answer to such a challenge is a show of strength. Such fights are to the death, and there are no rules as to how the battle is conducted once engaged."

"That's barbaric."

"It's the way things have been done among my kind for thousands of years. It has never changed, and I doubt it ever will. We are ancient creatures that live by an ancient standard.

It probably does seem barbaric by modern standards, but it is simpler by far than your bureaucracy of laws. Not to say there are no laws. That's why we have Masters in each region. My word is law and my lieutenants and I uphold the ancient laws of our kind. We police ourselves—which is another instance when partial shifts can come in handy. There are no jails that can hold us. Many infractions call for a death sentence and a quick death by combat is seen as more humane than staking someone out in the sun to die slowly. That is reserved for only the basest monsters. Usually we catch up with rogues before they earn that kind of punishment."

"I had no idea."

"Nor did I want to make you aware of the brutality of our existence, but I will have honesty between us. There is no other way for true mates. You will come to know all this soon enough."

He kissed the side of her neck, making her shiver.

"But come, we should make an appearance at the shifter party after they're done with their hunt. I want them to know who you are and that you are under my protection."

"Do you think they would try to hurt me?" She felt the undercurrent of caution in his words and the slight connection between their minds.

"Not if they want to live." For a moment, his gaze went flat with death. "But no. I don't think you have anything to fear from the *were*. In fact, I want them to know who you are so that they can keep an eye out during the day. Many of them prowl near your land. If they know you're here alone and unprotected during the day, they may help if they see something amiss."

"So you think I'm in danger? From what?" She didn't like the direction of this entire conversation.

"I didn't say that. I know of no direct threat against either myself or you, but having just found you, I can't bear thinking of even the possibility. Please indulge my overabundance of caution. In times past, mates were targeted by enemies of my kind for they knew without our mates, most of us would not go on. Without you, my life is over, Carly." He turned her in his arms and she searched his face.

"You're serious?"

"Utterly. We are One. Where you go—even into the next realm—I will follow."

"Oh, Dmitri." Fear struck her as she clung to him. She didn't want to be responsible for his death or even the contemplation of it. She would do all in her power to keep him safe, even if it meant making friends with a grizzly bear who could turn into a pimply teenager. "Let's get ready. We have a party to go to."

They went indoors, but it was some time before they got dressed in their party clothes. In between Dmitri had some very creative ways to dress her in silk scarves tied at her wrists and ankles. The man seemed to love tying her up, and she didn't mind in the least, even though she'd never experimented with bondage before in her life. Dmitri made her want to try new things and made her enjoy each and every one of them.

It was well after midnight when he ushered her into his car—hidden one level below her own spacious garage, which had originally been a small barn—and drove them down the deserted country road leading past her far pasture and into the woods. Every once in a while she saw animals running through the trees beside them. She even caught a few flashes of male wolves mounting females in a blatant display of animal lust. Why it turned her on, she didn't know. Then she caught sight of pale skin through the trees dappled with moonlight and realized she was watching a naked woman bouncing up and down over an equally nude man. And they weren't the only ones. As they drove, she saw more and more couples doing it out in the open, in the woods.

"I'm almost afraid to ask, but what sort of hunt were they doing tonight?"

Dmitri chuckled and she looked over at him. She didn't doubt he'd also seen the pairs in the woods. "Well, they call it a mate hunt, but it's more of a *mating* hunt. Few pairs find their perfect match during these kinds of events. Mostly they just hook up for the night. *Weres* are very open about sex. When they shift, they can't bring their clothes with them like we can, so they don't think much about nudity. It's a very open society. But when they do find their mates, they're as loyal to them as we are. I respect that."

"But not much else about them, right?"

Dmitri seemed to think. "No. There's a lot to be admired about the *were*. I suppose you're picking up on old prejudices I didn't even know I still had." He shook his head. "At one time, in the distant past, they say we were close allies. But after we won the struggle against darkness, our peoples drifted apart, or so the story goes. Like I said, I have more contact with *weres* than most of my kind because of where I chose to live. They're not bad people, but they can be stubborn about us. They aren't immortal, though they are long-lived. Still, few alive now remember what once was. It's kind of sad really."

"Well." She reached over and lifted his hand into her lap, offering comfort. "We can change that. That is, if you want to."

"All I want is their assurance that if they see anything strange on your land, they'll help you out. I think Jason is chivalrous enough to manage at least that. He and I have worked well together so far."

"Good. Then that'll be our goal for this meeting." She didn't see the fuss. She felt perfectly safe on the farm, but if it would make Dmitri feel better, she'd do whatever it took.

"For a minute there, I almost forgot you're a high powered business woman." Dmitri brought her hand to his lips for a tender kiss as he pulled into a long driveway. They shared a moment of silent communication, and she felt his admiration like a warm caress.

"Where are we?" she asked as they came out into a clearing

filled with cars in front of a large house with a gorgeous wraparound porch.

"This is the pack house. They use it for parties, meetings and other kinds of get-togethers. Members of the pack can live here too, if they have a need. Orphans, widows and such. They all look out for each other. Packs are like big, extended families."

"Impressive."

"I like their social structure. Of course it would never work with our kind. For one thing, none of us are related. Some have families—when mates have children—but few have extended families. There are rumors of some in the old world that have that kind of network, but those of us who chose to strike out to the Americas haven't had time to build anything comparable. We're still like pioneers, even centuries after the first of us came here."

"Fascinating. I just figured..." she drifted off as he looked for a good place to park. "I guess I hadn't really thought too much about it."

"We don't have children often or easily. I guess that's one of the many prices to be paid for immortality. But I have high hopes for your friends Lissa and Kelly. Atticus and Marc deserve a little happiness."

He parked the car, coming around to escort her out of the car. She blindsided him, leaning up to give him a hard, fast kiss.

"Not that I mind, but what was that for?" His laughing gaze sparkled down at her.

"You deserve a little happiness too, Dmitri."

"That's what I have you for." He pulled her into his arms and kissed her breathless.

A long, low wolf whistle reached Carly's ears and made her pull back. Her head was spinning when she looked around to find Jason striding out of the woods, buttoning his button-fly jeans and grinning from ear to ear. A stunning girl followed behind, tying her halter-top and holding what had to be Jason's shirt over one shoulder. It was more than obvious what they'd been up to.

"I would've invited you two to the hunt if I'd known you were keen enough to be making out in my front yard."

Chapter Nine

Carly half expected Dmitri to bristle at the werewolf's teasing, but he surprised her by laughing.

"Not that such an invitation wouldn't be appreciated, but we bloodletters tend to conduct our affairs in more private settings." He shot her a glance filled with mischief. "Most of the time."

Now just what the heck did that mean? Was he into exhibitionism in addition to bondage? And why did that idea make her squirm?

She licked her lips as she watched Jason stride right up to them. The men shook hands, and Carly watched the way Jason's bare muscles rippled all the way down his incredibly fit body.

"Watch it, mate. You're practically drooling over the puppy."

The voice in her mind made her gasp, but she could tell Dmitri was only teasing. He knew her heart well enough by now to know she wasn't interested in anyone but him. Still, she couldn't help but look when presented with such a feast for the feminine eye.

"Don't worry, baby. I know who brung me to the dance." She put a teasing, fake twang to her thoughts. *"But I'd have to be dead not to look at all that beefcake. Hubba hubba. If he weren't a dog, I'd love to set him up with Sally. She'd really go for a guy who could beat her at wrestling."*

"Sally's the cop, right?"

"*She's a detective now. And an expert martial artist. She's got that whole* my body is my temple *thing going on. She's gorgeous. And all the pervs who hit on her think she's a mindless bimbo. Too bad she can overpower them with her pinky. This guy, though, looks like he'd be able to give her a run for her money.*"

"*No doubt.*" She felt more than saw Dmitri trying to stifle a chuckle as he greeted the Alpha *were*wolf. He popped the trunk and the men walked around to the back of the car, leaving the two women to make their own introductions.

"I'm Carly." She made the first move toward the scantily dressed girl, holding out her hand in what she hoped was a friendly manner.

The girl took it and started, then sniffed loudly. Carly was about to take offense when she realized she was talking to a *were*wolf. More than likely, the girl could smell something about her. Carly decided to wait and see. She didn't want to cause trouble for Dmitri with these people.

"You're human." The girl sounded genuinely surprised.

"Um...yes." Carly didn't quite know how to answer. "I just moved here from California. What's your name?" She tried to sound upbeat but was at sea with this weird conversation.

"Oh, I'm Amy. Sorry. I was just surprised. I figured you'd be—" She broke off, blushing.

"Like Dmitri, you mean? Immortal? Well, that's not something we've come to yet in our relationship. To be honest, just the idea scares the hell out of me."

Carly could tell by the girl's reaction that she'd said the right thing. Amy loosened up and was all eager curiosity after that. She asked Carly about her software business, and they started talking computers. Amy, it turned out, was majoring in computer science at the university. She'd even had Dmitri as a professor during her sophomore year but was close to graduating now.

The men rejoined them, each carrying a box that tinkled as

they walked toward the house and Carly realized Dmitri had brought two cases of wine to the party. He was such a thoughtful man.

They led the way into the big house and Amy brought Carly with her. They were welcomed warmly, though Carly did sense a definite reserve in their attitude toward Dmitri. They were standoffish with her until they either got a whiff of her mortality or Amy clued them in. She became the center of attention for a while and made quite a few friends.

Some of Amy's friends were also into computers, and they ended up talking about the latest hardware for at least an hour while Dmitri watched from a corner where he was talking with the *were*wolf Alpha and some of the other higher ranked *were*s.

She was comfortable enough, after a few glasses of wine, to make the connection between their minds to ask a question.

"We haven't discussed it, but I'd like to keep my business. I worked too long and hard to make it what it is today, even if it was burning me out."

"I wouldn't ask you to give it up, my love. It is your decision."

"Well, I was thinking. A lot of these kids have the kinds of skills I need. Would you mind if I offered a few of them jobs?"

Dmitri seemed genuinely surprised. *"Not at all. In fact, I think it would endear you to their Alphas. Most of them wouldn't be able to find work at their level around here, and it's hard for* weres *to leave their families. Many would end up working in pack businesses in the area, not fully utilizing their educations. Your offer would probably be most welcome. I'll mention it to Jason and see what he thinks."*

Within minutes, Carly had the beginnings of a staff for her new headquarters. She hadn't intended to stay permanently when she moved here. She'd just been floating, really, drawn to the old farmhouse and unsure of where she'd go from there. But now she had a plan. She'd keep her office in California— she didn't have the heart to fire anyone—as a branch office, but she'd move her base of operations here. All she needed to do was find some office space.

"Or better yet, add on to the house and work from home. There's plenty of room on the farm. And I won't object to a work crew made up of weres. Jason has a construction business that does excellent work, as a matter of fact. If he knows he's building a place where his people can find employment, I bet he'll give you a break on the cost as well."

"This is all working out even better than I expected."

She didn't object to the way Dmitri entered her mind that time and listened in on her thoughts. Little by little, she was becoming more used to it, and it didn't startle her. Plus, she'd been the one to initiate conversation this time. She was beginning to see distinct advantages in being able to talk silently to him without anyone being the wiser.

She hung out with Amy and her friends most of the night, truly enjoying their company. They even managed time for a little girl talk.

"So...you and Jason?" Carly raised one eyebrow toward the hunky leader of the pack.

But Amy looked startled. "Me and the Alpha? No!" She laughed. "I'm nowhere near an Alpha bitch."

"Oh, sorry. When I saw you two coming out of the woods I just assumed."

"Nah. He was just being nice to me." She waved away the comment with an offhanded smile.

"Nice?" Carly wondered how screwing a girl in the woods was being nice to her.

"I forgot you're human. See, at the full moon the mating urge...well...it gets pretty intense. We get together at howls like this so we can all help each other. When the Alpha hunted me down in the woods tonight, he was doing me a big favor."

"I don't follow." Just when she thought things couldn't get any weirder, Amy dropped this new strangeness on her.

"Well, what would happen in a human high school if the

star quarterback suddenly started dating the nerdiest girl in school? People would start taking a second look at her, right? By hunting me tonight, the Alpha just gave my nonexistent reputation a big boost. Next time, some of the more suitable males will start sniffing around and I won't end up with the losers of the group, like I usually do. Jason's a good Alpha. He helps a lot of the younger girls like this when he can."

"I'll just bet he does." Carly couldn't help the judgmental tone of her voice as she looked at the Alpha asshole in question.

"Oh, no! You've got it all wrong, Carly. He really does help. Think of it this way. Instead of winding up with one of the other desperate singles like me tonight, I got to be with the primest of the prime Alphas. And I got to protect him too. By choosing me tonight—someone he could never mate—there won't be any speculation tomorrow about whether or not he intends to mate one of the Alpha bitches that have been sniffing after him all his life. We helped each other, you see?"

"I still think he's getting away with something here, but I'll take your word for it."

"Carly, my pack only has two bitches with Alpha potential right now." She pointed them out. One was a brassy blonde named, appropriately enough, Candy, and the other was a dour looking older woman with what seemed a perpetual scowl on her face. "I don't care to take orders from either one of them, which I'd have to do if they somehow managed to corner Jason and make him mate her."

"I didn't think that kind of thing could be forced."

"Not forced, exactly, but a desperate enough person could find a way to coerce it out of someone in a moment of weakness. And once mated, we're stuck for life. I wouldn't want to see Jason bonded to either one of those women and both have been hatching plans for some time to get him alone. During the full moon, we're all especially vulnerable. Even the Alpha. Being with him is certainly no hardship for me and if it keeps him safe from those designing bitches, it keeps me safe from having one of them as my Alpha as well. Everybody wins."

"Except those other girls." Carly chuckled, understanding a bit of what motivated this totally unorthodox attitude toward casual sex in the woods.

Amy laughed too and that was how Dmitri found them some time later, when they were about ready to leave. They'd agreed only to stay for an hour or two, leaving the *weres* to their fun.

Carly left the party with a plan for her company's future that looked bright indeed. Amy had already agreed to work for her part-time while she finished school, and Jason was sending someone by to give her an estimate for the addition to the house the next week.

They made love the rest of the night and when Dmitri left her just before dawn, he left her smiling.

She worked on business plans for the rest of the week and building plans as well. Things were moving along, but Dmitri still made time for the two of them to spend some quality time alone. He'd sit with her and watch movies or just talk. Sometimes he took her out on the town. They'd seen a few concerts, even dined in some of the local restaurants and attended a play at the university. She loved going out with him. It felt like dating, but there was none of the uncertainty. She knew Dmitri loved her, and she knew it was forever. She'd never felt so secure in a relationship or with a man. He was slowly but surely bringing her out of her nerdy shell and she loved him for it, and for his patience.

He hadn't brought up the topic of sharing their thoughts again, or of her becoming a vampire. She wasn't quite ready to face any of that yet, but Dmitri was waging a winning battle, wearing down her defenses and making her love him more and more. His patience was a gift, his passion a pleasure.

"You should mention me to your friends," Dmitri said out of the blue as they sat at a linen covered table. "It would be good to get them accustomed to the idea that you have a man in your life." He'd taken her to dinner at one of the cozy off-campus bistros. She ate while he drank a heady burgundy, and she felt more than a little guilty enjoying her medallions of beef while he watched.

She loved him so much. He was the best thing that had ever happened to her, yet she was still afraid. He would live forever and she...well, she didn't know what she wanted yet. It was one of the many puzzles in her mind, driving her batty.

"We're not on the phone every day to each other, but the next time I speak to one of them, I'll mention you. I don't think I'd be able not to." She laughed as she sipped her water. "My friends always want to know if I've met anyone and when they start asking questions—especially Sally—there's no way to avoid spilling whatever beans you're trying to hold on to."

"Good. I've spoken to Marc and Atticus, you know."

"Comparing notes?" She wasn't sure if she liked the idea that Dmitri knew her friends' husbands so well.

"They both send their congratulations and well wishes. Carly," his voice dipped lower. "There's something I've been meaning to ask you more formally and now, I think, is the perfect opportunity."

Her breath caught when he reached into his pocket and pulled out a small velvet box. It looked old, not like something he'd picked up from the corner jewelry store, but something he'd had in his possession for a very long time.

"This came to me from my cousin, who in her time was a czarina. I would like you to have it regardless of your answer to my next question." He opened the box and Carly was momentarily stunned by the sparkle of a large, square-cut sapphire in purest baby blue, surrounded by a row of twinkling diamonds. The ring was vintage, and she could easily believe it had been worn by royalty. It was elegant and lovely, with the delicate lines of a long-gone age. She loved it. But his words came back to her, raising her eyes to his searchingly.

"What question?"

He got down on one knee, right there in the darkened restaurant. "Carmelita, will you marry me?"

She was struck speechless as she gazed at him. This was the most romantic thing that had ever happened to her. The darkened room, the quiet corner where few could see them, the delicious food by candlelight and the most handsome man she'd ever seen, kneeling before her like some old fashioned knight, asking her to marry him.

The only thing wrong was the fear that crept into her heart. Fear that he would live forever while she would grow old and die. The alternative was something she couldn't quite envision. The idea of living forever, drinking blood for sustenance and never being in sunlight again frightened the bejeezus out of her every time the thought crossed her mind.

But his smiling gaze said without words that he understood her fears. She felt the reassurance he sent directly to her mind through the small window he kept only partially open by her request. He'd been so good to her. He'd shown her the best loving of her life, treated her like a queen and respected her wishes, even when she knew he longed to share their minds fully, all the time. He was the best thing to ever happen to her. So what other response could she give?

"Yes, Dmitri." Tears fell unheeded down her smiling face. "Yes, I'll marry you."

She launched herself forward, and he met her before she could join him on the floor, rising to embrace her where she sat in the dimly lit corner of the restaurant. She was aware of the people around them, but nobody was watching as he kissed her passionately. She knew in the back of her mind, where they were joined, that it was his doing. He had the ability to turn attention away from them, easily manipulating human minds.

But she also knew he would never use his power against her. This was her decision, completely and utterly, as it should be. She loved him for that and for so much more.

He drew back, placing the gorgeous antique ring on her finger. He smiled, raising her hand to his lips for a sweet kiss that stole her breath.

"I love you more than anything, Carly. You have made me the happiest of men."

"I love you too, Dmitri."

Chapter Ten

Carly floated around the house in a daze, trying to concentrate on answering her email and keeping her business running. About mid-afternoon, a desperate call came from the campus and she had to drive down to check on a faulty connection. She got into her car and headed for the distant campus, noting with interest the gently falling snow, but she had a sturdy SUV. She could get through a little snow.

"Carly!" He awoke in a sweat, knowing something terrible had happened to his mate. As soon as the sun sank low enough, he transformed himself and took to the sky.

He flew to the hospital at breakneck speed, entering unseen and finding his way to her room. She was alone and in bad shape. There were all kinds of tubes leading out of her small body, and the sight of them hurt his heart.

"Carly." His whisper was gentle as he took her small hand in his own.

"Dmitri. You're here."

"Anywhere you are, I must also go. How do you feel?"

"Like I got run over by a truck. Oh yeah, I did." Even in such pain, she tried to make a joke and it touched him. She was so brave. So strong. Yet so fragile and so...mortal.

"My love, I can't stand seeing you hurt. I would take all this pain from you if I could." He cursed under his breath. "But you know I can. I could easily make you like me. The process of the change would heal your hurts and bring you immortal life, but you would never see the sun again. Still, we could spend every one of our immortal years together." He grasped her hand. "I won't force this on you. You have to make the decision."

He would not tell her that without his life-altering bite, she would most certainly die. He had wanted her to choose him over the light, and she had. It set his frozen heart free.

Dmitri held his breath while she thought it through. He could see the consideration in her pain-filled eyes, the fear and most of all, the love.

"I would rather have eternity to share with you, Dmitri, than the sun. I can live without the sun, but I can't live without you."

He held her close, tears of blood leaking from his eyes. "I feel the same."

Tucking her close to his chest, he jostled her as little as possible in the pure white snowfield of the hospital bed as he bent to her throat. Feeling his fangs grow long and hungry, he sank them into her jugular, draining her nearly dry before moving back. She was so rich and perfect. How he loved her taste. How he loved her.

Ripping a wound in his wrist, he held it to her parched lips, massaging her neck to help her swallow. Her pale, pale skin began to take on more color as he fed her his blood, his life's essence. She would require time to heal but now, he knew, she would survive. They would have eternity to share together while he taught her the ways of the darkness. She would be with him always.

When she had fed enough, he pulled his wrist gently back and sealed the wounds. He would need to feed well this night so that he could provide for her when she woke again. For now, sleep would claim her while her body underwent the enormous change that would make her immortal.

Dmitri left her in the hospital bed, not going far. He had

much work to do and little time in which to do it. First, he changed the hospital records to show a remarkable recovery on her part and a late evening release. He found the few members of staff who would need to have their memories altered and took care of that within moments. He also took the time to feed just a little from each of the humans he cornered. Taking a little from each, he quickly built back his strength, leaving them none the wiser.

Within an hour he was back in her room, disconnecting her from the monitors and taking her in his strong arms as he left with her, through the fifth-story window. Shapeshifting quickly, he allowed large, leathery dragon wings to spread out behind him. He moved like the phantom he was through the dark night sky. There were few humans about at this hour, but he was darkness itself. None would see him. Or her, as he cradled her close in his arms.

He took her to the bedroom, two stories under her own bedroom in the house above ground. There he laid her gently on the rich fabric of his bed, tucking her under soft covers.

He sat at her bedside as he had for so many nights while watching her sleep. He dare not share the bed with her yet. She was still healing and changing, her body in pain as it reformed. He would keep careful watch over her for the slightest sign of discomfort. Only when she was well again would he take his place at her side, claiming her for all time. It was a moment he looked forward to with every fiber of his being.

Carly was bleary-eyed when she woke. The room was darker than she remembered, and her mind was in chaos, her body aching in so many new and different ways.

She became aware of eyes watching her from the chair beside the bed. A supreme sense of déjà vu came to her, as she recalled having this dream before.

"Dmitri? Is that you?"

The flare of a candle suddenly lit the darkness, causing her to squint.

"I'm here, my love."

He leaned closer, his dark eyes warming in the flare of the candle flame, taking their heat and pulling it within his irises. He was so beautiful. He was a miracle.

"Am I dreaming?"

He came down beside her and gathered her into his strong arms, wrapping her gently within his strength. His lips found the side of her neck, sliding up over her jaw to seek out the corner of her lips, then moved to kiss her, his tongue thrusting deep inside. Her pulse pounded and there was a roaring in her ears. Her body felt so strange.

Dmitri kissed her long and deep, and she felt an ache in her teeth as they seemed to grow in her mouth. He pulled back, mesmerizing her senses as he moved down to lick at her pulse, his own teeth scraping back and forth in a rhythm that had her pussy clenching in time.

"Are you hungry, my love?" His voice growled low near her ear.

"Ravenous."

"Do you recall what you said to me in the hospital? That you would rather have eternity as my bride than stand again in the sun?" She nodded as he pulled back to look into her eyes. "That was the most beautiful thing anyone has ever said to me."

He let her see the tears that formed in his eyes. She rose slightly to kiss them away. He was such a tender soul, such a strong man with a beautiful heart.

"I meant every word." He kissed her again and once more her teeth felt so strange. "Dmitri." She pulled away, shock in her voice. "What's happening to me?"

His expression warmed her insides and went a long way to calming her fears. He ran one sexy finger around her puffy lips, dipping inside to test the sharpness of her new fangs.

"You are becoming like I am, my love. Don't be afraid. Your

fangs are coming in for the first time."

"Fangs?" She was amazed, then amused. She hadn't really thought about what it meant to become a vampire when he'd asked. Suddenly it was all too real and kind of cool. "Who do I get to bite?"

"Only me, my love." His eyes were deadly serious. "I will provide all you need."

So saying, he climbed onto the bed, tearing off the covers in one harsh movement. She was naked underneath and ready for him. He moved faster than thought to remove his robe, his cock springing hard against her thighs as he kneed her legs apart. She was more than willing as he positioned himself, testing her only briefly and smiling with smug male satisfaction when he found her slick and ready for him.

He shoved home with a groan as he came over her, his gleaming fangs glowing in the fiery light of the candle. Rolling, he pulled her on top of him, baring his throat.

"Take me, my love. Take all of me!"

Carly bent over him and allowed new and exciting instincts to take over. Her body rode his as she licked her way up his throat to the strong pulse just under his ear. With an agonizing hunger, she sunk her newly formed teeth into his flesh, gently at first, then harder when the first streams of his sweet, coppery blood hit her tongue. It was ambrosia. It was heaven. It was love made flesh.

She rode him, feeling his climax as they joined body to body, soul to soul, for the first time. It would be like this from now on she knew in her heart. They would never be parted.

She ran her tongue over the wound, sealing them with instinctual caresses of her mouth as they came down from the pinnacle. She rested on top of him, his cock still within her though somewhat relaxed. She knew he would be up for more within moments, but this short time of quiet joining was precious to her.

"You are a miracle, my love." His satisfied rumble made its

way through her body to her newly enhanced senses.

"No, Dmitri, it's you." She kissed his chest with little nipping kisses. "I never thought I could feel this way. I never thought I could bite anyone." She giggled as he stroked her back. "But I love you. I'll be whatever you want, if only I can stay with you."

"You are my bride, Carly." He sat up slightly so he could look into her eyes. "We will always be together. Now and forever."

Her smile held the sun. "Now and forever."

About the Author

A life-long martial arts enthusiast, Bianca enjoys a number of hobbies and interests that keep her busy and entertained such as playing the guitar, shopping, painting, shopping, skiing, shopping, road trips, and did we say...um...shopping? A bargain hunter through and through, Bianca loves the thrill of the hunt for that excellent price on quality items, though she's hardly a fashionista. She likes nothing better than curling up by the fire with a good book, or better yet, by the computer, writing a good book.

To learn more about Bianca D'Arc, please visit www.biancadarc.com. Send an email to Bianca at BiancaDArc@gmail.com.

Nitro? Meet glycerin...

Biting Nixie
© 2009 Mary Hughes
A Biting Love Novel.

Punk musician Nixie Schmeling is a hundred pounds of Attitude who spells authority a-n-c-h-o-r and thinks buying insurance is just one more step toward death. So she really feels played when she's "volunteered" to run the town's first annual fundraising festival. Especially when she finds out it's to pay for a heavy-hitting, suit-wearing lawyer—who's six-feet-plus of black-haired, blue-eyed sex on a stick.

Attorney Julian Emerson learned centuries ago that the only way to contain his dangerous nature is to stay buttoned up. He's come from Boston to defend the town from a shady group of suits...and an even shadier gang of vampires. But his biggest problem is Nixie, who shreds his self-control.

Nixie doesn't get why the faphead shyster doesn't understand her. Julian wishes Nixie would speak a known language...like Sanskrit. Even if they manage to foil the bloodthirsty gang, what future is there for a tiny punk rocker and a blue-blooded skyscraper?

And that's before Nixie finds out Julian's a vampire...

Warning: Contains more eye-popping sex, ear-popping language and gut-popping laughs than can possibly be good for you. And vampires. Not sippy-neck wimps, but burning beacons of raw sexuality—this means passionate blood-heating, violent bloodletting, and fangy bloodsucking. Oh, and cheese balls. Those things are just scary.

Available now in ebook and print from Samhain Publishing.

Desire can strike without warning.

Storm Warning
© 2008 Sydney Somers
Shadow Destroyers Book 3.

Journalist Blair Murphy is on the trail of a hot lead when she meets an even hotter stranger. Charmed by Drew Reid's sexy smile and intrigued by his evasive answers, Blair puts aside her undercover investigation of a corrupt politician for an under-the-covers investigation of every inch of his incredible body. But even after Drew satisfies her in every possible way, he refuses to satisfy her curiosity. Especially about the mystery woman who keeps calling his cell phone.

As a burnt-out demon slayer, the last thing Drew needs is an inquisitive woman complicating his life, especially when she turns out to be the one woman who's strictly off limits—his partner's sister. He knows firsthand why it's important to keep loved ones at a distance, yet the fierce desire Blair arouses makes it impossible to stay away.

Just as Drew prepares to hang up his sword for a normal life, a vicious attack on Blair awakens a storm of powers inside her that rage beyond her control. As her emerging abilities become increasingly unstable, their searing passion could be her salvation—or destroy them both.

Available now in ebook and print from Samhain Publishing.

LaVergne, TN USA
31 January 2010
171606LV00002B/95/P